At first I could see nothing, but in a few moments the horse and rider emerged from the shadow of overhanging trees into the moonlight. The horse was a pinto and seemed smaller than most. So was his rider, from what little I could make out as he drew closer. He sat straight in the saddle, his face hidden in the shadow of his wide-brimmed hat, his body swaying with the rhythm of his horse.

My heart leaped to my throat, and I pressed back against the barn wall. Was this the Gray Angel of Death riding to meet me at a deserted barn, under a gibbous moon, and me without as much as a pocketknife to defend myself?

DEATH'S GRAY ANGEL

Fawcett Gold Medal Books
by James Sherburne:

DEATH'S GRAY ANGEL

DEATH'S PALE HORSE

DEATH'S GRAY ANGEL

A Paddy Moretti Mystery

James Sherburne

FAWCETT GOLD MEDAL • NEW YORK

A Fawcett Gold Medal Book
Published by Ballantine Books
Copyright © 1981 by James Sherburne

Library of Congress Catalog Card Number: 81-4468

ISBN 0-449-13131-9

First published by Houghton Mifflin Company. Reprinted by permission
of Houghton Mifflin Company.

Manufactured in the United States of America

First Ballantine Books Edition: July 1987

To Nancy Lee, Jenny and Jimmy
for the three very best reasons

Contents

1

Cognac and Claret

Jack Farringay was a good-looking man with curly brown hair, gray eyes, and a big square chin with a cleft in it. He looked as if he'd be as handy in a saloon as in a salon. He also had a gift for pithy speech, as he now proved.

"Have a drink, Mr. Mills," he said.

We were seated together in the Palace Car of a Kansas and Pacific express two hours out of Topeka. I don't usually find myself in the Palace Cars of trains, but this was a special circumstance, as will be explained in time.

I told him I would be delighted. He beckoned the white-jacketed attendant. "Two from your best bottle, George," he ordered with a smile that softened his imperious tone.

As we awaited our drinks he regarded me thoughtfully. "Mills," he said. "That's English, isn't it?" I told him it was. "You don't look English. Irish, I would have said. Irish, or maybe Italian. But English? You could have fooled me."

"Who knows? Maybe some mick tinker tied his mule outside Grandma's house sometime when Grandpa was away. Or maybe it was an organ grinder who tied his monkey. It's a wise child who knows his own father, as they say. Don't you agree, Mr. Farringay?''

He looked at me sharply. "Some men wouldn't find it easy to joke about their mother's virtue, or their grandmother's either, Mr. Mills.''

I assumed an abashed expression. "I'm afraid I find it easy to joke about too many things. My father thinks that's my problem—or anyway, one of my problems.'' I plucked at the nap of the green plush armrest in an apologetic manner. "He said it shows lightness of character, and lightness of character is a definite drawback in the business world.''

Our drinks arrived. Farringay tossed a silver dollar on the attendant's tray. "Keep the change, George—buy an annuity," he said jovially. He raised his glass. "To you, Mills, and to that stern father of yours.'' We both drank, and he set his glass down. "Let's see—you said he was in the publishing business, didn't you?''

"That's right. He's owner or part owner of a dozen newspapers.'' I plucked names out of the air, starting with the *Chicago Inter-Ocean*; the only name I was careful *not* to mention was *The Spirit of the Times*. "Then, besides all that,'' I went on, "he owns a book-publishing company in Boston and a printing company in Hartford, and I don't know what all besides.''

Farringay's gray eyes showed dancing highlights. He crossed his legs and inspected his gleaming patent leather oxfords for a moment, then raised his glass again. "A business like that really keeps you hopping, I bet," he suggested.

I nodded glumly. "I haven't been on my boat in a month. Missed the Block Island regatta and practically the whole Newport season. Not that that means so much—I know the whole world doesn't revolve around Newport, for heaven's sake—but a man has to have *some* interests outside of his work.'' I took a swallow and continued defensively, "Man doesn't live by bread alone.''

"Of course he doesn't," he answered. "A man without outside interests is only half a man. You mentioned a boat. What kind of a boat would that be?"

"A thirty-footer. I named her the Annabelle Two, after a girl I know. I mean the girl's name was Annabelle, not Annabelle Two. But this was the second boat I named after her. The first one was just plain Annabelle, without any number." I took a pull on my drink. "She was in the chorus at the Winter Garden."

Farringay nodded understandingly. "Boats are wonderful, and so are women. It's no wonder we enthusiasts name the one after the other. I remember a good story about that. It seems there was this English yachtsman—"

As he told the story I studied him from round innocent eyes. He was three or four years younger than I, I decided, which put him in his late twenties, although he acted with the assurance of an older man. His suit was of nubbly tweed, and the tailoring looked English. He was wearing a tie with regimental stripes, and the slender chain that crossed his waistcoat was obviously gold. He smelled of two things—lime toilet water and money.

He finished the story and I made a point of missing the point. It was really a very funny story, and it was hard to keep from laughing immediately, but I managed. We finished our drinks and Farringay ordered two more. The conversation moved from yachting to deep sea fishing, to dry fly fishing, to hunting, to golf and tennis and horse racing, and finally to pugilism. Farringay asked me what I thought of the new padded gloves and Marquis of Queensberry rules.

I frowned in concentration. "Why, I don't know—I guess they're all right. I mean, it's the humane thing, isn't it?"

Farringay shook his handsome head impatiently. " 'Humane' isn't a word I want to hear in the prize ring. Fighting is fighting, that's what I say. And a man fights with his bare hands, not with a couple of pillows." He smacked his hand on his armrest. "By God, when I put out my money, I want to see claret flow."

I nodded. "I see what you mean. More manly. I bet the fighters like the old-fashioned rules better."

"Of course they do. A pugilist is a fighting animal, and that's what a fighting animal likes to do—fight! When his blood's up he wants to bite and kick and gouge and whatever else it takes to win! This John L. Sullivan, this Boston butcher's boy, may be the boxer a lot of people say he is, but nobody will ever know if he's a real prizefighter or not if he stops working with his bare hands! Bare hands!" he repeated. "Bare hands, by God. That's the ticket!"

I agreed. He finished his drink and clapped his own bare hands together. "Talking about raw meat gives me an appetite, Mills. How about some dinner? You're my guest, of course! No"—he cut off my protests with an upraised palm—"no, I insist! It's not that often I get to talk with a true sportsman!"

We went forward through two swaying cars to the diner. Outside, the bare Kansas prairie lay under the pale spring sun like a sleeping pregnant woman, oblivious to the ripening within her. The engineer blew his whistle as we entered a curve, and one by one the railway cars tilted to the left. I was stepping from one car to another as the train shifted under my feet, and for a moment lost my balance. I clutched at Jack Farringay's arm. It was as firm as a block of wood.

The dining car was full, but just as we entered an elderly man arose from a table for two, dropped a bill on the tablecloth, and came down the aisle toward us. I glanced at his face casually and then found I was unable to take my eyes from it. It was patrician—proud, intelligent, ironic, capable of ruthlessness or compassion as the occasion warranted, but never, I thought, capable of a dishonest or dishonorable act. The hair was silver, the brow high, the nose aquiline, the lips thin and delicately curved. The eyes, half-hooded by relaxed lids, were the sudden startling blue-green of the Gulf Stream.

Instinctively I stepped aside to give him room as he passed, and he nodded his head in a brief but courtly gesture. His eyes rested on me a moment in kindly salutation, and then dismissed me.

I turned my head to watch his progress down the aisle, and Jack Farringay touched my arm. "There's an open table now," he said. "Let's take it before somebody else does."

We seated ourselves at the table for two. Before the waiter scooped it up I noticed the bill the elderly gentleman had left was a twenty. "Did you see that old bird, Jack?" I asked, raising my elbows to allow the waiter to replace the tablecloth.

"You mean the fellow who was sitting here? What about him?"

"He's a real tycoon, or I miss my guess. That was a twenty-dollar bill he left for his meal!"

Farringay raised his eyebrows. "Maybe he ate a lot," he said.

The waiter reset the table and offered menus. Before I could read mine my companion took it from my hand and placed it on the table. "Please, let me do this," he said with a smile. "It's my treat, remember, and I like to think I have a flair for the pleasures of the palate, among others. But first, let's have another drink."

We had two, as a matter of fact, and then Jack ordered for both of us. He was certainly more experienced on the à la carte side of the menu than I was, and he did us very well, with wines to match, and brandy and cigars afterward.

Farringay asked me what role I filled in my father's publishing business, and I tried to think of a way to make my answer sound both accurate and impressive. I told him that

in a sense I was like the prospector for a mining business—
it was my job to inspect possible acquisitions and make
recommendations as to which should be purchased.

Farringay exhaled a fat ring of tobacco smoke. "That
sounds like a mighty impressive job. Your father must have
a lot of faith in your judgment."

"Well, I guess I've earned it over the last few years,"
I said comfortably. Holding my brandy balloon in both
hands, I leaned back in my chair and stretched my legs
under the table. My foot encountered something that
moved. "Oh, I'm sorry," I said, thinking that I had
brushed against Farringay's shoe.

"What's that?" he asked.

"I'm sorry I stepped on your shoe," I said.

"You didn't step on my shoe."

"I didn't?" I raised the edge of the tablecloth and looked
under the table. Our feet were eight or ten inches apart.
Between them lay a leather wallet. I reached for it, grunt-
ing at the sudden constriction of my stuffed belly, and
brought it out into the light. "Hey, look at this! You think
there's enough here to pay for our dinner?"

It was a slender wallet of the billfold type, crafted from
supple Morocco leather, worn with use but undoubtedly
expensive. I saw it contained a number of bills of large
denomination as well as two or three folded pieces of paper.

Farringay leaned toward me. "Handsome wallet," he
said judiciously. "How much money's in it?"

I flipped through the bills. "Gad! There's almost a thousand dollars here!"

"Any identification?"

I withdrew the folded pieces of paper and dropped them
on the tablecloth. Among them was an engraved card. It
bore the simple inscription "C. Hamilton Yarnell." I read
the name aloud.

Farringay was unfolding one of the pieces of paper. He

glanced up with a frown. "Yarnell? Hamilton Yarnell?" he repeated. "That sounds familiar. Doesn't it to you?"

"Not that I remember. What have you got there?"

He flattened out the piece of paper on the table and studied it, his brow creased in concentration. After a few moments he handed it to me. "I'm not sure what it is. What would you say?"

I studied the short list of letters and numbers on the page. It looked like this:

March

P-AFCo	22	→	35
FarS	7	→	13
TolSec	—		14(S)
MWA	9	→	
Hth	3	←	7
IDRR	5	←	12
		→	9

I shook my head in bafflement. "Some kind of code. Could be anything. Say, you know what? I bet that old bird who was sitting at this table when we came in dropped it!"

Farringay nodded. "I think you're right. So he must be Hamilton Yarnell. And I tell you, Mills, I've heard that name before. Yarnell—Hamilton Yarnell." He shook his head impatiently. "I can't put my finger on it, but I've got the feeling he's somebody I should know."

We were still puzzling over the cryptic list when the conductor entered the dining car. Farringay beckoned him to our table. "Is there a Hamilton Yarnell on the train?" he asked.

"Mr. Yarnell? Yes, sir—he's in drawing room A, car twenty-two, that's two cars ahead." He regarded us respectfully. "Are you acquainted with Mr. Yarnell, gentlemen?"

"We have something that belongs to him," Farringay said in dismissal. He called for the check and we made our way forward through the cars. We stopped in front of a door marked A, and Farringay rapped sharply.

"Come in," called a voice within.

It was indeed the same elderly personage we had seen in the dining car. He was now wearing a dressing gown of maroon silk and matching leather slippers. He rose as we entered, putting aside the newspaper he was reading, which was, I was startled to see, *The Spirit of the Times*. "May I help you, gentlemen?" he asked in a brisk but courteous tone.

Farringay replied for both of us. "Mr. Yarnell?" The elderly man nodded. "I believe we have something of yours. We found it under our table in the dining car." He produced the Morocco wallet from his breast pocket.

Yarnell seized the wallet and pulled out the bank notes and the folded papers, an expression of sudden concern on his face.

Farringay spoke with an edge of offended dignity. "I'm sure you'll find all your money present and accounted for, sir."

"Money? Who gives a damn about the money? What about the papers?"

"The only papers we found we replaced. I'm sorry to say we unfolded one when we were looking for some identification, but we couldn't make head or tail out of what was written on it."

Yarnell's eyes, piercing as an eagle's, moved from Farringay's face to mine. I felt like a schoolboy called up before the principal. "That's right, sir," I added earnestly. "Not head nor tail. It might as well have been written in Sanskrit."

"Who else did you show it to?" Yarnell demanded.

"N-nobody! We folded it back up right away and put it back in the wallet!"

"And the wallet hasn't left my possession since then," Farringay added. "You can rest easy on that score."

"You're positive?" Yarnell pressed. Farringay nodded. With a sigh Yarnell tossed the wallet on the table by the window. "Gentlemen, I apologize. Deeply. Profoundly. There are great issues at stake here, but it was churlish of me to take my anxieties out on you when you have come to set my mind at rest. I am in your debt, sirs. Here—sit down, please. Take some refreshment with me. Have a cigar, and allow me the opportunity to express my appreciation." He took us each by the elbow and drew us to a double seat by the window, then offered us fat Havana cigars and cognac from a cut-glass decanter. It was very nearly the best brandy I've ever tasted.

We introduced ourselves, and Hamilton Yarnell was particularly interested to hear that my father was the Mills of Mills Publications. "Of course! I know him well—but only by reputation, I regret to say. Blue chip all the way! So you're his son, are you?" He looked at me in friendly appraisal, his sea-green eyes half-hooded, his sensitive mouth delicately curved. "If you're a chip off the old block, I imagine you had a hunch what those notes of mine on that piece of paper meant. Ehhh? Didn't you?"

I said I hadn't the foggiest notion. He chuckled unbelievingly. "Never saw the initials P dash A F Co before in your life? Never took a flyer on the I D R R? Come, come, my boy—we're all businessmen here. You don't have to pretend you were born yesterday!"

"I'm sorry, Mr. Yarnell, but I really don't have any idea what your notes mean," I repeated. He gave me a skeptical look as he withdrew the paper in question from his wallet and folded it down the center from top to bottom so that only the abbreviations were visible; the numbers and arrows were hidden on the other side.

"Taking you at your word, sir, allow me to elucidate," he said dryly. 'P dash A F Co stands for Pan-American

Fruit Company. The numerical information beside it—
which I am sorry I cannot share with you—indicates a bottom figure, at which it should be bought, and a top figure,
at which it should be sold. The arrow indicates the stock
should be played to rise." His slender forefinger moved
from the first to the second abbreviation. "I hope I'm not
going too fast for you," he said in gentle mockery. I assured him he wasn't.

"Far S stands for Farrier Shipping. Once again the arrow counsels a rising market." The forefinger moved again,
and continued to descend the page with each new identification. "Tol Sec is, unsurprisingly, Tolliver Securities. In
this case the notes tell me to expect a stock split when the
market value reaches a certain figure. Next comes M W
A—Martin-Williams-Amberson—a growth stock, to be held
indefinitely. Then Hth—Hammersmith—which I intend to
sell short. And finally the Iowa and Duluth Railroad, which
I plan to sell at a certain high point, then buy again at a
very attractive low, and finally resell at a second high."

He refolded the paper and put it back into his wallet.
"You gentlemen have done me a very great favor by returning these notes to me, and I wish I could repay you by
sharing with you the extremely valuable information they
contain. Unfortunately, however, it is not all mine to share.
Other parties are also involved, and all of us have sworn
to protect the confidentiality of our information." He raised
his shoulders slightly in a gesture of helplessness. "I won't
insult you by offering you money, so I don't know what
else remains but the brandy bottle." He raised the carafe
and refilled our glasses.

I settled back on the seat and sipped the ambrosial liquor. Outside the window the Kansas prairie continued to
unroll, as featureless as drifted snow. Hamilton Yarnell
was asking me a polite question about the publishing business when Jack Farringay, sitting beside me, interrupted
with an ejaculation. "Now *this* is what I call interesting!"

I saw he had picked up a leather-bound album and was leafing through its pages, which appeared to contain mounted newspaper clippings and pictures. I leaned toward him for a closer look. The pictures were of pugilists and the newspaper articles were descriptions of prizefights.

"Oh, you're a follower of our modern gladiators?" Yarnell asked.

"I should say I am! Mills and I were talking about the sport just before we found your wallet!" He turned pages enthusiastically. "Why, this is a fascinating collection, sir!"

"Just a few of the lads I've had the pleasure of seeing in the flesh. That bruiser you're looking at"—he tapped an illustration of an unappetizing brute in black tights—"Boston Bobby O'Flynn, went thirty-five rounds with the bare knuckles last week in Denver." He chuckled in reminiscence. "His face came to resemble extremely juicy beef tartare."

"And you were there?" asked Farringay with a touch of awe.

"Oh, yes. Perhaps too close—I had a new suit somewhat, ah, bedizened; don't know if the cleaners will ever get the stains out." He smiled gently, as if mocking himself for a human but amusing peccadillo. "Worth it, even if they don't, however. I won seventy-five hundred on the fight."

"A bare-knuckle fight, Mr. Yarnell?" I asked. "I understood bare-knuckle fighting was illegal everywhere in the country."

He smiled tolerantly. "It is, almost everywhere. Which is not to say you can't find a likely match if you put your mind to it. 'Illegal' and 'unobtainable' are two entirely different words, Mr. Mills."

Farringay turned the pages of the album and asked questions about various pugilists, which Yarnell answered graciously. I interrupted to point out, "All the fighters in the pictures have gloves on."

"Of course they do," the silver-haired man answered. "Also all the descriptions here are of absolutely legal prizefights—the promoters and participants in bare-knuckle boxing are hardly anxious for publicity. But rest assured, young man—most prizefighters are happy enough to take off their gloves if the purse is right. And the purses are; there's often more money to be won without gloves than with them." He smiled slightly and concluded, "And that goes for the bettors as well as the fighters."

"A first-class bare-knuckle fight—by God, I'd love to see one again!" Farringay exclaimed. "Eh, Mills? Wouldn't that be a treat, though? To see a little claret flow before we're too old to enjoy it!"

With an eager smile I said, "You bet it would!" I assumed a boxer's stance, fists cocked aggressively before me. "Take that, you bloody scoundrel! Pow, pow! There goes your nose!" I pantomimed two punches at an invisible opponent. Yarnell and Farringay smiled in approval, and then Yarnell raised his hand commandingly.

"One moment, gentlemen! I may have just had one of my better ideas!" He began to pace back and forth across the narrow compartment, two steps each way, his slim body as dynamic as a piston stroke. "Now, I am in your debt, very deeply in your debt, and feel an obligation to repay you for your courtesy and consideration. No, no!" he silenced us as we began to remonstrate. "No, I'm quite serious about this, so hear me out. Now, I believe you both indicated an interest in witnessing an exhibition of bare-knuckle fighting. Correct?" He paused and Farringay and I both nodded. "Very good," he continued. "Then perhaps you would allow me to arrange for you to be at the ringside for an old-style championship fight between Kid Slaughter and Tim the Tiger O'Meara, just three days from today!"

I gasped, and Farringay cried out, "I'd go across the country to see that!"

"You won't even have to go across the state." Yarnell chuckled. "But wait a minute. That's only half my offer. Here's the other half." He refilled our glasses again from the cut-glass carafe, then raised his glass in a toast. "I guarantee you both will win at least ten thousand dollars on the fight," he said, and emptied his glass.

I drank the glorious cognac with thanksgiving in my heart.

2

Columnist in Lamb's Clothing

I have to make one thing clear. My name is not Mills.

It is Paddy Moretti, and I am, more often than not, a columnist for the weekly sporting newspaper *The Spirit of the Times* ("A Chronicle of the Turf, Field, Sports, Aquatics, Agriculture, and the Stage"). I am thirty-two years old, six feet tall, and fifteen pounds overweight. I was born and raised by an Italian father and an Irish mother in Corbo County, Ohio, and attended Goshen High School until my devotion to racehorses precluded continuation of classroom studies. I followed my four-legged idols from county fairs to state fairs and thence to the great commercial tracks, working in any job that would keep me alive and allow me to stay near them. Along the line I learned the California Job Case and found an occasional job setting type for small-town newspapers. The day came when I set a story about a horse race that I had written myself; the editor liked it and asked for more of the same—and I discovered I had become a sports writer.

During the following decade, while other reporters covered the Hayes-Tilden election, Garfield's assassination, and the Haymarket Massacre, I described horse races. Also baseball games, prizefights, field sports, and boat races—but primarily horse races, which led to my present position as racing columnist for *The Spirit of the Times*—a job which is my glory and my despair.

Two months before the occurrence of the events described in the previous chapter, I returned to the editorial office after a brief free lunch at McSorley's Old Ale House. My eye was immediately caught by my editor, Otto Hochmuth, who contributes very little to the glory of my job, but much to its despair.

"Moretti, if I might intrude upon the period normally spent in the contemplation of your digestive processes, would you give me a moment of your time?"

Hochmuth always spoke in a low voice, but somehow it could be heard in the middle of a Tammany Hall picnic. All eyes followed me as I crossed the crowded room to the editor's desk. "Yes, Mr. Hochmuth?" I asked.

Hochmuth was wearing a green eyeshade, which gave his normally pasty skin a reptilian hue and turned his yellow eyeballs chartreuse. He eyed me without favor. "Moretti, you're wanted in the Owner's office," he said.

I raised my eyebrows. Summonses to the sanctum of the Owner—a word that was always spoken as well as written with a capital O—were rare events in the lives of senior staff members, and virtually unknown to the working press.

"The Owner's office?" I repeated. "What for?"

"Perhaps he intends to elevate you to a fitting position in the corporate management. Then again, perhaps he wants the pleasure of firing you for chronic incompetence and alcoholism. Or perhaps there is a third possibility we haven't considered. Why don't you go and find out?" He returned to the galley proofs on his desk with elaborate unconcern, but I knew his eyes were on me as I continued across the editorial room.

I gave my name to the Owner's secretary, a rabbity young man in blue serge, and he scurried through the heavy teakwood door, to reappear a few seconds later and beckon me on. I entered a room smaller than the New York Stock Exchange, paneled in walnut and leather-bound matched editions, enlivened with dim oil portraits of ancestors, and furnished with leather chairs and a massive desk that seemed lost in its immensities.

Four men were present. Three, standing at parade rest in front of the desk, I recognized as staff members of *The Spirit of the Times*; one was Bigglestaff, *The Spirit*'s theater critic; the second was Freddy Moore, our only Harvard man and our specialist in the diversions of the rich; the third was Clem Harber, baseball writer and general troubleshooter. The fourth man, seated behind the desk, was of course the Owner—Frederick Follinsbee Monk III. He was a short, fat man whose hairless scalp and apoplectically red complexion made him resemble an animated Gouda cheese. He was speaking as I entered, but paused to glare at me.

"Pardon me, sir, but I understand you want to see me. I'm Moretti, and I wish you a very good day, Mr. Monk." I smiled in a comradely but respectful manner.

"You the horse-race man?" he barked. I told him that such was my good fortune. "Know anything about prizefighting? Or confidence games?"

I shook my head. "No more than anyone else who follows the sporting life, I'm afraid."

"Well, they don't either"—he jerked his head contemptuously at the three men across the desk from him—"so we'll just have to get all of you educated together. Fraley or McBride can tell you all you need to know about prizefighting, and I'll have Chief Byrnes send over somebody from the bunco squad to explain the confidence racket to you. Then, by God, we'll make the bastards sorry they ever messed with the Monk family!"

Bigglestaff, the dramatics man, only partially concealed a shudder. "I'm sorry, Mr. Monk, but I don't understand what possible connection a theater critic could have with pugilism and swindling. Not that I'm not willing and eager to do anything I can—''

"You travel a lot, don't you?" Monk interrupted. "All four of you travel a lot. You spend half your time on trains—I should know, since the paper pays all your transportation costs. Well, that's where these bastards work— the Pullmans and Palace Cars out of Chicago. That's where they pick up their lambs for the fleecing. Well, from now on, by God, I intend to have my own lambs out there waiting for them!"

"Us being the lambs?" Clem Harber asked in his nasal voice.

"Well, you're the men in the right place to make contact, shuttling back and forth to baseball games and horse races and play openings and what not. All you have to do is keep your eyes open and act ten percent dumber than normal."

"And a hundred percent richer," said Freddy Moore dryly.

For a moment Monk looked disconcerted, and then he reassumed his expression of resolution. "That's right— you'll have to look like wealthy men. You'll have to eat in the dining car and buy a drink occasionally. But that doesn't mean you have a license to throw away money!"

"You want us to buy new suits and charge them to the paper?" Harber asked.

"Certainly not! Plenty of rich men wear suits as shoddy as yours—if you're wealthy it's considered a harmless eccentricity! Looking rich isn't a matter of clothes, for God's sake, it's a matter of attitude! Just tell yourself you're superior to all the clods around you, and everyone else will think you really are!"

I coughed deferentially. "Excuse me, Mr. Monk, but I'm feelin' like a man who's just opened a book in the middle, and can't make head nor tail of the story at all.

I'm wonderin' if you can't explain a bit more, so I can get it straight in me head.''

The Owner looked sternly at me. "Do you always talk in that ridiculous brogue?''

"Only when I'm a trifle unsure of meself—of myself. It's when my nerves get jumpy that I seem to remember the speech of my mither with the most perfect clarity. Somehow in moments of stress the language patterns of the auld sod—''

"Shut up,'' the Owner suggested.

I obliged, and after a moment he began to tell the story from the beginning, speaking slowly with a controlled rage that brooked no interruption. His nephew Boffie, full name Theodore Allwyn Buffington, only son of his younger sister Edwina and her husband Ned Buffington, had been bilked of five thousand dollars by a pair of confidence men working out of a fight store in Council Bluffs, Iowa. (I opened my mouth to ask what a fight store was, and then thought better of it.) The contact had been made on a train heading west out of Chicago, and soon afterward Boffie had rendezvoused with the swindlers at a hotel in the Iowa town. From there he had wired his bank for funds, and had received five thousand dollars through Wells Fargo. Twenty-four hours later the swindlers were gone, and so was the money.

"And he had trusted them!'' Monk cried, his voice shaking. "He trusted them, and they took advantage of him! Why, the poor boy takes after his father—he hasn't got enough sense to pour piss out of a boot!'' He shook his head. "Well, they'll find out they took on more than they bargained for! Because that boy isn't all Buffington—fifty percent of him is pure Monk!''

We talked for another twenty minutes in the sanctum sanctorum, and when we four writers left, it was with the realization that apprehending the bilkers of Boffie was not only a responsibility but an opportunity as well; if any one of us could provide assistance to the police in the arrest of the miscreants, his future career at *The Spirit of the Times* would be blessed by the Owner's approval.

The four of us spent an hour discussing prizefighting, both the legal and illegal varieties, with the paper's resident expert, Knobs Fraley, arranged for a meeting with Lieutenant Costigan of the bunco squad the next morning, and then adjourned to McSorley's Old Ale House. Bigglestaff would have preferred the gilded taproom of a fashionable uptown hotel but, being outvoted, came along grudgingly. When he received his stein of ale from Old John McSorley, he held it with the tips of his fingers, as if fearing it would soil his fawn gloves.

We sat in the back room under the life-sized portrait of Peter Cooper. We had the room to ourselves—all the other patrons were seated around the pot-bellied stove in front. I munched on dry cheese, savage onions, and stale soda crackers, and Bigglestaff leaned as far away from me as possible. Clem Harber probed his teeth with a gold toothpick and Freddy Moore studied his pewter mug thoughtfully.

Harber broke the silence. "Well, gentlemen, the obvious question before us is, do we or don't we share whatever information each of us happens to come up with? In other words, do we enlarge our chance of tagging these lads at the cost of a certain amount of individual glory? Or does each of us hoard his information selfishly, with the probable result that nobody succeeds in nailing the buggers?" He lowered his toothpick and raised his stein, swallowed, wiped his mouth, and continued: "I for one believe in cooperation all the way."

Freddy Moore nodded judiciously. "I agree. Pooling our information will make us four times as likely to pick up a lead, and we'll all share in whatever success comes out of this."

"Oh, absolutely—this is no time for grasping individualism,'' Bigglestaff agreed. "We should take our theme from the Bard: 'We few, we happy few, we band of brothers.' " He shot his cuffs.

I swallowed a mouthful of dessicated cheddar cheese with difficulty and said, "We're all in agreement, gentlemen. It's one for all and all for one. *E pluribus unum.* In unity there is strength." I raised my mug.

"We put selfish desires behind us," said Harber.

"We work together," said Moore.

"We share our knowledge," said Bigglestaff.

"We trust one another," said I.

We left a few minutes later, each determined to keep any scrap of information he was lucky enough to gain strictly to himself.

3

Making a Killing at the Fights

All I had ever heard about Cogswell, Kansas, was that some unpleasantness occurred there during the late war. If anyone had asked me at the time which side committed the unpleasantness and what form it took, I would have smiled and changed the subject.

Jack Farringay and I arrived a little past eleven in the morning. One of the thrill-seekers assembled to watch the train come in directed us to the Barnard Hotel. Since no transportation seemed to be available, we picked up our valises and set out on foot.

Cogswell was a typical small prairie town, consisting of one very wide street and a dozen narrower ones, all unpaved; an impressively ugly courthouse and a three-story hotel; a newspaper office and a livery stable; four churches (one Catholic); a grimly institutional building identified over the front door as the James H. Lane Public School; fifteen or twenty stores and businesses; Masonic and Odd Fellows halls; two illegal saloons; and (as I later discovered) an extremely hospitable whorehouse known through much of south-central Kansas as Moll Sweeney's House of Delights. Most of the buildings along the main street were brick; the residences that lined the other streets were white frame. The population, officially listed as 5500, was for the most part industrious, sober, and God-fearing, to judge by the specimens we observed on our walk to the hotel.

"What a hick town!" I exclaimed to Farringay. "Who'd ever believe one of the biggest prizefights in the world was going to take place here?"

Farringay frowned at me warningly. "Careful, Mills! Remember, that's ten thousand dollars' worth of information you're bandying about!"

The Barnard Hotel was indistinguishable from a thousand other small-town hotels. The lobby smelled of cheap cigar smoke and rancid cooking grease. All the chairs were occupied by men who looked like hardware or corset drummers and who were entertaining themselves by reading newspapers, lying to one another, and spitting in the tarnished brass spittoons that dotted the floor like metallic fungi. They all stopped what they were doing and watched us as we crossed to the desk.

We signed for a double room, which the clerk assured us we were lucky to get. "We're just bustin' out our seams," he said proudly. "Can't remember ever seeing so many traveling men in town."

Farringay grunted noncommittally. "Has Mr. C. Hamilton Yarnell registered yet?" he asked.

"No, sir. Mr. Yarnell wired for a reservation, but he ain't come in."

Yarnell had said he would meet us in Cogswell before we had separated on the Palace Car the day before. "I imagine he had some business in Wichita, and will be in on a later train," Farringay said to me. He glared at the clerk. "Are we supposed to carry our own bags up to the room?"

"Oh, no sir, no sir!" He tapped the bell on the desk. " 'Bednego, get over here!"

A black man not over four and a half feet tall materialized beside us. "I'm here, Mister Alfy," he said through pink gums. He picked up our bags without bending over, and led the way to the broad stairway at the rear of the lobby.

Our room on the third floor was everything I had expected—garish floral wallpaper against which pious chromos of biblical scenes vibrated like an optical toothache; a brass-steaded double bed with a sagging mattress; a threadbare carpet, two comfortless chairs, and a washstand.

'Bednego set the two valises on the floor and shuffled to the window, where he pulled one curtain back from the grimy glass and let it fall again. "Window, sah," he said. He moved to the washstand and raised the pitcher. "Water, sah," he said. Neither Farringay nor I made a movement toward our pockets, so he crossed to the bed and plucked at the coverlet. "Bed, sah," he said hopefully.

I dug out a quarter and flipped it in the air. "How would you like to get us a bottle of good whiskey, 'Bednego?"

Farringay snorted. "You're out of luck, Mills. Kansas is a dry state. It's in the state constitution."

"My understanding is that it's dryer in some places than in others." I regarded the diminutive Negro questioningly. "How about it, 'Bednego? You suppose you could find a man who knows a man who knows a man?"

His eyes followed the rise and fall of the quarter. "I've heard tell there's a man named Mole, he sometimes fixes gentlemen up. I'll be glad to ask him to pay you a call, sah."

I tossed him the quarter. "You do that." He shuffled quickly from the room, closing the door behind him. I dropped on the bed. It was as uncomfortable as it looked. "My God, it feels like the Pennsy roadbed," I complained. "Two days here is going to seem like two weeks. You suppose Yarnell will get here soon? I hope he hasn't abandoned us in this primitive isolation. How long till our friend Mole appears with the old indispensable, that's the first question.''

Jack Farringay took off his coat and vest and hung them neatly in the closet. ''Yarnell will be here soon—don't worry. Meanwhile, brother Mills, think about the approaching exhibition, and even more importantly, think about that big ten thousand dollars waiting out there!''

''Oh, I am, I am!'' I assured him. ''Only I think better with a glass in my hand.''

Ten minutes later there was a knock at the door. It was Mole; I would have identified him anywhere. Soft, downy black hair grew so low on his sloping forehead it almost merged with his heavy eyebrows. His eyes, dark and moist, blinked into the light. His shoulders were broad and sloping, his arms long, his hands large and wide, with very short fingers. He moved a step into the room on bowed legs and raised the carpetbag he was carrying.

''The coon said you wanted to see me,'' he said in a husky voice.

I inspected his wares. Five or six bottles had labels purporting to identify their contents as rye whiskey, bourbon, or blended whiskey. Two jars were unlabeled, and contained a liquid as colorless as water. I unscrewed one of the jar lids and sniffed; the smell sandpapered my nasal passages and squeezed water from my eyes, and I screwed the cap on again.

Farringay watched with an ironical smile as I negotiated for a quart of bourbon and paid the Mole the two dollars he demanded. ''Better make sure he comes back tomorrow,'' he suggested. ''It wouldn't do to run out without a replacement handy, would it?''

''Say, you're right, Jack—thanks!'' The bootlegger agreed to stop by the following day, and replaced his stock in his carpetbag. He started out the door, then paused with his hand on the knob.

''Anything else you might be needing, gents?''

I looked blank. "Like what?"

"Like some fun for tonight. Like a game, say. Or like a good cockfight. Or like some girls—some real high kickers." His eyes gleamed wetly from under his shaggy brows. "There's lots to do in Cogswell."

"Well, now that you mention it—" I began.

"We'll send for you if we need you," Farringay interrupted. After the bootlegger left he went on: "We have to remember our priorities, old man. There'll be plenty of time for that kind of thing after the fight—and plenty of money for it, too."

"If Yarnell ever shows up, that is."

"I said not to worry, didn't I?" Farringay snapped. "With a man like Yarnell, his word is his bond. And even if he doesn't show up, I'm sure we can locate the fight ourselves with a few judicious questions. Meanwhile, what do you say to a little luncheon, if we can find a place that won't poison us?"

The restaurant was next door to the hotel, but there was a connecting door in the lobby. We seated ourselves at a table by the window, and Farringay inspected a rash of spots on the tablecloth. "I see the specialties of the house are stew and scrambled eggs," he said. "Taken with a good deal of tomato ketchup, I would imagine."

A waitress arrived, her apron appearing to confirm my companion's analysis. "What'll it be, gents? The special today is beef stew. Or, if you want, there's liver and onions. Or we could fry you up a couple of steaks, or scramble a mess of eggs."

"Which we would then cover with ketchup? No, I think I'll go with the favorite. Bring me the stew," Farringay said. I concurred, and she disappeared into the kitchen.

We talked idly as we waited for our food. I was in the middle of a pointless anecdote designed to reinforce my supposed character of feckless playboy, when I suddenly stopped in midsentence, my mind emptied of words.

Through the street door, on the arm of a tall young man with blond hair and a vacuous expression, appeared the young woman responsible for this mental evacuation. She too was blond, but where her escort's hair seemed colorless, hers was a concentration of all colors, vibrant with dancing highlights of silver and gold. She was small in stature, probably less than five feet tall, and her body seemed constructed entirely of curved lines—gentle curves that outlined her neck and arms, flowing curves that shaped her shoulders and waist, swelling curves that formed her firm round breasts. Her face was rounded but not plump, her nose slightly retroussé, her mouth small but full, and her eyes an incredibly bright cornflower blue. She swam before my eyes like a mirage.

"My God!" I breathed.

"My God!" I heard Jack Farringay gasp.

I glanced at him, expecting to see an expression of stunned reverence on his face. Instead, to my surprise, he was staring past me toward the door connecting the restaurant with the hotel lobby. Two men were entering; one was a somewhat imposing personage with split whiskers, striped pants, and a Prince Albert coat, and the other was smaller and younger, with slicked-back black hair and quick, small eyes. Compared to the vision who had just entered the other door, they seemed unremarkable, and I switched my attention back to its previous focus.

The young woman and her escort walked to a table across from us, nodding to other diners as they passed. He drew out a chair for her and she thanked him with a charming smile. Her teeth were as white and even as I would have expected. He sat down facing her and said something, and she replied with a pretty shrug. Then the waitress arrived at their table and cut off my view.

I turned back to Farringay. He was frowning at the tablecloth. I noticed that the two newcomers who had entered by the lobby door were now seated and engaged in conversation. "She's a stunner for a fact, isn't she?" I asked.

Farringay looked at me blankly. "Who?"

I laughed. "You must have a lot on your mind, Jack. At the table by the wall—the blonde. The one that lights up the room."

"Oh." He looked where I directed and grinned in simulated lechery. "Ah, yes. Delectable. A morsel to tickle the most discriminating palate, yes indeed."

Our waitress arrived with our plates of stew. It was surprisingly good. We suspended conversation while we ate, and I kept a surreptitious eye on the blond beauty. Afterward, as we waited for our dessert, Jack excused himself. "Have to make some room for the pie," he said with a wink. He went through the door into the hotel lobby.

A few moments later the man with the slicked-back hair rose from his chair, said something to his companion, and also went through the lobby door.

The waitress brought our apple pie and refilled our coffee cups. My eyes met those of the girl across the room, and I felt burning coffee splash my fingers as we both looked quickly away. I took a bite or two of pie. In a few moments Farringay returned and sat down. Shortly thereafter the man with the slicked-back hair returned to his table.

"Do you know that fellow?" I asked. Farringay raised his eyes questioningly, and I nodded toward the black-haired man.

"Never saw him before in my life. Say, this pie is dandy, isn't it?"

After lunch we took a brief constitutional along both sides of Cogswell's main street, and then returned to the hotel. The desk clerk said that Mr. C. Hamilton Yarnell had arrived and was in his room.

Yarnell received us warmly and pressed cognac and cigars on us. "Gentlemen, the exhibition is set for tomorrow night," he said. "As I believe I told you on the train, it will be between Kid Slaughter and Tim the Tiger O'Meara, two of the pluckiest maulers in the world of fisticuffs. As I also indicated, the outcome is something less than unpredictable.'' He drew contentedly on his Corona-Corona. ''I trust you gentlemen are amply supplied with the wherewithal for wagering on a sure thing.''

''I'll have to wire my bank, Mr. Yarnell,'' I said. ''I didn't want to do it until I talked to you and was sure everything was set.''

''Well, you better trot on down to the telegraph office, Mr. Mills. I wouldn't want you to miss out on a chance to shake the money tree.'' He turned to Farringay. ''How about you, sir? Are you well supplied?''

Farringay replied that he had better than five thousand dollars with him. Yarnell nodded approvingly. ''Just right,'' he said. ''The odds will favor O'Meara, two to one. That five thousand will win you ten. You have them send you five thousand too, Mr. Mills—I'd tell you to get more, but I'm afraid that's all the traffic will bear.''

I headed for the door. ''I'll send a wire right away, Mr. Yarnell.''

''Fine, fine.'' He gave me a courtly little bow. ''Meanwhile, perhaps Mr. Farringay and I can become better acquainted. Another brandy, Mr. Farringay?''

I had more than one thing to do in Cogswell that afternoon, and it was after four when I returned to the Barnard Hotel. Farringay was in our room. He seemed impatient. ''Everything go all right? Did you get the money?'' he demanded as I took off my jacket and picked up the bottle of Mole's Choice Stock.

I poured a dollop and filled the glass with water. ''It's wonderful to have a well-disciplined bank. I think they're afraid I may complain to Papa if they're not obliging.'' The whiskey tasted even worse than it had before lunch. ''Matter of fact, the shoe's on the other foot. I'd hate to have to explain to the paterfamilias that I pulled out five thousand to bet on a prizefight." I giggled. "Of course I won't ever have to—I'll get the five back into the bank and keep the ten for myself, and nobody'll ever be the wiser."

"Good thinking, Mills," Farringay approved. "A real stroke of high finance."

"Yes, it is, isn't it?" I lay down on the bed and held my glass up to the light. The liquid seemed to contain many small floating particles. I decided to ignore them. "What about the fight, Jack? Is it all set? Where do we go, and what time?"

"Mr. Yarnell says it will be tomorrow afternoon at three, at a farm a mile from town. The farmer's name is Eakins, and the fight's going to be in his barn. A man named Tommy Tompkins is in charge." Farringay fingered his slender gold watch chain. "Yarnell says there'll be plenty of money there—big money. People from Kansas City, Topeka, Wichita, all willing and anxious to put down their greenbacks—mostly on Tim the Tiger." He grinned engagingly. "And at two to one, we'll accommodate them, won't we?"

I raised my glass. "Accommodation is my middle name," I answered.

The balance of the afternoon, the evening, and the following morning dragged by at a leaden pace. Jack Farringay didn't let me out of his sight—the usual procedure among confidence men once the mark has provided himself with the necessary funds. We had dinner, read the newspapers in the lobby, and retired early. The next morning we ate breakfast, took another constitutional, and stopped by Mr. Yarnell's room for a visit. While he offered cigars and poured brandy he regaled us with accounts of prizefights and wagers won and lost. He really was an entertaining man, and I hoped he would join us for luncheon, but he pleaded the press of business, so Jack and I lunched with each other in the hotel restaurant. Midway through our meal the gentleman in the Prince Albert coat and his companion with the slicked-back hair entered and took a table. They ignored us, and since Farringay carefully looked the other way, I ignored them.

The blond vision failed to appear, to my considerable disappointment.

We returned to our room and waited. Jack buried himself in *Harper's Weekly* and I leafed through the pages of *Police Gazette*. The accounts of nefarious criminals and bloodcurdling crimes lacked their usual appeal, and I found my attention straying even from a three-column illustration of the current Toast of Broadway, clad mostly in black net tights. "Isn't it about time, Jack?" I asked.

"Patience, my friend. To everything there is a season, and a time to every purpose under the heaven." He wet his finger and turned a page.

I returned to the current Toast, considering her every purpose. The time dragged on. Finally Jack consulted his watch and grunted in satisfaction. "Up and at 'em, Mills," he said as he put his magazine aside.

We hired a gig at the Cogswell livery stable and headed out the Carrsville Road, following directions that Yarnell had given Farringay. We found the Eakins place without difficulty; it was an unkempt farmhouse with an unpainted barn behind it, communicating an impression that its owner had given up the struggle. Two other gigs and five or six saddled horses were tethered beside the porch. As we arrived Mr. Yarnell appeared with another man at the barn door and waved to us. "Over here, gentlemen," he called. "I want you to meet my friend Tommy Tompkins, to whose entrepreneurial enterprise we are indebted for today's festivities. Tommy, may I present Mr. Mills and Mr. Farringay, two gentlemen to whom I am considerably beholden."

The prizefight promoter was a big, florid man with gray hair, careful eyes, and a mobile mouth. He smiled broadly and extended his hand, which was large, soft, and muscular, like a masseur's. "Good meeting you, gents," he said in a rich bass-baritone. "Any friend of Mr. Yarnell, and so on."

"Come inside," Yarnell invited. "There are some other devotees of the sport I want you to meet."

We entered the barn. In the center, raised a foot above the dirt floor, was the ring—a platform twenty feet square, canvas-covered and enclosed by triple ropes attached to four wooden stanchions. Two stools faced each other from opposite corners, both presently unoccupied. A dozen or so spectators sat on improvised benches—boards laid across wooden boxes and barrels—or stood beside the ring. Their voices were raised in lively discussion and argument, and the air was heavy with tobacco smoke.

Yarnell introduced us to a number of the spectators, who appeared to be uniformly affluent, bloodthirsty, and partisan to Tim the Tiger O'Meara. After we shook hands with one especially outspoken enthusiast, Farringay winked and whispered, "Truly, they are geese for the plucking!"

Standing a bit apart from the other spectators were two men I recognized: Prince Albert Coat and Slicked-back Hair, from the restaurant. Yarnell guided us toward them. "Mr. Mills and Mr. Farringay—Mr. Magruder and Mr. Wheeler," he intoned. "I believe you gentlemen will find you have much in common." I sensed a hint of mockery in his voice.

Magruder, the Prince Albert coat, nodded to us condescendingly. "I suppose you both are great supporters of O'Meara, like all the rest of them," he said.

"Not I," Farringay snapped back. "I have a bit of money that says Kid Slaughter will tan the Tiger's hide for him."

I nodded vehemently. "That goes for me too," I said. "So if you're looking for a wager—"

Magruder looked at us more carefully, as did Mr.

Wheeler. "I should say not—not against Kid Slaughter I'm
not. So you like the Kid too, do you? Hell, I thought I had
the field all to myself." He turned to his companion. "How
do you like that, Wheeler? We've got competition."

The black-haired man pursed his thin lips. "I wouldn't
worry, Magruder. I think there's enough here for all of
us."

"I hope you're right," Magruder said. He lowered his
voice. "These people here, they're so anxious to get money
down on O'Meara they're giving two-to-one odds. I hope
you won't upset that with a lot of injudicious talking and
betting."

Farringay rubbed his square chin thoughtfully. "Yes, I
see what you mean. It would be a shame to ruin those
handsome odds, indeed it would."

"Particularly when you don't need to," Wheeler said.
"I'll tell you what to do. Don't suggest any bets yourself—
just mention that you like the Kid, conversational-like, and
let the other fellows bring up the bet. Let *them* persuade
you, see? You just act the least little bit reluctant, and
they'll push those odds on you!"

Yarnell nodded judiciously. "My recommendation exactly." He put one hand on Farringay's shoulder and the
other on mine. "By the way, friends—when you make a
wager, it's customary to ask Tommy Tompkins to hold the
stakes until after the fight. It prevents bad feelings, we've
found. All right?" We nodded our agreement, and he excused himself to join another group. Mr. Wheeler produced
a silver flask and we four partisans of Kid Slaughter toasted
one another. He returned it to his breast pocket. "Well,
Magruder and I still have a few simoleons to get down on
the Kid—" he said.

"And so do we," Farringay interrupted. "We better get
a move on, Mills."

He drew me toward three spectators who were standing
beside the ring and arguing about which round would see

the Tiger knock out Kid Slaughter. When we expressed our belief that there would be no such round, they pressed us to back up our opinion with money—at, gratifyingly, 2-to-1 odds. Tommy Tompkins was glad to hold four thousand dollars of theirs and two thousand dollars of ours.

No sooner was that bet placed than two other spectators challenged us to offer them the same opportunity. Other sportsmen joined in, waving money and insisting on accommodation. "I'll take five hundred of that," shouted one red-faced bettor, waving the greenbacks under my nose. "A thousand here! Give me a thousand!" another cried, pushing the money into my hand.

"Gentlemen, gentlemen!" Farringay shouted over the clamor. "We'll take everything we can afford! Mr. Tompkins, will you come here?" Tompkins appeared again, and Jack and I gave him the balance of our money—eight thousand dollars in hundred-dollar bills. Tompkins then collected from the other bettors and jotted down a column of figures in a small notebook, which he returned to his pocket. He folded the money into a roll as thick as a baseball and stuffed it inside his coat. "All right, gents, your bets are placed!" he called.

Almost as if on signal, the fighters and their handlers entered the barn, followed by a shabby man carrying a doctor's black bag. Tommy Tompkins joined them and escorted them to the ring, pushing his way through the spectators with proprietary dignity. First came Tim the Tiger O'Meara, wearing a crimson silk dressing gown over a broad, heavily muscled body that seemed too massive for the thin ankles and small feet that supported it. He had the face of a neighborhood bully who has grown up enraged because the magic of his fists is not always successful, and other alternatives have eluded him. His two handlers followed on his footsteps; one was a small bald man with nervous hands and an odd, sidling gait; the other, carrying towels and a bucket, was an impassive Scandinavian.

Kid Slaughter and his retinue followed. The five thousand dollars I had just wagered upon him, even though it was not my own, nevertheless increased the curiosity with which I studied him. He was wearing a bottle-green dressing gown, and it was easy to see that the body under it was considerably less bulky than that of his opponent. His hair, cropped short, was carrot-red, and his skin was a startling milky white. His features were over-large and quite expressionless, so that the effect of his appearance was of a face crudely chiseled from stone. The moment I saw him a thrill of revulsion ran through me, and I was glad that our eyes had not met.

The Kid's handlers, a short fat man in sleeve garters and a six-foot black man carrying towels and bucket, followed him into the ring. The seventh man in the procession, he of the black bag, took a seat beside one of the neutral corners.

Tompkins climbed through the ropes and raised his arms. "Gentlemen, welcome to an exhibition of old-style boxing, staged for your edification and amusement, and featuring two of the greatest pugilistic champions in the history of the manly art." He introduced O'Meara and Slaughter in turn, and each gave sulky acknowledgment to the cheers of the audience, which were considerably louder for the Tiger than for the Kid. "With your kind permission, I will act as referee," he went on, "and the medical responsibilities of the day will rest in the capable hands of our local Aesculapius, Doc Rolf Bennigsen." He gestured to the shabby man with the black bag, who seemed not to hear his words, but continued to stare straight ahead from pouched and bloodshot eyes. There were groans and catcalls from the audience.

Tompkins responded, "A little more respect, gentlemen! I happen to know Doc hasn't had a drink in fifteen minutes! No, seriously, Doc is well qualified to give emergency medical attention in the unlikely event that any such is required—a necessary precaution, gentlemen, in a state where old-style boxing is illegal, as I'm sure you will understand upon reflection."

He meant that if one of the fighters was killed during the bout everyone in attendance could be charged with conspiracy resulting in reckless homicide—a point that Jack Farringay had already emphasized to me.

I yawned to indicate that I was undisturbed by the possibility.

Tompkins briefly listed the rules—there were very few—and summoned the fighters to the center of the ring. Tim the Tiger, wearing crimson silk drawers, hunched his broad shoulders and bounced up and down on his lithe and muscular legs. Kid Slaughter assumed a boxing stance, ducked his head behind his left shoulder, and advanced on his opponent. The two men touched their bare knuckles together, and the crowd roared.

It was an exciting fight, and one with more science and less gore than I had expected—at least at the beginning. O'Meara had fifteen pounds of weight and an inch or two of reach on the Kid, but Slaughter was faster. He relied on his counterpunching ability, which meant he had to stay out of the way of O'Meara's murderous fists and dart in behind them with swift and less damaging jabs. His hope of winning appeared to lie in wearing down his more powerful opponent before too many of O'Meara's cannonballs connected.

For five minutes the Kid had things his way, dancing and weaving between the Tiger's punches, driving straight rights and lefts at the bigger man's head and belly. O'Meara's partisans grew restless; one called, "Show some spunk, Slaughter—stand up to him!" and another cried, "What's the matter, Kid—yellow?" I cupped my hands and shouted, "Thataway, Kid, keep working on him! Let's see some claret!" The red-headed boxer continued his dart-

ing attack, oblivious to critic and supporter alike, and
O'Meara shook his head in baffled frustration.

Farringay grabbed my arm, his handsome face aglow
with satisfaction. "He's going to turn that big bull into two
hundred pounds of ground meat, Mills! I wish we had another ten thousand down!" I nodded and yelled, "Kid!
Stick your thumb in his eye!"

Then suddenly the situation changed. The Kid ducked
under a swinging left to jab his own left at O'Meara's
cheek. The blow missed, and before the Kid could recover
Tim the Tiger caught him with a thudding punch just under
the breastbone. The Kid's knees bent, his guard dropped,
and for a moment he stood unprotected. O'Meara launched
a powerful left hook at his head, which exploded over his
eye and sent him stumbling back against the ropes. The
Kid covered his head with his hands and O'Meara smashed
deliberate blows into his body—a left, a right, another left,
another right. The Kid began to sink, his back sliding down
against the ropes. A pink flush stained the dead white skin
of his torso. O'Meara stepped close to him, cuffed his pro-
tective hands away from his face, and smashed a fist into
his jaw.

A howl of joy burst from the O'Meara supporters as the
Kid's buttocks hit the floor. He lay at the edge of the ring
with his hands again covering his face, one knee raised,
the heel of his shoe scuffing ineffectually against the canvas. Tompkins, arms spread, stepped between the fighters.
"Time! That's the end of round one!" he called. O'Meara
backed slowly to his corner and lowered himself to his
stool, while the Kid's handlers sprang through the ropes
and helped their fighter to his feet. Slaughter shook his
head from side to side as he was half-carried to his corner.

I raised my voice so Jack Farringay could hear me above
the boisterous chortles of the O'Meara backers. "You think
they'll get him out again for the next round?"

Farringay's expression was grim, but he answered confidently, "Of course, O'Meara hardly touched him." He leaned close to my ear. "This is all play-acting. You wouldn't want it to look too easy, would you? Somebody might smell a rat."

"That's mighty fine play-acting," I said doubtfully. "I'd hate to play-act that hard."

"Don't worry about a thing. Mr. Yarnell guaranteed it, didn't he?"

The Kid's handlers worked over him furiously, the short white man pressing salts against his nose as the huge black man kneaded his shoulder and neck muscles and slapped his body until it glowed. The doctor entered the ring and bent over the fighter, apparently checking for damage serious enough to end the contest. After a few moments he caught Tompkins's eye and spread his hands in a gesture signaling consent to continue. Tompkins nodded and called, "Gentlemen—seconds out of the ring! Take your places for round two!"

O'Meara moved into the center of the ring confidently, his guard high and a crooked smile of anticipation on his face. Kid Slaughter was slow leaving his corner. His oversized features were set in an expression of determination. He no longer danced and weaved, but moved in short, careful steps.

O'Meara feinted with a left and drove his right hand at the Kid's head. The Kid ducked and pushed his hand into O'Meara's face. O'Meara moved closer and smashed two blows at the Kid's belly. The Kid blocked them with his elbows, counterpunched, and scored a hit above O'Meara's eye. O'Meara stepped back to launch a knockout punch at the Kid, and the Kid followed him, placing two more fast jabs in O'Meara's face. O'Meara shook his head angrily and stepped back again. Again Kid Slaughter followed him instantly, and again two fast jabs exploded in O'Meara's face. This time blood showed at the corner of his left eyebrow.

"Claret, by God, here comes the claret!" Jack Farringay giggled with genuine joy. *There*, I reflected, *is a man who enjoys his work*.

In the few seconds since the second round had opened the balance had shifted, and Kid Slaughter was regaining the initiative. He moved cautiously, taking no chances, his body beginning to weave once more, his eyes hooded, his mouth a lipless slit, his bare-knuckled fists moving in circles before him. A shadow of apprehension passed across O'Meara's face as he stepped backward again.

"You've got him on the run, Kid!" I called. "Keep your hands in the big ox's face!" Farringay and the Kid's two other supporters, Magruder and Wheeler, joined my exhortations; the other spectators were silent as the Kid moved after his opponent, and as his fists lashed into the other's face again. The cut above O'Meara's eye widened, and he wiped away blood with the back of his hand. He moved back again, and again Slaughter followed him as closely as his shadow, fist jabbing like a striking snake. O'Meara covered his head, and the Kid pounded him twice in the body. This time when O'Meara backed up, he stumbled.

"He's breaking up!" Farringay shouted in my ear. "Kill him, Kid!"

And now, for the first time in the fight, Kid Slaughter, apparently sure that the victory was within his grasp, slowed down to launch a deliberate knockout blow, drawing his right hand behind his shoulder and raising his left elbow as a counterbalance. His body was uncovered to O'Meara's desperate sudden thrust.

The Tiger's fist struck the Kid over the heart with a thud that could be heard over the gasp of the crowd. For a moment the Kid stood flat-footed in the center of the ring as his hands dropped to his sides. Then his chest convulsed, and to the sound of a groaning cough, a great gush of blood burst from his mouth and poured down his chin and neck, divided into two crimson streams separated by his left nipple, and continued down his white belly to darken his bottle-green silk drawers. His head lolled over on his shoulder, his knees buckled, and he fell heavily to the floor.

O'Meara, mouth agape in stupefaction, backed slowly away from Slaughter's immobile body, and Tompkins dropped to one knee beside him. "Doc! Doc Bennigsen! Come quick!" he cried. "I think he's hurt bad!"

Doc Bennigsen climbed awkwardly between the ropes and knelt beside the prostrate fighter. His fingers checked Slaughter's pulse as he brought an ear close to the open lips. He remained motionless for several seconds; the barn was as still as a forest after a snowfall. Then he dropped the Kid's wrist and rolled up one eyelid with his fingers.

He looked up at Tompkins and said in a low but perfectly audible voice, "He's dead—that wallop in the chest must have stopped his heart."

The silence of the crowd continued another second, while the news sank in. Then the spectators erupted into a babble of exclamations. "He can't be dead!" "But he is!" "Jesus Christ, what'll we do?" "They could call this murder!" "Hell, it was a fair fight, wasn't it?" "But it's against the law!" And then, from three or four different men, "I'm getting out of here!"

Tompkins raised his arms. "Gentlemen, one moment, please!" The clamor of dismay diminished momentarily and the promoter continued. "There's been a terrible tragedy here, and it won't help to have any of you involved in it. I have all the bets, and I promise you men who backed O'Meara that your money's as safe as if it was in the bank. You'll always be able to reach me here in Cogswell. But right now, for heaven's sake get out of here!"

The audience began heading for the door. I saw Wheeler hustling Magruder along. Jack Farringay grabbed my elbow. "Hurry, Mills! You don't want to be caught here with a dead man, do you?"

It was the moment I had waited for. I smiled at him as I took out a silver whistle from my pocket and raised it to my lips. "Oh, I don't really mind," I said—and blew.

The shrill note cut through the yammering like a wind through tall grass.

In the silence that instantly fell I gestured toward the doorway and announced, "It's my pleasure to introduce Sheriff Alf Bybee, a man with whom you'll have many things to discuss. Come in, Sheriff!"

Sheriff Bybee, a barrel-shaped man with nicotine-stained mustachios and a nose like a lump of red clay, entered the barn, followed by two other men. All three wore gunbelts. "Whitey, you stay by the door," the sheriff ordered. "Don't let nobody out till I tell you." He advanced toward the ring. "Now, who wants to talk?"

Before anyone could answer I stepped up on the platform and indicated the scene with a sweep of my arm. "It's a confidence game, just like I told you yesterday, Sheriff— and we've caught them dead to rights! They're running a fight store here—Tompkins manages it. The con men work the trains, roping marks. They bring 'em to Cogswell, to bet on an illegal bare-knuckle boxing match. The match is supposedly fixed, and they understand they're betting on a sure thing."

Tompkins interrupted shrilly. "I don't know what he's talking about, Sheriff. You know me! Why, I'm a Cogs- well boy!"

Bybee motioned him to silence and regarded me through small, slightly asymmetrical eyes. "You're telling it," he said.

I continued eagerly, buoyed by the expectation of scor- ing a journalistic coup, confounding my co-workers, and securing my future at *The Spirit of the Times* beyond the malicious reach of my nemesis, Otto Hochmuth. "The way they work it, the fighter the mark is betting on is just about to win when he's accidentally killed. So not only does the mark lose his money, he's so scared of being involved in a manslaughter case that he tucks his tail between his legs and skedaddles. He doesn't worry about the money he's lost; all he can think about is how lucky he is to get out of it without going to jail.''

Bybee's gaze flicked to the supine form of Kid Slaughter. "That feller on the floor there—he's the one supposed to be killed? How come he's got all that blood on him?''

I laughed confidently. "That's chicken blood, Sheriff! It's a trick con men call the cackle-bladder. You take a little bag made from a pig's bladder and fill it up with chicken blood, and keep it inside your mouth until it's time to play dead. Then you bite down and *whoosh*—out comes what looks like a gallon of blood.''

Sheriff Bybee stepped into the boxing ring and looked down at Kid Slaughter. "So this feller is faking it, is he?'' he asked.

"Why, sure,'' I chuckled. "Come on, Kid, rise and shine! The masquerade is over.''

The Kid didn't move. Sheriff Bybee bent over him and checked his pulse, just as Doc Bennigsen had. Then he straightened and looked at me thoughtfully.

"What you say is mighty interesting, son,'' he said, "except that this man is as dead as Wild Bill Hickok's grandpappy.'' His right hand moved easily to the butt of his holstered pistol. "And everyone in this barn is under arrest.''

4

. . . Nor Iron Bars a Cage

I have always disliked jails, even under the best of circumstances—assuming that there can be a "best of circumstances" where jails are concerned.

My first experience with durance vile occurred in the Corbo County Jail in my hometown of Goshen, Ohio, on the Halloween night of my twelfth year. My cronies and I were engaged in a somewhat unsavory prank involving a neighbor's privy when we were apprehended and hustled to the lockup. Our parents were notified, our protests and promises notwithstanding. One by one the fathers appeared to escort their sons home to the expected and accepted punishment; the boys left with at least the reassurance of returning to the devil they knew. Finally I alone remained, impatiently counting the minutes until my father arrived to claim me.

I remember how my heart leaped when I saw his swarthy, saturnine face in the opened door. "Papa—" I cried in sudden relief.

The jailer was with him. "That's your boy, ain't it?" he asked.

My father studied my face with disapproval. "He's-a the criminal that knock over the shit-house?" he asked coldly.

"He shore is one of 'em—we caught 'em red-handed," the jailer replied.

My father studied me a moment longer, then turned away. "You keep-a him here where he belong," he said—and left.

My sense of loss that night—my sense of *deserved* loss—was almost unendurable. I wept for hours; I probably would have gone on all night if the man in the next cell—it was the town drunk, Tubbo Wall, sobering up—hadn't distracted me by teaching me the words to "McCann He Was a Rounder" and "God Damn the Lane Hotel."

The next morning, of course, my father appeared again and saw to my release. Neither he nor my mother chastised me physically, and the incident was never spoken of again between us. The message that was communicated to me was that boys are spanked, but lawbreakers are jailed, and if I continued as a lawbreaker, jailing would be my inevitable fate.

Now, in Cogswell, Kansas, the grim irony was that I was jailed even though I, probably alone of the fifteen-odd men in the holding cell, was completely innocent of any lawbreaking. I would have been a good deal more comfortable if I *had* been guilty of something illegal—it would have made my fellow prisoners regard me with less aversion.

The cell door had no sooner clanged shut than Farringay and Yarnell cornered me. "All right, Mister Mouth, who are you?" Farringay demanded.

I saw no advantage in trying to huddle behind the shreds of my assumed identity. "My name is Moretti, and I'm a reporter for *The Spirit of Times*," I answered stoutly, "—and it's happy I am to meet you in my own person, so to speak." I extended my right hand.

"Jesus, a reporter!" Farringay groaned. "I ought to break your goddamned head for you."

"Easy, Jack, that won't do us any good now," Yarnell said. He looked at me as though inspecting an unusual first edition in his leather-lined library. He raised one eyebrow, touched a finger to the tip of his patrician nose, and asked gently, "All right, Moretti, you son-of-a-bitch, why did you sandbag us?"

I explained about Mr. Monk's nephew, Boffie Buffington. When I finished Farringay said to Yarnell, "Yeah, we heard about that one, remember? It was the Hot Stove Kid, working with Samuelson out of Council Bluffs."

"I remember—and watch the names, Jack." Yarnell continued to regard me with cold blue-green eyes. "Of course Jack and I had nothing to do with the Buffington touch, Moretti. We've never worked out of Council Bluffs in our lives. You must have known that."

I acknowledged that I did.

"And yet you deliberately set out to entrap us. With malice aforethought. To worm your way into our confidence, to expose us to the police, and to rob us of our liberty. Why, Moretti? Two men who had never done you any harm, who had, in fact, offered you the hand of fellowship—why would you deliberately return that fellowship with betrayal?" I opened my mouth to speak, but he continued. "When I called you a son-of-a-bitch before, Moretti, I slandered all female dogs everywhere."

"Now, wait a minute!" I cried. "You roped me and branded me and were just about to skin me of five thousand dollars! What are you talking about with that hand-of-fellowship malarkey?"

"The truth is, you were willing to sacrifice us for your own journalistic advancement, weren't you? Who was really the entrapper? Who was really the victim? What price the next step up the ladder, eh, Moretti? Ah, the wages of ambition!"

I was so unprepared for his attack that I stammered. "B-but you're confidence men! Y-you were trying to rob me!"

"Perhaps, although it hasn't been proven. But what has been proven is that *you* set out to rob *us* of our God-given freedom to walk the face of the earth in search of our daily bread—solely so you could advance an inch on the wretched treadmill of your profession. Do you deny it?" He leaned toward me, his aquiline nose as stern as a judge's warning finger.

"Why, yes—I mean no! I mean of course I planned to expose you—that's my business! Why should I deny it?" I was aware that my voice was rising in pitch.

"You can't deny it," Yarnell accused. "Because you know that in every important, every *meaningful* way you are as much motivated by ruthless greed as the most unprincipled criminal in America!" He turned to Farringay. "Right?" he asked.

Farringay nodded judiciously. "Right," he agreed.

I spread my hands wordlessly. Yarnell continued to glare at me for a moment, and then his expression changed to one of impish amusement. "All right, relax, Moretti," he said lightly. "All I wanted to establish is that we're all whores working in the same house, and that all we differ about is price. Agreed?" As I gaped at him he went on. "I just had to get rid of your holier-than-thou attitude, that's all. Otherwise you won't be worth a damn to us."

"Why should I be worth anything to you?" I asked in bewilderment.

Yarnell and Farringay glanced at each other in commiseration. Yarnell continued. "Look, Moretti. Somehow Kid Slaughter got killed this afternoon, and he had no business being killed. Jack and I are in jail and will be staying here for I don't know how long, and so will all the other boys from the fight store. There's no possible way any of us can find out what happened at the barn today. But you, Moretti, you'll be outside in no time. Probably the only reason Sheriff Bybee put you in here at all was to scare you a little so you'd be sure to tell him everything you know when he gets around to asking you."

"Well, I hope you're right—"

"Oh, I'm right, don't worry. Now, this is the important thing. Once you're outside, find out all you can about Kid Slaughter's death."

"I plan to—but I don't see much mystery about it."

Yarnell's eyes narrowed slightly, as if to balance his broadening smile. "Paddy," he said. "You don't mind if I call you Paddy? Good. Now, Paddy, let me point out something to you: what Tommy Tompkins said back in that barn was gospel. If a prizefighter gets killed in an illegal fight, the law can call it reckless homicide, and everybody involved is an accessory."

"Looking at a five-year stretch in the calaboose, most likely," Farringay interjected.

Yarnell put his arm around my shoulder. "However, if the cause of death predates the fight—if, in other words, the fighter didn't die specifically because of what happened to him in the ring, but because there was *already* something wrong with him, something which would have killed him anyway—then a good lawyer could make mincemeat out of a homicide charge."

"You mean something like a history of heart disease, for instance?"

"Heart disease, water on the brain, epileptic seizure, ptomaine poisoning—anything that's satisfactorily fatal." He smiled paternally. "Paddy, before I forget, I want to apologize for my uncomplimentary remarks a few moments ago. I was carried away by the stress of the moment, and I'm sorry, and I certainly wouldn't want you to hold it against me—or against Jack, either."

I said that if I kept track of everybody who called me a son-of-a-bitch I would have one of the most extensive filing systems in contemporary journalism. Yarnell and Farringay greeted this sally with great appreciation.

Then Yarnell resumed. "Of course we wouldn't expect you to help us for nothing. As the Physician reminds us, the laborer is worthy of his hire, eh, Paddy?" He raised his hand as if to silence any argument. "No, no, let's be businesslike about this." He leaned closer and lowered his voice. "You find something we can use in court to show that Kid wasn't killed in the ring, and Jack and I will guarantee to pay you two hundred dollars."

"Two hundred dollars?" I cried incredulously. "Two hours ago you were clipping me for *five thousand* dollars!"

"Right!" Yarnell agreed. "But remember—a: You'll be getting that five thousand back from the sheriff; b: It's not really your money anyway, but our two hundred will be; and c: We can't afford to pay any more—we just don't have that much fall money."

"How about it?" Farringay asked. "Will you do it?"

I looked from one to the other admiringly. "I've heard of bare-faced effrontery, but this has knobs on it!" Yarnell nodded calmly and they continued to await my answer. "I'll tell you what I'll do," I went on. "I'll find out everything I can about Kid Slaughter's death—I'd be doing that in any case. If anything I find out helps you in court, and if you feel grateful about it, you might think of delivering a case of Irish whiskey to a certain sports reporter in New York who can't ordinarily afford the stuff. I won't take any money from you, but I'm helpless to prevent other forms of overpowering generosity."

Time passed slowly in the holding cell. After my talk with Yarnell and Farringay I tried to strike up conversations with other prisoners—Wheeler and Magruder, Tommy Tompkins, the two men who had handled Kid Slaughter in the ring—with no success. They either turned away from me with a curse, or stared through me as though I didn't exist.

I couldn't understand Magruder's attitude. Everyone else in the cell was obviously part of the confidence game, but the big man with the split whiskers, the striped pants and Prince Albert coat was in the same position I was. He was a mark brought in to be fleeced. It seemed to me we had a good deal of common ground, particularly since I had arranged for the intervention of Sheriff Bybee, thereby preventing the loss of his money as well as my own.

Apparently he did not agree. When I approached him with a pleasant "It's a shame they're holding a couple of innocent men like us in the same cell with these bunco artists, isn't it?," his complexion darkened and the hairs of his beard stiffened as if electrified.

"Keep away from me, you bungling fathead," he snarled.

I regarded his wrathful expression with hurt surprise. "It's a fathead I am, then, for saving you five thousand dollars? If it had been ten thousand, would that have made me an imbecile? And if it had been twenty thousand, the complete Idiot of the Western World?" He looked as if he were about to speak again, then thought better of it and turned his back on me. "Next time I'll try to regain your respect by letting you lose everything you own," I said to his shoulder blades.

A little later the cell door opened and the deputy called Whitey put his head in. "Magruder—is there a Magruder here? Sheriff wants to see you." Magruder stalked through the door without a glance at his cell-mates, the very picture of outraged dignity.

Whitey opened the door wider and said, "All right, you two galoots get on in there now. Move, you hear me?" Two men sidled past him and entered the cell. "And try to behave yourselves, for God's sake!" he said as he slammed the cell door behind them.

Both the newcomers wore faded jeans stuffed into fancy high-heeled boots, and both had bow legs, but there the similarities between them ended. One was at least six foot three, with massive shoulders and a broad chest that swelled into a belly so vast that his studded belt could only form a tangent to its bottom arc. The other, who was almost a foot shorter, reached his maximum breadth at the level of his ears; his neck descended straight into his shoulders, his shoulders straight into his chest, and his chest straight into his hips without any lateral movement whatever—he was in effect a bifurcated tube.

Coincident with their arrival came a smell apparently compounded of rank sweat, horse, cheap liquor, vomit, fried onions, liniment, creosote, and sulphur, which, in its full odorous synthesis, is beyond my ability to describe. It seemed to emanate more from the large man than the small, but this was no doubt because there was more of him for it to emanate from.

The large man strode to the center of the cell, followed by his companion. He put his great hands on his hips, set his features in a ferocious frown, and declaimed, "For them as ain't never had the privilege, I'm Sidewinder Sam Sallee, and this short order of humanity here is my pard Charlie Moon. Them as want to take issue with me is welcome, but I don't recommend it. I've killed men from the Yukon to the Brazos without it ever cost me a wink of sleep. I'm the greatest bronc fighter the world's ever seen—there ain't nothing wearing hair, hoofs, and hide that I can't fork and quirt and spur from his snaky head to the root of his tail. I've reached down into a panther's mouth and pulled him inside out. I've fought grizzlies to a standstill, till they was crying for mercy like babies. White men fear me, greasers and Injuns avoid me like the plague, and there ain't no limit to the number of women I can satisfy and delight. Ain't that true, Charlie?"

Charlie Moon nodded his head in solemn confirmation. "Every goddamned word," he declared. He drew a once-red bandanna from his pocket, moved it through his fingers until he found a flexible inch or two, and blew his nose. The result seemed to satisfy him, and he refolded the bandanna carefully and returned it to his pocket.

Sidewinder Sam Sallee inspected his fellow prisoners, his gaze falling first on Yarnell and Farringay. "And just what are a pack of dudes like you doing in a lowdown lockup like this?" he demanded.

Yarnell and Farringay glanced at each other, and Yarnell shrugged. "The sheriff seems to have some idea we were involved in a confidence game," he answered.

"I guess I don't have to ask if you were," Sidewinder Sam said, scratching his belly.

Yarnell smiled gently. "*Honi soit qui mal y pense,* my friend."

The big cowboy's eyes swept across all our faces. "Honey swackied Mally pants," he repeated. "I wouldn't put it past her, if we're talking about the same Honey. Whatever it was she done, it's just about her style." His eyes rested on me. "You, there—yeah, you, the one that's trying to look like he ain't here—are you one of these confidence fellers too?"

I straightened my shoulders. "Paddy Moretti's my name, and I work for a sporting newspaper. I'm a writer."

Instantly Sidewinder Sam's expression changed from bullying contempt to something approaching awe. "A writer! Did you hear that, Charlie? This hombre's a writer!" He extended a pawlike hand to me and gave me a handshake that put my knuckles in jeopardy. "I'm plumb tickled to death to make your acquaintance, Mr. Moretti. A writer! Well, I'll be dogged! I been wanting to get together with a writer since I forget when!" He released my hand and put his arm around my shoulders. "I reckon you're a friend of Ned Buntline and Stuart Lake and them *Police Gazette* fellers, ain't you?"

I had once had Ned Buntline pointed out to me in a restaurant, and I often perused the *Police Gazette* when time permitted, so I answered modestly, "Well, we swim in the same waters, you might say. It's a small world in the writing game."

Few of the half-truths I've told in my life have had more momentous effects.

Sidewinder Sam hugged me to his armpit. "Goddamn, Charlie, we done fell into the thundermug and come up smelling like a rose. Our friend Moretti here is going to make us famous in every barbershop in the United States!"

With the first twinge of misgiving I asked, "I am?"

"Course you are? What was Bill Cody before Ned Buntline got aholt of him? A damn buffalo skinner, that's what! What about Bill Hickok? Nothing but a card-sharping backshooter! What about Wyatt Earp and Doc Holliday? They was both pimps, and Holliday was the worst shot in the Arizona Territory to boot. The O.K. Corral? Hellfire, Moretti, it wasn't a patch on the Sawdust Stable Shootout! You ever hear the true story of the Sawdust Stable Shootout?"

"No, I don't think I have," I said as I tried ineffectually to draw away from him.

"Goddamndest bloodletting in the history of the American West. I was there in the thick of it, Moretti, with a hogleg Colt and a fifty-caliber carbine, and both of them so hot they scorched the hide offn my hands! The Maxey boys and Colley Walsh was up in the left, see, shooting down over some bales of hay; Little Jimmy Mattoon and the Poncho Kid was in a horse stall covering the front door; and Herb Fessenden and a couple of other boys, I disremember their names, was laying up in a wagon and shooting over the tailgate."

"A mighty interesting story, Mr. Sallee. I have no doubt of it. But I'm afraid it's a bit out of me line, what with me writing for a sporting newspaper." I smiled in commiseration. "I wish I could help you, indeed I do."

He continued as if he hadn't heard a word I said, and his bear hug around my shoulders abated not one foot-pound. "There I was, backed up by the sheriff and one deputy so scared he was dripping wet from the waist down. I stand behind the barn door, where they can't see me from inside, and start to swing it open. I yell, 'Clayton Maxey! Will Maxey! If you boys want to stay alive, throw down your guns and come out with your hands up!' "

"Moretti? Somebody here named Moretti?" the deputy named Whitey called from the cell door.

" . . . Their reply is a blazing volley of lead," Sidewinder Sam went on. "Bullets are buzzing through that stable door like a swarm of mud daubers. 'My God, Sam, no man alive can stand up to fire like that,' the sheriff says. 'Here's one that can, when it means standing up for the right,' I says . . ."

"Moretti? Are you in there?" Whitey called again.

"Here!" I cried, finally managing to struggle free of Sidewinder Sam's gorilla embrace. "I'm Moretti. What is it?"

"Come on with me. Sheriff Bybee wants to see you."

I made my way past a dozen scowling confidence men to the cell door. Behind me Sidewinder Sam shouted, "I'll tell you the rest when you get back!" As I passed Yarnell and Farringay, the older man nodded and said, "What did I tell you? You'll be out on the street in half an hour."

"Just remember our deal," Farringay said.

I said I would, and followed Whitey to the sheriff's office.

Sheriff Alf Bybee sat at a battered roll-top desk whose pigeonholes were stuffed with bills, letters, wanted circulars, boxes of bullets, brown bottles, lengths of rope, old newspapers, half-eaten sandwiches, a rattlesnake skin, and something hairy that might have been a human scalp. He was leaning back with his short legs wrapped around the chair legs. Standing facing him, imposing in his black frock coat, was my fellow confidence victim Magruder. On the other side of the room the doctor, Bennigsen, held his shabby black bag in both hands, as if it represented his credentials and his badge of office.

Apparently the sheriff was concluding a conversation. "All right—as long as we understand each other, Mr. Magruder. Just make sure to keep me informed. Wouldn't like no big surprises. I hate surprises."

Magruder nodded curtly. "Don't worry, Sheriff." His eyes flicked to me. "Barring fatheads, I'm sure everything will turn out just fine."

"I hope so. I truly hope so." Bybee turned to me as Magruder left the office. "Don't take that fathead comment personal," he said. "He probably wasn't talking about you at all."

"I don't care if he was or not!" I retorted. "It's a terrible thing when a friend of law and order, as well as a member of the working press, finds himself incarcerated with felons! Why, Sheriff, if it hadn't been for me—"

"If it hadn't been for you I wouldn't have a dead man on my hands—is that what you was going to say?"

"Not precisely. What I was going to say was that if it wasn't for me you wouldn't have bagged the whole fight store setup, the whole kit and caboodle of them. And as far as Kid Slaughter being dead is concerned, it just gives you a heavier charge to lay against them—conspiracy resulting in reckless homicide, isn't that it? Why, you can put them away for years, if you want to!"

Sheriff Bybee regarded me from his asymmetrical eyes. "When you first come to see me, Moretti, all we was talking about was a confidence game. That's all very well and good, but what we got now is a dogie with a different brand, you might say." He glanced at Bennigsen. "Ain't that right, Doc?"

Bennigsen clutched his bag tighter as he nodded. "That's right, Sheriff. That sure is right," he said in a whiskey baritone.

"All right—but what's that got to do with me?" I demanded. "The only reason I'm in Cogswell is to get a story, and I've cooperated with you all the way! I was the intended victim, for heaven's sake—there's no way you can say I was involved in any conspiracy!"

Bybee shrugged. "Maybe you mean there's no way *you* can say you was involved." I opened my mouth to protest, and he raised a hand. "No, no, Moretti. Hold your horses— I ain't saying I'm going to keep you in jail with the rest of these coyotes. I know you helped me out, and I ain't an unreasonable man. You'll be back in your room at the Barnard Hotel in fifteen minutes, so hear me out." He waved his hand at Doc Bennigsen. "You might as well mosey off, Doc. Get yourself a drink."

Bennigsen bobbed his head and shuffled toward the door, his black bag held protectively in front of him. At the door he turned and looked back at us, as if to reassure himself he had permission to leave. His putty-colored face was slack, and his red-veined eyes seemed in hiding behind their pouches. "Sheriff . . . Mister . . ." he said, bobbing his head again. Then he left.

"Okay, Moretti, I reckon you're hot to get to the telegraph and send off your story tellin' how you captured the confidence men and all. Well, I got no objection to that. My name's spelled B-Y-B-E-E, by the way. First name's Alf, for Alfred—but I guess you already know that." I nodded to indicate that I had committed this important fact to memory. "So send off your story," he continued, "but stay in town, d'you hear? I want you to be able to testify when I take these bunco artists to court."

"When do you think that will be, Sheriff?"

"Well, I can't rightly say—I got some sorting out to do first. Then I'll have them bound over till the judge gets here next week on the circuit. And then we'll have us our trial."

"So you want me to stick around for another week? I don't think my editor's going to like that very much." I shook my head ruefully. "They're not even the same bunch of con men I was supposed to find."

"Well, they're the ones you ended up with, so I guess you'll just have to live with it. Come back and see me tomorrow, Moretti—may be something more for you to tell your friends in New York."

Outside, a raw prairie wind sang a harsh falsetto along Cogswell's main street. Particles of grit sneaked between my tightly squeezed eyelids and expanded to the size of marbles as they struck my eyeballs. The sky was leaden gray, and empty except for three circling hawks or buzzards in search of their next meal. The temperature must have fallen twenty degrees in the past few hours.

I leaned into the sharp-edged wind and headed along the sidewalk toward the Barnard Hotel. On the first corner was a two-story brick building bearing the name DROVERS STATE BANK in gilt letters across a plate-glass front window. I felt a slight tremor of recognition down deep in my brain— hadn't I heard of a Drover State Bank somewhere? Something to do with violence, with war perhaps? But just then another boulder caromed between my squinting eyelids and I thought no more about it.

The Barnard Hotel's lobby still smelled of cigar smoke, the chairs were still filled with corset drummers, and the brass spittoons still mushroomed up from the threadbare carpet. The dining room off the lobby was dark, and I realized I was too late for supper. A dispiriting thought.

I checked the desk for messages, but there were none. I asked the clerk if it were possible to order a sandwich. He referred my question to the dozing bellman, 'Bednego, whose minuscule body was propped in a corner behind the desk. 'Bednego opened his eyes slightly and allowed as how it was.

"What kind of sandwich can I get?" I asked.

"Hoss cock, sah?" 'Bednego suggested hopefully.

The clerk coughed apologetically. "He means bologna, don't you, 'Bednego?"

"If you says so," 'Bednego agreed.

I requested a bologna sandwich and a couple of hard-boiled eggs, if available, and went up to my room, where I threw myself on the comfortless double bed. *All right, the time has come, me boyo,* I told myself. *What are you going to tell that spalpeen Hochmuth?*

My problem was this: because of my zealous entrapment of a confidence gang, I was now confined to Cogswell, Kansas, for an indefinite period—with my expenses footed by *The Spirit of the Times,* an institution not noted for its reckless generosity. Furthermore, the confidence gang I had entrapped was, in all candor, not the confidence gang I had been ordered to entrap. Then, too, the stories that I should be covering during the next few days would have to be covered by another staffer, thereby doubling the expenses to the newspaper, as well as depriving its columns of the journalistic flair that I would have contributed.

I considered the difficulties of the problem as I poured three fingers of Old Mole into a tumbler and added a soupçon of water. The implacable Hochmuth would use my present embarrassment against me, I had no doubt; it seemed unlikely that Monk, the Owner, would exert himself to protect me, even though I had gotten myself into this predicament solely on his behalf. *An example of the ingratitude of mankind, surely,* I thought, wincing as the alleged bourbon clawed a path down my throat.

But then again, was my hand totally bereft of trumps? Had I not unmasked a bogus sporting enterprise? Were not the criminals responsible now languishing in jail? Hadn't a man died in an illegal fight, and wouldn't other men pay for that death in ways still to be determined in a court of law?

Bereft of trumps? How could I have ever thought so! Why, it was only a question of playing my cards in a confident manner, I decided as I poured three more fingers of Famous Mole into my empty glass and added a tad of water. Why, I could spin a yarn that would have our readers sitting on the edges of their seats! Hochmuth would see it; if the wretched man was anything at all (which indeed he might not be) he was a newspaper man!

I began to compose a telegram:

OTTO HOCHMUTH EDITOR SPIRIT OF THE TIMES NEW YORK NY

HAVE PENETRATED CONFIDENCE RING AND PUT SWINDLERS BEHIND BARS STOP VAST FIGHT STORE OPERATION DESTROYED STOP WITNESSED FIGHTER KILLED IN RING BEFORE HORRIFIED SPECTATORS STOP MUST REMAIN HERE FOR NEXT FEW DAYS AS AM STAR WITNESS AGAINST CRIMINALS STOP FULL EXCITING STORY FOLLOWS

MORETTI

When I finished I read it over and felt so pleased with the results I had another taste of Mole's Special Reserve before I went to the station and had the telegrapher send it off. Then I ate my sandwich and went to bed.

5

The Annals of the Gray Angel

The next morning I awoke to find the sun shining brightly through the window, the insides of my eyeballs only slightly grainy, and only the gentlest of headaches agitating my cerebellum. I stretched voluptuously, reflecting that I was able to do so only because Jack Farringay had done *his* night's sleeping in jail. This thought added an extra touch of satisfaction to my matinal musings.

I whistled as I performed a sketchy ablution and dressed in my rumpled suit. When I surveyed myself in the streaked mirror over the washstand, I decided my appearance was not entirely unprepossessing.

In short, I had that feeling of fatuous self-confidence that is almost always unjustified by coming events.

I descended to the lobby and crossed to the dining-room door, through which wafted the aroma of fresh coffee and frying meat. With pleasant anticipation I realized I was hungry. The waitress waved me to an empty table, and I tucked a napkin under my collar and ordered flapjacks and honey, beef bacon, fried potatoes, and black coffee. When it arrived, there were side dishes of applesauce and cottage cheese as well. A Lucullan feast.

I ate until my belt bit into my stomach, and then fished the remaining two-thirds of the cigar Hamilton Yarnell had given me from my breast pocket. Wreathed in fragrant smoke, I considered my plans for the day.

I had promised Hochmuth an exciting story, and I would deliver one. I reshuffled what I had decided were my trump cards the night before and decided they were still strong. But they would be stronger if I could buttress them with additional facts, background information which would indicate a history of criminality or at least raciness in Cogswell, Kansas—something that would cause my readers to place this apparently unexceptional cow town in the direct line of descent from Sodom and Gomorrah.

And for that, I decided as I knocked my cigar ash into my empty coffee cup, I needed to visit the local newspaper office.

The *Cogswell Free American* was quartered on the second floor of a swaybacked frame building a few doors down the street from the Drovers State Bank. Access was by means of a steep stairway on the outside of the building. I climbed the stairs and opened the door.

Inside was a single room that ran the length and breadth of the building, but still seemed cramped by everything that was crowded into it—two printing presses, one large and one small, an assortment of type fonts, barrels of printer's ink, piles of (mostly inky) cotton waste, stacks of exchange newspapers and other stacks of back issues of the *Free American*, envelopes full of clippings, coffee cups, odds and ends of clothing, and other detritus that defied quick classification. The room had two occupants: a man in a black printer's apron lay on his back on a mattress of newspapers, snoring through a thicket of unkempt whiskers; and in the far corner of the room, behind a desk whose pigeonholes were even more cluttered than Sheriff Bybee's, a man with the green eyeshade and sleeve garters of an editor blinked at me and called querulously, "All right, I see you. What do you want?"

I told him my name and identified myself as his brother in the great fraternity of journalism. He swore and spat into a pile of waste. "You're the one that blew the whistle on the confidence men? Well, that wasn't a bad day's work, even if there are a few solid citizens around here who wouldn't agree with me. Come over here where I don't have to yell at you. Don't step on Oscar there—I don't need him awake for another two hours, and if he wakes up now he'll be drunk again by ten o'clock."

I stepped over the sleeping printer and threaded my way to the editor's desk. He indicated a chair, and I removed three books from it and sat down. He folded his hands behind his head and put his feet on his desk. "My name's Hamp Wyeth, Moretti, and I'm the owner, publisher, editor, head reporter, and columnist of this mighty organ of public opinion. I bid you welcome."

I said I was glad to meet all five of him. He smiled, which made his face look like that of a fifty-year-old schoolboy. "I don't suppose you'd like a drink, would you?" he asked.

"Well, even though it's a bit before my usual hour—" I began.

"I'm sorry to say I don't have a drop on the premises. Can't afford to—Oscar there would find it and drink himself to death." His expression became monitory. "Besides, drinking in the morning is terrible for you; it's those precious hours of sobriety between breakfast time and noon that separate the productive citizen from the souse." He reached into one of his pigeonholes and produced a jar of unappetizing candies. "Forget your craving and have a peppermint."

I popped one into my mouth with small enthusiasm. "Thank you," I said obediently.

Wyeth helped himself to a drop and shoved the bottle

back into its pigeonhole. "All right, Moretti," he said briskly, "now do you want to tell me what *really* brought you to Cogswell?"

"Why, just what you said—to blow the whistle on a couple of confidence men who were unwise enough to fleece the nephew of the owner of my paper."

"And that's absolutely the only reason you had for coming here?"

"What other reason could I possibly have?"

He sucked on his peppermint drop noisily and answered my question with another question. "In that case I imagine you'll be leaving town as soon as you've sent off your story about Kid Slaughter and the fight store, won't you? There wouldn't be anything else to keep you here, would there?"

"Should there be?"

He studied me for a moment. "All right, Moretti, what do you want from me?"

"Whatever you can tell me to make Cogswell sound interesting. To put it bluntly, all the dirt you can think of."

He considered my words for a moment. "All right, if that's the way you want to deal 'em," he answered. "Okay, I'll give you what I have, but you have to remember I only go back to eighteen-seventy. That was the year I bought the *Free American*, so I can't tell you too much about the massacre or the bank robbery."

"Massacre? Bank robbery?" I asked. I felt the same tremor of half-recognition that had occurred when I had first passed the Drovers Bank.

Wyeth frowned in disbelief. "The Cogswell Massacre. General Warren Quarrles, the Angel of Death. The missing hundred and ten thousand dollars. The fight at Hunter's Creek ford. And you never heard of any of it, I suppose?"

It came back to me then, all of it that I was familiar with. It was one of the war stories I had heard when I was growing up in Corbo County, Ohio, and which I had remembered because it was bizarre and bloody, like the Petersburg Crater, the McAndrews locomotive chase, and the business at Fort Pillow. I nodded. "Of course I remember now. The Confederate Angel of Death—that's what he called himself. He was proud of it. He must have been one of the worst butchers of the war, and it was here in Cogswell that he did his worst butchering." I shook my head ruefully. "Of course I remember."

"He was bad enough, I reckon," Wyeth agreed. "Want me to refresh you on the details? Like I said, I wasn't here then, but I've learned a good deal about it since I came."

I said I would, very much, and he leaned back in his chair, looked up at the ceiling, and began. "Quarrles came out here from someplace back East in the early fifties. He was a schoolteacher, taught in the school here in Cogswell for two years, until he got a girl in trouble and had to skedaddle. He was lucky not to get the tar and feathers. The whole business gave him an unfriendly feeling toward Cogswell, which, not being a forgiving man, he carried with him from then on.

"Things were bad in Kansas in those days. The rest of the country was still three or four years away from the War Between the States, but Kansas was smack dab in the middle of it. Free-state sodbusters were pouring in from the North, and pro-slavery border ruffians from Missouri were trying to intimidate them. Well, that state of affairs was just dandy for Warren Quarrles, who apparently figured he had a higher destiny than just being a small town ex-schoolteacher.

"Quarrles was pro-slavery. I don't know why, seeing as how he came from Ohio or Indiana or someplace like that, but my theory is he liked to think of himself as a member of a superior race, and how can you be superior if somebody else isn't inferior? Anyhow, he went to Missouri and joined up with one of the gangs, along with such worthies as Cole Younger and Frank and Jesse James."

I crunched my peppermint drop between my teeth, and

Wyeth immediately offered me another. "No thanks—I know my limit. Go on. How did the schoolteacher become the Angel of Death?"

"Well, at least partly because of that maniac John Brown. After Brown killed five men in cold blood at Pottawatomie, there was a bull market for guerrilla leaders in Missouri; with any plausibility at all, a small boy with a slingshot could recruit a regiment of dedicated ruffians. So Quarrles went into business for himself, you might say— got himself a gang of cutthroats and started raiding across the border. He had built himself a reputation by the time the war broke out, so Jeff Davis sent him a commission in the Confederate cavalry, so he could murder and rob in a pretty gray uniform instead of civilian clothes."

"And then he raided Cogswell?" I asked.

"Not until eighteen sixty-three. By that time he wasn't flying the Confederate flag anymore; he and his men were riding under the black flag. That's right"—he nodded at my unspoken question—"the black flag of anarchy, that means you don't obey any laws but your own. When Quarrles came to Cogswell he was no longer under the control of the Confederacy, even though he and his men still wore Confederate uniforms. He was known as the Angel of Death by that time—it sounds like the kind of name he would have thought up for himself—and I reckon he deserved it if anybody did."

Wyeth paused and shook his head, as if he were reminded of more cruelties, more brutality and death, than he cared to remember. Then he began to describe the Great Cogswell Massacre.

Warren Quarrles and his band of approximately eighty guerrillas had ridden into Cogswell shortly after nine in the morning. Quarrles had divided his forces outside of town, and the raiders came from two directions, part from the northeast, part from the south. By the time they met outside the Drovers State Bank they had already killed twelve peo-

ple. Quarrles led a half-dozen men into the bank while the
rest of the band wreaked havoc outside, racing back and
forth along the streets and firing at everything that moved.
While their leader was inside the bank they killed eighteen
people and wounded twenty more. Most, but not all, of
the dead were men; one was a nine-year-old boy shot as
he stared saucer-eyed from a second-story window.

Quarrles emerged from the bank with a sackful of money
over his shoulder and two captives stumbling behind him,
prodded by the pistols of his men. One was the president
of the bank and the other was the assistant cashier, and
both their faces were dead white in the morning sun.
Quarrles ordered them mounted with their hands tied behind them. He busied himself stuffing his saddlebags with
the bank's currency, and told his lieutenant to burn the
town.

By this time most of the guerrillas were in Cogswell's
largest saloon (Kansas was wet in those days) and there
were only a handful available to act as incendiaries, which
explains the survival of a large part of the town. However,
the livery stable, the jail, the general store, the dry-goods
store, the barbershop, two other saloons, and a dozen private homes were burned to the ground. Among the dozen
people incinerated in the fire were a deranged woman and
her paralyzed husband, and three small children.

Quarrles and his officers succeeded in persuading their
troopers to leave the now-smoldering barroom, and soon
the guerrillas were remounted, most with open whiskey
bottles in their hands. The band and its two hostages set
off down Main Street toward Carrsville, twelve miles to
the south. On the way out of town they killed three more
times—first when an eighty-nine-year-old man was struck
in the head by a thrown whiskey bottle, second when a
teen-age boy injudiciously leaned out of his front door to
see the dashing cavalrymen and took a bullet in the lungs,
third when a young wife screamed in outrage at a guerrilla

as he rode her husband down, and received a bullet in exchange.

Quarrles left the command half a mile south of town, after ordering his second in command to proceed to Hunter's Creek ford, where he was to halt the men and wait for him. The guerrilla band continued six miles to the ford, where they amused themselves for half an hour by stringing up their hostages and using them for target practice.

Then they were approached, not by their commander, but by two troops of Union cavalry and a hundred or so mounted and armed civilians who had followed them from Cogswell. A few of the guerrillas escaped across the creek, but most of them were surrounded by their pursuers; as they were outnumbered and fuddled with alcohol besides, their resistance didn't last long.

The Union cavalry commander looked at Quarrles's black flag and decided to turn the prisoners over to the Cogswell civilians for custody. The civilians waited until the troopers were out of sight and then murdered the lot of them.

But Quarrles had escaped. The Gray Angel of Death was still loose, still on horseback, with a fortune in stolen money to finance new outrages against bleeding Kansas. For forty-eight hours the countryside shook with the tumult of sheriff's posse and vigilante band, as well as the bugle calls of the army.

They captured him in a barn twenty miles west of the Missouri line. He offered no resistance. The saddlebags had disappeared. He was taken to the nearest army guardhouse and locked up to await his trial and inevitable execution. According to his guards, all he would say was that the money was hidden where no one would find it until he, Quarrles, was ready for it to be found—and that the town of Cogswell had not seen the last of the Gray Angel of Death.

Two days later, in a manner that has never been explained, he escaped. He was never seen again, in Kansas or, as far as anyone has reported, anywhere else.

"Although I have a hunch," Wyeth concluded thoughtfully, "that he's out on the West Coast somewhere."

"What gives you that idea?"

"My theory of the universal migration of malcontents. Did you ever hear of any Huns or Goths or Conquistadors moving *east*?" He answered his own question with a shake of the head. "Fat chance. There's a natural compass needle in the human race that points toward the setting sun. If you have to pull up stakes to find God or keep from being hanged, then you head west. It's a kind of winnowing process that's been going on since the beginning of history—what Darwin calls natural selection." He brooded a moment. "God knows what kind of population the state of California is going to end up with."

"How much money did Quarrles get away with?"

"You really don't know?" I said I didn't, and he shrugged his shoulders. "The bank said a hundred and ten thousand," he answered. "Of course there were the usual whispers that the figure was set high to cover up a shortage, but I've never heard anything to make me believe it."

"Is it possible to stuff a hundred thousand dollars into two saddlebags?"

Wyeth raised his eyebrows. "As a matter of fact, it is, as long as most of it is in twenties or larger."

"And nobody's seen any of it since then? No little kids toddling up to the candy counter to buy twenty dollars' worth of licorice whips?"

"Nary a one. Not a trace I've heard of in the twenty-odd years since it happened."

We sat quietly for a few moments, listening to the snores of Oscar the printer on his mattress of newspapers and thinking about the Gray Angel of Death. I had the uneasy feeling I often get when I reflect on the War Between the States—as if it is simultaneously ancient history and as contemporary as the Oklahoma land rush and the incandescent lamp, as if its veterans are middle-aged men yarning about half-forgotten battles, and yet the hatreds it generated are as real as hot breath on the back of your neck.

I changed the subject. "When I first came in, Mr. Wyeth, you said something I didn't understand. You said, 'Blowing the whistle on the confidence men was a good day's work, even if there are a few solid citizens who wouldn't agree with me.' What exactly did you mean by that?"

Wyeth snorted. "Moretti, Tommy Tompkins has been here in Cogswell for over a year now with no known legal means of support. Most of that time he's been running his fight store. There's been a steady stream of pugs, grifters, and marks through the Barnard Hotel. Anybody who hasn't noticed them must be looking very carefully the other way."

"You mean like Sheriff Bybee? You think he's being paid off?"

Wyeth looked shocked and sucked audibly on his peppermint drop. "Paid off? Alf Bybee? Why, he'd let daylight through you if you offered him a five-cent cigar! No, Alf couldn't be bribed—but he could very easily not notice certain goings-on that were bringing money into town, especially if he thought the victims had it coming anyway. Cogswell can use all the money it can get."

"When I went to see him he was glad enough to cooperate on a raid."

"I guess he figured too many people had gotten to know about Tompkins's fight store—it had gotten too big to ignore any longer, with a reporter from a New York newspaper nosing around. So Alf decided to come down on them. Of course he had no idea he was going to find a dead body in the ring."

"What other 'solid citizens' wouldn't agree with you about blowing the whistle?"

He shifted his lanky body in his chair and reversed the position of the large feet crossed in front of him on the desk. "Why, the people who were making the most money out of the business—like Wally Stebbins and his wife Flo, who own the hotel. And like Elwood Flocker, who runs the Drovers Bank. And of course Moll Sweeney, at the House of Delights, and Mole, who does most of the bootlegging business around town. Our night-life entrepreneurs, you might say."

"I've met Mr. Mole and sampled his wares," I admitted. "But Miss Sweeney's offerings are still an untapped reservoir to me. If you've some suggestions in regard to her personnel, I'd take it as a great kindness to hear them."

Wyeth took his feet off his desk and leaned forward. "Well, this is only secondhand information, you understand, but I've heard some fascinating things about a brassy-haired filly named Billie Mae who came to Moll's a couple of months ago." He leaned closer and lowered his voice. "Now I'm no expert on unusual biological and physiological endowments of females, but would you believe it possible for a woman—"

"If I ever saw two men talking about something they had no business to talk about, it's you two!" cried a melodious soprano voice behind me. I turned guiltily and found myself staring into the bright cornflower-blue eyes of the blond vision I had first seen in the hotel restaurant when I was dining with Jack Farringay. Her white-gold hair glowed in the room's dull light, and the gray skirt and powder-blue shirtwaist she wore, while not chosen to advertise the appetizing curves within, certainly did nothing to conceal them.

"You keep pussyfooting around," Wyeth growled with affectionate sternness, "and you'll hear things that you've got no business to hear, and that's a fact! Moretti, this is my daughter Ellen. Ellen, this is Mr. Moretti, the big New

York reporter that busted up Tommy Tompkins's bunco game.''

The corners of Ellen Wyeth's eyes crinkled as she smiled. She put out her hand to shake mine. Her fingers were small and cool. ''That wasn't a bad day's work, Mr. Moretti,'' she said.

''That's exactly what your father said—although to be sure it sounds sweeter coming from you than it did from him.'' I bowed over her hand, which I fancied she allowed to rest in mine a fraction of a second longer than politeness required.

''So now I suppose we'll be reading about Cogswell in the New York newspapers. Well, I just hope you spell our names right, Mr. Moretti.''

''Ah, it's not likely I'll be forgetting how to spell the name of Wyeth, not after the pleasure of meeting you, Miss Ellen.'' My accent had become as heavy as Irish soda bread, and there didn't seem to be anything I could do about it.

Ellen's smile broadened, and a dimple appeared in her left cheek. She cocked her head to one side and considered me. ''You have a way with the blarney, Mr. Moretti.''

''Me first name is Paddy, which I hope you'll call me by, if I'm not presuming on too short an acquaintance.''

''Since Daddy introduced us, I'm sure it will be perfectly respectable.'' She turned to her father. ''What I need from you, sir, is some money. There's an absolutely mouth-watering green silk taffeta that's just come in at Tuttle's. It will make up like a dream, and it's only thirty-one cents a yard, and I need ten yards. And there's a lovely black silk braid for trimming, and it's seventeen cents a yard and I need at least six yards. And they've got a gray seal plush—''

Wyeth interrupted with a groan. ''This is worse than the Chinese water torture. Can't you just give me a figure for the complete damage?''

"With careful management I can get by for five dollars. Just consider it my reporter's wages for this week."

"Reporter's wages? Whoever heard of a reporter spending his wages on black seal taffeta plush or whatever?" He fumbled around on his desk and found a decrepit leather wallet. "A Chinaman can feed a family for a year on five dollars," he said as he passed her the money.

"I'll remember that as I'm throwing your money around," she replied primly. "Good day, Mr.—Paddy. I hope I see you again before you leave Cogswell."

"Your daddy and I have about finished here. Maybe you wouldn't mind if I joined you while you walk to your store," I suggested with attempted casualness. "We might even have a bit of lunch if you've a mind to."

Ellen glanced dutifully at her father. He shrugged. "Don't see why not," he said. "Nice to meet you, Moretti. If I can do anything else for you—whatever it is you're after—let me know." As we began to work our way between the piles of newspapers he called after us, "Oh, step on Oscar on your way out, will you? I guess it's late enough."

6

In Quest of Quarrles

We descended the stairway outside the *Free American* building. Ellen Wyeth turned to face me at the bottom of the stairs. "I'm sorry if this is an indelicate question, but I have to know," she said in a voice edged with anxiety. "Was my father drinking with you this morning?"

"Why, no," I answered in surprise. "Quite the contrary—he gave me a temperance lecture. About how sober mornings were the difference between the productive citizen and the souse."

"Then why were both of you sucking on those peppermint drops?" she demanded, her blue eyes dark with suspicion.

"I presume because your father likes them. He had a jar in his desk. Why, are you worried about him?"

"Oh, no—" she began, shaking her head in denial. She hesitated, then continued in a lower voice, "I'm worried to death! He's promised to stop, but I don't know if he will. It's gotten worse and worse during the last few months, and now it's hurting the paper. Names misspelled, stories not covered, deadlines missed—I do what I can, but it's not enough to make up for him when he's—when he's under the influence.''

"I see,'' I said uncomfortably. ''Well, for what it's worth, I'm reasonably sure he hadn't been drinking this morning. Although I can't say the same for Oscar the printer.''

"Oh, Oscar—'' She waved one hand in dismissal. ''Well, forgive me for burdening you with my problems, Mr. Moretti—''

"Paddy.''

"Paddy.'' She smiled, and the dimple appeared in her cheek. ''If you're going to walk me to Tuttle's, we better get started.''

Ellen Wyeth shopped with the painstaking relentlessness of an ambitious music student running scales. Even though she had decided on her purchases before entering the store, she nevertheless inspected every other bolt of material on the shelves, her lovely face set in a frown of concentration. Every so often she would appeal to my judgment with a ''How do you think these would look together?'' or a ''Do you think this is too young (or old) for me?'' and I would reply that they would be bewitching together, and of course they didn't look too young (or old).

When she finally paid her money and I tucked her neatly wrapped bundle of material under my arm, it was noon and time for luncheon. We stepped out into the harsh wind and headed toward the Barnard Hotel. Ellen walked with short, quick steps, and I felt like a Clydesdale as I lumbered along beside her. I made small talk about Cogswell and the West in general.

"Oh, I think the West has left us and moved farther on,'' she said. ''At least we're not what they call the Wild West anymore.''

"Your father said much the same thing. He said it was due to a natural compass needle in all malcontents that points toward the setting sun.''

She pursed her pretty mouth. "You don't have to explain it. I'm an authority on all my father's theories." She stopped and pointed to the wall of the building we were passing; it was the Drovers State Bank. "Do you see those holes there? They're bullet holes, from the Quarrles raid, the famous Cogswell Massacre. I grew up in this town hearing stories about robbings and killings and lynchings, showdowns and backshootings, cattle rustling and barn burning, crooked card games and drunken brawls, and sometime during those years it changed from the way things *are* to the way things *were*, and that suits me just fine. Cogswell may not be very exciting anymore, but it's a place where a person can plan ahead and look forward to making a life for himself."

I thought that a woman with Ellen Wyeth's face and figure could make a considerably more interesting life for herself in Chicago or New York City. "There was a fair amount of excitement out at the Eakins place yesterday," I pointed out to her.

"Of course there's always *some* excitement—but that boxer's death was an accident, and all those people out there were outsiders, except for Tommy Tompkins, and even he's not what you'd call a real Cogswellite."

I took her arm and helped her over a curb. "What do you mean, not a real Cogswellite?"

"I understand he's a local boy who grew up here before the war. But he didn't come back until last year, when he started bringing those fighters and gamblers here. And he's never really been part of the town. It's as if he's—*extraneous*—like the treasure hunters who descend on us every summer."

We paused as a farm wagon crossed our path, the horse's hoofs and then the creaking wheels splattering mud on our shoes. "Treasure hunters?" I repeated.

"Looking for the Drovers Bank money that Quarrles stole. The famous hundred-and-ten-thousand-dollar saddlebags. They're supposed to be hidden somewhere around here, you know, where the Gray Angel left them before he was captured."

"And lots of men come here looking for them?"

"Oh, we get forty or fifty every summer—in spite of Quarrles's curse." She gave a little laugh. "If it wasn't for the curse, I guess we'd have hundreds."

"You mean what Quarrles is supposed to have said after they caught up with him—that nobody would find the money until he was ready for it to be found, and that Cogswell hadn't heard the last of him? That has cut down the number of treasure hunters?"

"That and the accidents," she replied. At my look of inquiry she went on. "Oh, there have been a number of accidents among those people during the last few years. All perfectly natural, perfectly ordinary, but unfortunately enough to cause some superstitious talk."

"Such as?"

Her tone became impatient. "Oh, I don't know! A drowning in the creek, a horse rolling over on a man, a case of food poisoning. Last year two men were camping together and got into a fight and shot each other. Nothing supernatural, I can tell you that!"

"Then why do you sound like it upsets you?" I asked placatingly.

She hesitated, and then smiled ruefully. "I guess because things like curses belong to the way Cogswell was, not the way it is now. Why, today we have four churches and not a single legal saloon, and twenty years ago it was just the opposite. We have a Ladies' Literary Society and a chapter of the Eastern Star, and for the last two summers we've had our own Chautauqua!" Her voice took on the rhythm of recitation as she continued. "Cogswell is the commercial center for an area of over a thousand square miles of diversified agricultural and stock-raising interests—"

I raised my hand. "I believe it! Surely we're in the exact geographical heart of Utopia. I never doubted it for a minute!"

Ellen laughed in embarrassment. "I guess I sounded like—like some businessman or something."

"Well, certainly like an enthusiast." I saw we were in front of the Barnard Hotel. I took her arm and said, "Let's get something to eat before we fall swooning of starvation." We crossed the lobby of the hotel and entered the restaurant door. The room was nearly full, and I believe every male eye in the establishment fixed itself upon Ellen Wyeth with unwinking intensity. She either ignored or was unconscious of the interest she aroused; as we took our seats and awaited our waitress she focused her attention entirely upon me.

Who knows where a man may find perfection? I asked myself. *Roses bloom on dungheaps. Cinderella was at home with mops and buckets before the Ball. Why shouldn't I find the girl of my dreams on the Kansas prairie?*

I regarded her pink-and-gold loveliness a moment before regretfully pulling my thoughts back to business. "Your father told me Warren Quarrles lived here in Cogswell before the war. Are there many people around who knew him then?"

"Oh, I don't think so." She paused to give her order to the waitress and waited while I gave mine, and then continued. "Everything has changed so, and it was so long ago . . ." She frowned thoughtfully. "Of course, there's Miss Carrie Heckman—she taught at the school the same time as he did. She retired five years ago. She's an old maid, and lives with a cousin here in town." She gave me an address, which I jotted down in my notebook.

"Then there's the brother of the girl"—she hesitated and gave a little cough—"the girl with whom he was involved. Her name was Sally Kilpatrick. Harve Kilpatrick runs a lumberyard on the north side of town.'' She gave me directions and I wrote them down.

"Oh, of course," she continued. "There's Elwood Flocker—he's the president of the Drovers Bank. They say that he and Warren Quarrles were best friends back before the war. And then that they became particular enemies."

"How did that happen?"

"Well, you understand this is all gossip—but I understand that Sally Kilpatrick was Mr. Flocker's girl first, and that Warren Quarrles betrayed his friendship." She lowered her eyes as I said, "Aha."

I wrote down Flocker's name. "Anyone else you can think of?"

She mentioned three more people, whom I dutifully jotted down. One was a retired Methodist preacher named Hardie, the second was a railroad employee named McGerr, and the third was a farmer-stockman named Henderson. That was the crop.

I put my notebook in my pocket. Ellen looked levelly at me. "Now *you* tell *me* something," she said. "Why do you want those names?"

I sighed. "I honestly don't know, Ellen. Mostly, I think it's because I have a thin story to fill out, and Warren Quarrles is the most interesting thing that ever happened in Cogswell, and maybe if I can borrow some of that interest for my story it will keep a carnivorous editor from eating me alive." As she continued to regard me questioningly, I added, "It's me intuitive Celtic and Latin blood, no doubt."

Our food came. Ellen ate daintily, but with good appetite, and between bites questioned me about the enchantments of a reporter's life in New York City. Did I attend the opera and the theater? Did I dine at Delmonico's and Rector's and Sherry's? Had I met the Vanderbilts and the Astors? My answers were somewhat equivocal; I failed to tell her that I was considerably more at home in Tony Pastor's Bowery vaudeville theater than in any opera house, and that the only time I ever ate at Sherry's I almost had my brains blown out by a killer with a derringer. I don't believe I mentioned the free lunch at McSorley's Saloon, either.

"Don't let's talk any more about me, macushla," I said. "Let's talk about *you*, and what you plan to do with the rest of your life."

"Oh, there's nothing to tell about me," she began. Then her eyes widened, her lips parted, her bosom swelled, and her hands clapped together. "Oh, I was hoping I'd see you!" she cried.

"Ah, the feeling is mutual, to be sure!" I replied eagerly.

"I've had a long morning over the account books," said an irritable voice behind me, "and I thought I owed myself a good meal."

I turned to see the tall young man with the colorless hair and vacuous expression who had been with Ellen the first time I saw her in the restaurant. He was wearing a dark suit that had apparently been purchased from a mail-order catalogue, a celluloid collar, and a black string tie. His mouth-breathing suggested overdeveloped adenoids, and there was a pimple under one of his large ears. His expression was perhaps a shade less vacuous than the last time I had seen him.

"How are you, Ellen?" he asked as he lifted an unoccupied chair from a nearby table and sat down beside us. "What's good today?"

From the expression on her face I would have thought we had been joined by Maurice Barrymore. "Oh, sit down with us, Harold," she cried unnecessarily. "Harold, I'd like you to meet Mr. Paddy Moretti from New York City. Mr. Moretti, this is Harold Anspaugh. Harold is our local pharmacist—he's a graduate *cum laude* of the Briggs School of Pharmacology in Kansas City, and he makes up all the prescriptions himself!"

Harold Anspaugh favored me with a cursory glance. "How do, Mr. Moretti. I tell you, Ellen, it's hard lines for a man that wants to make something of himself in this world. I added up columns of figures till I thought my eyes were going to fall out of my head, honest to Pete." He reached over to another table for a napkin and unfolded it in his lap. "I'll be glad when we're married and you can do my bookkeeping for me."

Ellen blushed and lowered her eyes demurely.

The waitress came and Harold Anspaugh ordered his luncheon. She asked if Ellen and I wanted dessert. My appetite had disappeared like water in dry sand, but Ellen attacked her tapioca pudding with suddenly increased enthusiasm and prattled on to Harold while he ate pot roast and I drank a cup of coffee.

I couldn't stand it. I called for the check. Harold, his cheeks bulging like a squirrel's, said thickly, "Now, I don't want you paying all the bill, Mr. Moretti. You just figure out what you and Ellen had and let me pay the rest."

"That's very liberal of you, Mr. Anspaugh." I bowed to Ellen. "Forgive me for rushing off, but I have a story to write for a very unsympathetic editor, and it's past time I was getting at it. Thank you for bringing a bit of grace and beauty to a lonely man's repast."

As I walked out of the restaurant I thought disconsolately, *A druggist! A druggist who values her principally for her abilities as a bookkeeper! My God, she's only a mortar to his pestle!* It was a metaphor I immediately regretted.

In the lobby I stared toward the stairs and then hesitated. Rather than begin work on my story, I decided to put the list of names Ellen had given me to use. Something told me that the trump cards that I thought I had discovered in my hand the day before would turn out to be considerably less potent than they had seemed—that when I sat down to satisfy Hochmuth, I would need a good deal more than I had.

Miss Carrie Heckman lived in a back bedroom in a cousin's home. The cousin's wife admitted me into the house and showed me up the stairs. "I don't know how much longer she's going to be with us," she said in a voice loud enough to be audible throughout the house. "She's got something growing inside her, some kind of tumor, I expect. Her belly's all swole up." She paused in front of an open bedroom door. "She's in there. Don't be surprised if she don't make any sense. She's going downhill." She put her head in the door. "Here's a man to see you, Miss Carrie. Name of Moretti, from New York."

I thanked the cousin's wife and entered the small room. A tiny woman wearing a blue satin bed jacket over her nightgown sat supported by pillows in a narrow bed. Her hair was so thin her scalp reflected light through it, and her face was eroded by a web of wrinkles, but her eyes, which echoed the bright blue of the bed jacket, were alert. Her skeletal hands were folded over a protuberant belly that looked as if it weighed as much as all the rest of her together. There was a sweetish smell of decay in the room.

"Yes, I remember Warren Quarrles," she said in answer to my question. "He wasn't the kind of man you forget— it wouldn't be safe to forget him. If you did, he just might come back and teach you a lesson.

"I remember one day not long after he started teaching here, one of those long, hot September days when it's all you can do to keep your eyes open through the afternoon. There were two rooms in the schoolhouse; I had my little ones in one room, and taught the bigger children in the other. Well, all of a sudden I heard this crashing noise from Warren's room, along with yelling and carrying-on like an Indian raid. I thought someone was being murdered. I ran in and saw Warren and this big boy—he must have been

eighteen years old, and a good three inches taller than Warren—rolling on the floor and punching and gouging each
other." She shook her head in remembered wonder. "It
seems the boy had dozed off while Warren was demonstrat-
ing the extraction of square roots. An unforgivable insult."

"Who won?" I asked.

She laughed, a sound like an ear of corn being husked.
"Oh, Warren, of course. Warren always won—he couldn't
have stood not to. I think at one time or another he fought
every boy in his class who was bigger than he was, and
beat them all. I believe it was necessary for him to prove
to his students that he surpassed them in all ways. Not just
intellectually—they expected that, of course—but physically, morally, in will, in ambition, in tenacity—in every
way that was important to them." She laughed again.
"Not, however, in humor or tolerance, I'm afraid."

"It sounds as if he was already practicing to be a mili-
tary leader."

"It's hard to know what Warren planned. He always
seemed to be looking ahead to a future that was different
from anything other people expected." She shifted her body
against the pillows and pressed her fingers into her stomach. "You're from New York, Mr. Moretti? Why does a
gentleman from New York want to know about Warren
Quarrles?"

"He's quite a famous man, as I'm sure you must know,
Miss Heckman," I said.

"Infamous, I think you mean," she corrected. "Oh, yes,
I know. The dashing General Warren Quarrles, the Gray
Angel of Death." She glanced toward one corner of the
room. "There's a framed picture of him on the wall there.
Would you like to see it?"

I took the small picture down from its nail and brought
it over to the bed. It was an illustration from a magazine,
Harper's or *Leslie's* probably, neatly matted and framed
under glass. It showed a man in the uniform of a Confed-

erate cavalry officer standing, one gauntleted hand on hip and one jackbooted knee bent, amid a half-dozen soldiers of lower rank. The officer had dark, oriental eyes and a drooping black mustache, and was shorter than most of the men around him. The drawing was unsigned, but it could have been by Winslow Homer.

I studied the picture and then handed it to her. She gazed at it a moment, her bloodless lips pulling down at the corners. "He was always a handsome man, although not as tall as he would have liked to be," she said reflectively. "It was one of the things he had to compensate for, I think." She put the picture against her stomach and folded her hands over it and looked at me coolly with her bright blue eyes. "We were engaged to be married once, you know."

"No, I didn't know."

"Oh, yes. At the end of his first year at the school—that would have been the spring of 'fifty-seven. Everyone thought we were a lovely couple. We had very serious conversations about art and literature and politics, particularly politics, because Warren was thinking about running for office."

"As a Democrat?"

"Oh, goodness no. He was very much a Free-Soiler in those days. It was the coming thing, he said." She smiled. "He was very convincing. I began to see myself as a senator's wife, sweeping through Washington society on the arm of a man of destiny."

"What happened, Miss Heckman?" I asked gently.

"Oh, nothing too surprising, I expect. I was older than Warren, you see. Before he came to Cogswell most people thought of me as an old maid. They were surprised when an attractive bachelor popped the question to a thirty-five-year-old spinster. Which made them just that much more ready to say 'I told you so' six months later." Her eyes narrowed, as though she were squinting into a glaring light.

"Warren and I were very close to another couple during our courting days; we used to picnic with them often, and read poetry aloud together, and sing songs around the harmonium—"

"Sally Kilpatrick and Elwood Flocker," I said.

She didn't seem to notice the interruption. "—and did all the things young people did together in those days," she continued. "Her name was Sally, a beautiful young girl, very soft-spoken and considerate, but with a will of her own. She was much younger than I, not more than nineteen or twenty. I liked her very much. I won't mention her beau's name, because he's quite an important person in Cogswell now, married to another woman, with a fine family and a lovely home.

"As I said, both couples were engaged. Our relationships were chaste, Mr. Moretti. Warren respected me and Sally's beau respected her. Both men were gentlemen, and gentlemen do not establish physical relationships with ladies outside of holy wedlock. Or so I believed.

"It came as a considerable shock to me to learn that Warren and Sally were physically intimate. It also came as a considerable shock to Sally's beau, who discovered the pair in a compromising position in a barn on Sally's farm."

"What did El—what did Sally's beau do to the scoundrel?"

She made a dry sound, which could have been either a chuckle or a cough. "First he tried to thrash Warren, but I believe was not successful at it. Then he wanted to challenge him to a duel, but was persuaded not to by his friends, who were apprehensive of Warren's marksmanship. Finally he armed himself with a horsewhip and led a group to Warren's house, with the intention of first whipping him and then tarring and feathering him and riding him out of town on a rail."

"What happened?"

"Warren left before they got there. Unlike some other men who later became Confederate leaders, Warren Quarrles had no enthusiasm for lost causes." She was silent a moment, and when she spoke again her thin voice was weaker than it had been, and unsteady. "I never saw him again, Mr. Moretti. And I'm afraid that's all I can tell you about General Quarrles."

"What about the girl, Sally?" I asked.

"She left three months later—when she started to show." A grimace of pain crossed her face and she closed her eyes. When she opened them again she said, "You must excuse me now. I think I will rest for a few minutes."

I rose and thanked her for seeing me. Reaching out my hand, I said, "I'll be glad to hang that picture back on the wall before I leave." She handed it to me, and I pointed to the face of a burly corporal who towered over Warren Quarrles in the drawing. "By the way, Miss Heckman—do you recognize this soldier here?"

She glanced incuriously at the picture. "No. Should I?"

"Oh, no." I replaced the picture on its nail, said goodbye, and closed the bedroom door behind me. As I descended the stairs I reflected on the curious fact that one of the Gray Angel's noncommissioned henchmen was indubitably the same man I had seen die in the prize ring in Eakins's barn—Kid Slaughter, twenty-five years younger.

Kilpatrick's Lumber Yard was ten minutes' walk from the center of Cogswell. In the cool spring air the odor of new-cut white pine was almost intoxicating. I breathed deeply as I skirted a pile of bright new planks and entered a one-room office building.

Two men were working inside. One, stooped and white-haired, sat at a desk stacked with ledgers near the door. The other, a man of about forty-five with a florid complexion and a pitted skin, was studying a blueprint at another, larger desk. He lowered the sheet and looked up at me. "Yes?" he asked in a harsh voice.

I told him who I was. "I'm interested in anything you can tell me about General Warren Quarrles," I said.

"Jervis, get the hell out of here. I'll call you when I want you back." The white-haired man rose and left the room without a word. Kilpatrick rolled his hands into fists and leaned forward on them. "Now, just what the devil do you mean walking in here and mentioning that son-of-a-bitch's name?" he demanded.

I said I was sorry if the subject was a sensitive one, but the newspaper I worked for was interested in Quarrles and the Cogswell Massacre, and I'd like to ask him a few questions if he didn't mind.

"Well, I do mind. I mind a hell of a lot. Quarrles was a traitor and a murderer and a thief, and the sooner everybody in this country forgets about him the better off we'll be. Now tell me something: who gave you the idea of coming to me?"

"You must know, Mr. Kilpatrick, it's common knowledge that your sister and Warren Quarrles were—" I began. He came around the desk faster than I would have believed possible, with one fist raised above his shoulder at full cock. His face was as dark as raw beef. I was barely able to slip around the clerk's desk before he reached me. Keeping the desk between us, I said reasonably, "Now what's the point of this, Mr. Kilpatrick? Beating me up isn't going to change what happened here thirty years ago, is it? What's done is done, and nothing in the world is going to change that."

For a moment he stood glaring at me with his chest heaving and his fist poised. Then he lowered his arm and released his breath in a long exhalation. "You're right—nothing in the world is going to change that." He looked at the floor for a moment, then he raised his eyes and said with an apologetic smile, ''Sorry if I got a little hot under the collar. Ask any questions you want.''

''I'm trying to find out as much as I can about the kind of man Quarrles was. I know you don't like him, and with good reason, but I'd appreciate any specific facts you can give me.''

Kilpatrick walked back to his own desk and sat down. He rubbed his knuckles and spoke in a quiet, even voice. ''I was five years younger than my sister Sally. She was keeping company with Elwood Flocker, and Quarrles was courting Miss Carrie Heckman, the other schoolteacher—at least that's what people thought. Well, I wished it was the other way around. I thought Flocker was a big drink of water—still do, as a matter of fact. And I thought Warren Quarrles would have made the best brother-in-law in the world.

''I hero-worshiped the man. I thought he was the smartest, gamest, resourcefulest bastard that ever lived. Sometimes he'd let me go along with him and Elwood when they went varmint-hunting; he could track like a Cheyenne, and never tried a shot he wasn't sure of making. Old Elwood, he couldn't hardly hit a cow with a broom at five paces. Or if we were fishing Quarrles would show me where the lunkers were, and he was always right. He'd hardly ever wet a line and not pull out two or three good ones before he was finished.

''And all the time he'd be telling us all kinds of things nobody else in town knew anything about—stuff about politics and science and foreign countries, and about the white man's duty to be the leader of mankind.'' Kilpatrick frowned at me as if I had contradicted him. ''That's right—the leader of mankind. He talked a lot about leadership. About how it wasn't a privilege, it was an obligation. He said if you were one of the few who was destined for leadership and you didn't take it, then you were sacrilegious, because you were opposing God's will.''

"If you're one of the chosen few, it's a good idea to let yourself be chosen," I said.

"That's right. I thought it was really unfair that I was going to get Elwood Flocker for a brother-in-law instead of a destined leader like Warren Quarrles. Particularly after he saved my life."

"Warren Quarrles saved your life?"

"Yes. We were swimming in the creek near our farm, and I got caught in an underwater tree-branch. I cracked my head when I dived in and I would have drowned if Quarrles hadn't come down after me and pulled me out. I came to on the bank, with Warren and Elwood looking down at me."

"Didn't Elwood help get you out?" I asked.

His mouth twisted in contempt. "Elwood? Elwood was scared of the water. Hell, if I'd waited for Elwood to pull me out, I'd still be under the creek today! No, it was Warren Quarrles saved my life, and I was so grateful I couldn't stand it. I thought what a wonderful, brave, intelligent, fine fellow he was—and all the time the sneaky son-of-a-bitch was screwing my sister in the barn!" He shook his head as if, three decades later, he still had difficulty comprehending the fact.

"One thing I don't understand, Mr. Kilpatrick. Obviously Sally and Quarrles were attracted to each other—why didn't they just break their engagements and get married? Particularly after Elwood caught them in the act?"

"Because Miss Carrie Heckman had inherited some money, and the Kilpatricks were as poor as Job's turkey and getting poorer by the day! The farm was Mama's—it had come down to her from her father—and Daddy didn't have any gift for farming. He owed the bank more than he could pay and everybody knew it. No, Warren Quarrles was too much a man of destiny to marry into a family that didn't have two dimes to rub together."

I thought for a minute. "After Quarrles left town, did

Sally hear from him? Did you think she went somewhere to meet him, after—"

"After she started to stick out in front? I don't know. I never have known. From the day she ran away, I've never heard a single word from her. As far as I know, nobody else has either."

Kilpatrick was silent, his lips pressed together as if he were tasting bitter memories. "After that," he continued, "things got worse for us. We weren't hardly able to clear enough to get us through the winter, let alone for the seed we need in the spring. Then Daddy come down with a case of the bloody flux that kept him in bed for a month.

"And then the barn burned down.

"That was the straw that broke the camel's back. After he got out of bed Daddy just sat on the porch all day and stared out over the farm like it was some kind of dangerous animal that had to be watched. I tried to keep things going, but it was too much for me. So we moved into town. Mama did sewing and took in washing, and I got a job clerking at the store. It was better than the farm."

"And you never did hear anything from Sally?"

He shook his head. "Never a word."

"Were you in Cogswell when Quarrles raided the town, Mr. Kilpatrick?"

"No, I was in the army by then—the Union army. We were chasing Pop Price all around Missouri. But Mama was here, and saw them ride right past this house, drinking out of whiskey bottles and shooting at anything that moved. Her next-door neighbor, Mr. Huberman, was on his front porch, and they shot him dead. Mama told me she saw them ride a man down in the street, and then one of the raiders pulled up and started riding back and forth over the man's body, and when a woman started to cuss him out, the Reb shot her down in cold blood."

"Did your mother see Quarrles?" I asked.

"Oh, yes. He was out in front, sitting as stiff as a ramrod

and looking straight ahead like he was on parade. Like he had nothing to do with what was going on around him. And right behind him the two hostages from the bank that he was taking along to hang." He glared at me. "By God, I'd give anything in the world if I could been there with a navy Colt in my hand when he rode by."

"If you had been, you wouldn't be here now to tell about it," I pointed out. "Tell me something, Mr. Kilpatrick. You grew up around here. Have you ever heard of a family named Slaughter hereabouts? Or of a man named Kid Slaughter?"

He shook his head. "Not that I can think of."

"How about Tommy Tompkins? I understand he was a local boy."

"Tompkins? The fellow that's been putting on those bare-knuckle fights?" He rubbed his square chin thoughtfully. "Wait a minute. There was a Tommy Tompkins in Cogswell before the war. He was a few years older than me. Never finished school—dropped out and did odd jobs for anybody who'd pay him. He ran with some pretty wild boys, if I remember. You mean he's the same Tompkins that's here now?"

"He may be. I guess everybody who's named Tompkins has Tommy for a nickname." I put out my hand. "Thanks for seeing me and talking to me."

He shook my hand. "Hope you get what you need for your story, even if I don't know why anybody'd want to read it. Who you going to see next?"

"Your friend Elwood Flocker," I answered.

"Shit. Send that bookkeeper in on your way out. Can't afford to let him waste the whole day."

The private office of the president of the Drovers State Bank would have been more appropriate to Wall Street in New York than Main Street in Cogswell. It was a large room with walnut paneling and heavy brocade curtains over the windows, so dark that even in midafternoon it took the combined efforts of three lamps to make the pictures on the walls visible. The pictures all seemed to be of Elwood Flocker—Elwood Flocker shaking hands with politicians, Elwood Flocker posing beside an assassinated grizzly bear, Elwood Flocker on horseback and on shipboard, Elwood Flocker in the bosom of his family. Identification offered no problem because the original sat behind a massive teakwood desk and observed me across silver-mounted inkwell, calendar, and fountain pens as I waded toward him through deep piling of the rug. He made no move to rise.

"Whatever it is you want, Mr. Moretti, I'll give you five minutes for it—not a second more," he said in a voice that was both low-pitched and querulous.

I introduced myself as I had to Kilpatrick, as a reporter for a New York newspaper interested in Warren Quarrles. As I talked I studied the man. He was tall, and carried too much fat on a narrow-shouldered frame. The fat tended to bunch up in certain places like his cheeks and jowls rather than distributing itself evenly over his face and neck, and I imagine it did the same under his clothes, swelling in tallowy bulges on his breasts, hips, and thighs. His graying hair was thin and carefully combed over his balding crown. He wore a massive gold signet ring on one finger.

"All right," he said when I finished. "I don't know what I can tell you, but ask away."

"Well, sir, when Quarrles and his men robbed the bank here, what was it like? Did you see him and talk to him?"

"Oh, I wasn't here that day, Mr. Moretti." He was toying with a silver letter opener, bending the slim blade between his fingers. "I was home with an earache. I suffered terribly from earaches as a young man, although for some reason I haven't had one for the past ten years." He considered the bent letter opener and then released the blade. "I've often wondered what would have happened if I *had* been there that day."

"How do you mean, sir?"

"I kept a pistol in my desk drawer," he answered significantly. "I might not have been able to get them all, but by Godfrey I could have put a bullet through Warren Quarrles!"

"You would have shot Quarrles, Mr. Flocker? Even though you and he had been best friends before he left Cogswell?"

His eyes narrowed and the letter-opener blade bent dangerously. "Where did you hear that?" he asked harshly.

I told him it wasn't hard to put together the story of Quarrles and Sally Kilpatrick and Carrie Heckman and Elwood Flocker. I repeated my question. "And you would have shot your friend Warren Quarrles, for a fact?"

"Of course I would have shot him! I would have shot him as a rebel, and a thief, and a—" He paused.

"And a fornicator," I concluded for him. "A fornicator who seduced his best friend's fiancée. That's fair enough, isn't it?"

"Mr. Moretti, you apparently want me to believe that you are concerned with thirty-year-old gossip," he said firmly, "but I'm certain it has no legitimate part in any story your newspaper plans to run on Warren Quarrles. And I remind you that the press is governed by the laws of libel in this country."

"Of course we are, and I thank you for reminding me of it," I said. "Now if we can get back to the day of the robbery, sir—what's your understanding of how much money Quarrles got away with?"

The banker stiffened. "I know exactly how much it was, because I did the audit the next day. It was a hundred and ten thousand dollars, give or take a hundred or so."

"And as far as you know, none of that money has ever reappeared?"

"That is correct—as far as I know." He shrugged. "Of course there's no reason why I *would* know. Twenty-five years is a long time, and a hundred thousand isn't really all that much money."

I looked at the heavy gold ring on his finger and wondered how much it had cost. "When was the last time you heard from Sally Kilpatrick, Mr. Flocker?" I asked.

The flesh on his neck swelled like the gills of a fish struggling to breathe. "Moretti, I am married to a fine Christian woman, and I am blessed with three lovely and accomplished daughters. My home is the show place of the county, and I paid an architect from Chicago a thousand dollars to design it for me. As you can see from the pictures on the wall, I am the friend and confidant of many of the leading men of the age. I direct the affairs of a bank that influences the economic lives of thousands of my fellow citizens. And if you think I will allow an irresponsible scribbler from New York to tarnish my reputation, you've got another think coming."

"You refuse to tell me the last time you heard from her, Mr. Flocker?"

He narrowed his eyes and leaned closer to me. "You know and I know you don't give a damn about Sally Kilpatrick, Moretti. I know what you're here for, and it hasn't anything to do with that little slut. But for your information, I never heard anything about her after she left Cogswell. Good riddance to bad rubbish is the way I feel about it."

"Oh? And what am I here for then, Mr. Flocker?"

He opened his mouth to answer and then thought better of it. Instead he withdrew a turnip-shaped watch from his vest pocket and consulted it. "Your five minutes is up," he announced.

"Sally Kilpatrick was pregnant when she left town," I

mused aloud. "Are we *sure* it was Warren Quarrles who put her in that condition?"

Flocker's neck swelled again and his face paled to the color of pipe clay. "By God, if I thought you'd ever hint at anything to the contrary—" He rose to his feet and leaned over his teakwood desk. "Now get out of here, Moretti!"

I rose and slipped my notebook into my pocket. "Thanks for the gift of your time, sir. It's an honor meeting someone as important as yourself."

I was halfway to the door when he said, "Have you heard about our local superstition, Moretti? Quarrles's curse? Nothing to it, of course—but some funny things have happened to people who came sniffing around Cogswell looking for the money he stole. They died."

He was still standing behind his desk watching me as I left the office.

7

A Ride in the Country

Back in my room I helped myself to an ounce or two of Mole's anodyne and took a look at my trump cards. I jotted them down on a sheet of paper:

1. In 1863 a Confederate general raises hell and steals $110,000, which he hides somewhere.

2. He puts a curse on the town and on anybody who tries to find his money. (?)

3. Twenty-five years later a pug dies in an illegal boxing accident. Was he one of Quarrles's raiders?

4. Some con men, caught perpetrating a swindle, now reside in the local jail.

5.

When I got to 5 I stopped and refilled my glass. My trump cards seemed to be deuces and treys of the wrong suits. How could I have deluded myself they would justify the cost and inconvenience of my stay in Cogswell to the Owner and Otto Hochmuth? A chilly awareness of approaching doom began to radiate outward from the pit of my stomach.

There was a knock on the door.

I stopped my hand in midair, where it hovered over the whiskey bottle like a spider over a trapped fly. "Come in," I called.

The door opened to reveal the diminutive figure of 'Bednego the bellman. "Mr. Moretti, you got a message, and I come up here it give it to you," he said, in case I didn't realize he was standing at my door.

"Thank you, 'Bednego. What is it?" Dutifully I searched my pockets for a coin.

"Sheriff Bybee, he say if you still interested in that prizefighting gentleman who got hisself killed out at the Eakins place, you better come over to the jail directly."

"Oh?" I felt a tentative flutter of hope as I located a dime and handed it to the tiny Negro. "Did he say why?"

"No, sir—only that somebody's fixing to take the body away." He pocketed the coin and withdrew carefully, closing the door behind him.

Outside the jail was a weatherbeaten farm wagon pulled by a swaybacked old mare whose bowed head had borne all the sadness of life. She was tethered to the hitching post. The tailgate of the wagon was down.

Sheriff Bybee was in his office, sitting at his roll-top desk. His left foot was bare, his left boot was on the floor beside his chair, and he was carefully darning a large hole in his sock. He glanced up as I entered. "Never learned how to do this till I was forty years old," he said. "Always figured why bother? Pretty soon I'd marry me a wife and she'd take care of my socks and so on. Well, all of a sudden one day I realized that I didn't know one woman in the world that would have me and probably I never would, and meanwhile I was throwing away a hell of a lot of socks. So I got me some needles and thread and a darning egg and started practicing. And you know what?" He held up the half-darned sock proudly. "There ain't all that many women can do as neat a job as that!"

"It's a beautiful job. What's this about somebody claiming Kid Slaughter's body, Sheriff?"

Bybee contemplated his sock a moment, then resumed his darning. "That's right," he said. "It's old lady Korshak, Anna Korshak and her boy Anton that ain't quite right in the head. They come in twenty minutes ago and asked if they could look at the body. I took 'em down to the basement where he's laid out, and Anna says she wants to be alone with him, so I come back here to darn my sock. Then in a couple of minutes she comes in and says she wants to take the body away with her. I says there's some paperwork I got to do first, and sends word to you at the hotel."

"Then she and her son are down in the basement now, with the mortal remains?"

He nodded. "I thought you might want to have a word with Anna before she packs it away."

"Thanks, Sheriff. Did she say why she wanted the body?"

"Anna Korshak ain't what you'd call real talkative. The only thing she said was 'I think he someone I used to know.'"

"Doesn't she have to be a relative or something to claim the body?"

"We ain't saving it for anything special. Anybody wants to take it off our hands is welcome. Saves the price of a pine box and digging the grave. Course whoever takes it has to bury it—they can't leave it laying around once it starts to stink. That'd be a violation of the law."

"But as far as you're concerned, the authorities have finished with the body?"

Sheriff Bybee raised his sock to his mouth and bit off the thread. "That's right," he said.

I heard someone moving in the hall outside the office,

and an old woman appeared in the doorway. Under the kerchief tied around her head, her face was as wrinkled and coarse as a persimmon. Watery blue eyes, barely visible between squinting lids, flicked past me to the sheriff. "We take him away now?" she asked in a hoarse, uninflected voice.

Before Bybee could answer I took a step toward her. "Mrs. Korshak, my name is Moretti, and I'm a reporter. I wonder if I might ask you a question or two."

She continued to look past me at the sheriff as she repeated her question. "We take him now?"

"Was Kid Slaughter a member of your family?" I asked. "Why do you want to claim the body? Do you have any feelings about the way he was killed?"

She ignored me as she waited impassively for the sheriff's answer. He gave it to her with a nod. "Yup, take him away, Anna."

She turned and gestured to someone in the hallway. Immediately a hulking figure in bib overalls appeared behind her. He was carrying a sheet-wrapped object in his muscular bare arms. One glance at the man's features revealed the reason for the Korshaks' interest in Kid Slaughter's remains—he looked enough like the boxer to be the Kid's twin brother.

Still ignoring me, Mrs. Korshak gave a formal nod to Bybee and preceded her son through the street door. I waved to the sheriff and followed them out. Mrs. Korshak stood by the tailgate of the wagon as Anton gently slid the sheet-wrapped object along the warped boards of the wagon bed. It came to rest between a keg of nails and a worn horse-collar, and Anton raised the tailgate and fastened it in place. Then with an incongruous courtliness he took his mother's arm and helped her up to the wagon seat; after unhitching the sad old mare he took his place beside her.

"Mrs. Korshak!" I cried as the wagon began to move. "Was Kid Slaughter your son, Mrs. Korshak?" Anton shook out the reins and snapped them across the mare's rump. "Did you know he was a bare-knuckle boxer? Do you know any of the men he was working with? Was there anything wrong with his health, Mrs. Korshak?"

The wagon creaked down the street. Neither the mother nor the son gave me a glance as I stumbled along beside them, shouting the questions. The old woman might have been carved from sandstone; the man beside her seemed barely in control of his emotions—eyes wide, nostrils flared, lips working.

My ankle turned in a rut in the road and I fell to my knees. When I rose again, wincing against the pain, the Korshaks' wagon was thirty yards away. I hobbled back to the sidewalk, swearing under my breath, and leaned against a building while I massaged my ankle.

"Don't guess they wanted to talk to you, Mr. Moretti," said a flat voice beside me. I looked up to see Harold Anspaugh standing in an open doorway, his mail-order suit jacket off and his striped shirt and string tie protected by a white apron.

"No doubt it seemed that way to you," I replied ambiguously. "Is this your pharmacy, Mr. Anspaugh?"

"Well, I wouldn't say it was *mine* exactly, but I manage it," he said, with a touch of smugness. "Want to come in and have a prescription filled?"

"Not today, thanks." I wouldn't have bought quinine from the wretch if I had been dying of malaria. "I think I'll just saunter back to the hotel and take care of one or two business matters." I gave him a cool nod and started out along the sidewalk. My ankle immediately turned again and I almost fell; humiliatingly, I stayed on my feet only by clutching Anspaugh's arm. "Jesus, Mary and Joseph, God damn the House of Orange!" I groaned.

"What you need is to rub some liniment on that ankle and wrap it tight in a good strong bandage," Anspaugh said authoritatively. "You better come in and get the weight off your foot, and I'll fix you up in a jiffy."

The idea of this prairie pill-pusher ministering to my pain like Our Savior washing the feet of a leper was more than I could bear. I released his arm and eased my weight back onto my traitorous ankle. "It's nothing at all, really, only the slightest twinge. I'll be strolling along now, thank you."

I walked away from him as casually as it is possible to do while maintaining an upright posture by leaning on the nearest wall.

At the hotel I hesitated a moment to gather my strength before beginning my slow walk across the lobby. Immediately the desk clerk called, "Oh, Mr. Moretti, this just came for you." I saw he was holding a telegram in his hand.

There was only one person it could be from, and not for the first time I marveled at Otto Hochmuth's ability to reach me when my defenses were weakest. I stuffed the envelope in my pocket and limped across the lobby and up the stairs.

I read the telegram when I had the last of my Ancient Mole in a glass by my elbow:

PADDY MORETTI, BARNARD HOTEL, COGSWELL, KANSAS

PLEASED TO HEAR YOU HAVE APPREHENDED MISCREANTS STOP SORRY THEY ARE THE WRONG ONES STOP HOWEVER YOU WILL BE GLAD TO KNOW YOUR COLLEAGUE CLEM HARBER HAS SUCCEEDED WHERE OTHERS HAVE FAILED AND CORRECT CONFIDENCE MEN ARE NOW BEHIND BARS STOP OWNER AND I AWAIT YOUR FULL EXCITING STORY STOP MILTON'S ADVICE QUOTE THEY ALSO SERVE WHO ONLY STAND AND WAIT UNQUOTE MAY NOT BE SOUND GUIDE TO SUCCESS IN JOURNALISTIC CAREER

HOCHMUTH

I allowed myself the time it took to sip my whiskey to brood over the injustice of my situation and to curse the selfish sycophantism of Clem Harber. So much for his promise at McSorley's to pool any information he received! I vowed I would never trust a baseball writer again.

I reread the telegram. There was no doubt about it: Hochmuth's macabre tone served notice that my time was running out. With a sigh I set my empty glass aside and took up my pencil.

As I wrote I realized my story was neither as rich as I had hoped nor as thin as I had feared. Told in narrative form, beginning with my roping in the Palace Car of the Kansas and Pacific Express, continuing through my arrival in Cogswell, scene of Warren Quarrles's legendary massacre and perhaps still under the shadow of his curse, through the bare-knuckle fight and the death of Kid Slaughter, and concluding with the incarceration of the bunco artists, it was a passably entertaining yarn, and one which was far enough from the usual fare of *The Spirit of the Times* to qualify as a novelty. However, it was light on detail. Who *was* Kid Slaughter? If he was, as I suspected, a Cogswell native whose name was once Korshak, what fate brought him back to his hometown? What weakness caused him to die in the ring? Who *were* the other members of the confidence ring—Yarnell, Farringay, Tompkins, Tim the Tiger O'Meara, and the others?—and why did they choose Cogswell for the location of their fight store? Because Tommy Tompkins had lived here before the war? Because Kid Slaughter had? What about the other mark, Magruder, he of the Prince Albert coat and damn-your-eyes manner, what had he meant by those few cryptic words he had spoken to Sheriff Bybee in the office at the jail? And why, I remembered with irritation, had he called me a fathead?

I continued with the draft of my story. After half an hour there came a knock on my door.

"Come in," I called.

The door opened and 'Bednego's head appeared four feet from the floor. "Mr. Moretti, I was wondering if you might be wanting to see Mr. Mole again sometime soon," he said solicitously.

I laid my pencil down. "I'm tempted to believe you are an agent of some Higher Power, 'Bednego. The answer is yes. Trundle him up here and accept your usual *pourboire*."

'Bednego said, "He's done trundled, sir," and swung the door wide to reveal Mole, dressed in a bright green shirt and two-inch-wide lavender suspenders, cradling his carpetbag in his simian arms. His eyes gleamed under his mossy brows as he stepped into the room.

"Ready for another trip to the well?" he asked huskily.

I looked through his bottles and selected another one filled with alleged bourbon. "Well, I lived through one of these—I guess I can take a chance on another. Still two dollars?"

"Two and a half. Expenses have gone up," Mole said.

"You mean it costs more to boil old boots in turpentine? Ah, well—the gracious niceties of life have never come cheap." I produced two dollars and a half for the bootlegger and a quarter for 'Bednego. As Mole was repacking his carpetbag I asked conversationally, "Oh, by the way, friend, the other day you were mentioning some of the varied pleasures of Cogswell after dark. Is one of the spots on your recommended itinerary Moll Sweeney's House of Delights?"

Mole frowned while he was translating my question to himself, and then nodded cautiously. "Yeah. You want to go to Moll's?"

"Why, I don't know. If time hangs heavy on my hands tonight I thought I might take a stroll around town and see the sights. How would I recognize Moll's if I happened to find myself standing in front of it?"

"You go out Center Street—that's the street that goes to the station. Cross the tracks, and there's a warehouse, and then another house with a flight of steps up to the front door, and green shutters over the front windows. That's Moll's."

"And I suppose the correct procedure is to knock twice and tell them Mole sent me?"

"Knock as many times as you want. Any time after dark."

"Well, I doubt if I'll be in the neighborhood, but it's nice to be assured a welcome in case I am," I said airily.

When 'Bednego and Mole had left, I opened the new bottle and poured myself a finger and a half, and noted that the quality had not risen at the same rate as the price. Then I returned to my story.

Five minutes later I threw my pencil down in frustration. There was no doubt about it—I needed more facts. I stood up and tested my ankle cautiously. It seemed to hold my weight without undue pain. I decided to see if it would get me as far as the livery stable.

At the stable the hostler explained that the gig Farringay and I had rented was undergoing repairs and no other was available. "You want a horse?" he asked. I said I did. He looked at me doubtfully. "Easterner, ain't you? Don't reckon you can tell a fetlock from a flapjack."

The walk from the hotel had done my ankle no good at all, and I was in no mood to accept the condescending comments of this hayshaker. "As a matter of fact I earn my living by studying the fine points of horses," I said coldly. "I am probably the shrewdest judge of horseflesh that Cogswell, Kansas, has ever seen. So rustle up your animal and set your mind at ease."

He studied me speculatively, his jaws chomping regularly on his chewing tobacco. "Reckon I'll let you have Rowena," he said. "She's like a rocking chair, and she'll bring you home safe whether you're asleep, drunk, or dead. Just ain't no way you'll get into trouble on her."

I considered a crushing retort and decided it was beneath me. He led out a small chestnut mare with a white blaze on her chest, and saddled her while I waited. Rowena and I exchanged speculative looks. Neither of us was, I believe, totally reassured by the other. I patted her nose and said, "Hello, Rowena—that's a pretty name for a pretty girl." She pulled her head away, rolled her eyeballs, and watched me from the corner of her eye.

I paid the hostler a dollar for the balance of the afternoon, and he handed me the reins. "Now, how do I get to the Korshak place?" I asked. He gave me directions: go south out of town on Main Street, keep going till I came to a single box-elder tree on the left, then turn right at the next road and follow it for about a mile. Cross a creek, take a left at the fork, pass a burned-out barn, and take the next lane to the right—that was the Korshak place. I repeated it all back, and then put my foot in the stirrup and swung up on Rowena's back.

I had never ridden on a Western-style saddle before, and although the high cantle cradled my buttocks with welcome reassurance, the cruel horn that threatened to unman me more than evened the score. Surreptitiously I dropped my hand to cover the top of the pommel to ameliorate the goring I expected to receive.

After a minute or two the giggles and pointed fingers of two urchins on the sidewalk called my attention to the fact that my trouser bottoms were working their way up my legs. I tugged the cuffs down to cover my pale and hairy calves, only to find that the friction between fabric and leather immediately caused them to rise again. As I was rapidly leaving the town behind me, I decided to ignore it.

My squirming in the saddle apparently communicated a sense of uncertainty to Rowena, for after a measuring backward glance she began to edge toward the side of the road.

I was inattentive, and before I knew what she was planning she made a good try at wiping me off on a tree trunk.

The rough bark scraped across my bare leg just as an overhanging branch swept toward my head. Instinctively I bent forward, and the saddle horn pressed sharply into my abdomen. The branch whistled over my head, my leg came clear of the tree, and Rowena glanced back hopefully to see how much damage she had caused.

I swore at her in Italian, which somehow seems more appropriate with animals than Irish, and dragged her head to the left until she was in the middle of the road again. My knee was deeply scratched and bleeding, but my trousers were undamaged, due to the fact that the cuff was now riding up on my thigh, with the rest of the pants leg wadded above it. Sometimes things work out in mysterious ways.

Rowena and I proceeded carefully along the road south of town until we came to the lone box-elder on the left—a great circus tent of a tree, sixty feet high and at least that wide, with enough shade under it to keep half the citizens of Cogswell comfortable. Fifty yards beyond it a road, or more accurately a rutted track, cut off to the right. I turned into it and followed it for a mile over rolling open fields until I approached a line of trees that marked a creek.

I became aware that I was being watched before I reached the bridge. It came to me as a certainty, even though I had seen no living creature since I left the town. I felt it first as a chill that ran up my spine, as if I were sitting in a sudden draft. A moment later Rowena shied and tossed her head in apparent sympathy. I patted her shoulder and turned to study the empty skyline, broken only by occasional stands of trees and a circling hawk in the distance. Was the watcher following me, or was he ahead of me, waiting? Was he a friend or a foe?

What was it Hamp Wyeth had told me in his office? That Warren Quarrles had said the town of Cogswell hadn't seen the last of the Gray Angel of Death.

Saints preserve us, I told myself, *next thing you know, you'll be populating the prairie with Confederate spooks.*

I continued watchfully along the trail toward the trees. Rowena was definitely uneasy, and I talked to her in a soothing voice and stroked her neck and withers. She was so preoccupied she automatically crossed the creek by the bridge, rather than trying to dupe me into letting her take a drink from the water so that she could roll on me, as I am sure she would have done under normal circumstances. I saw no one in the grove beside the creek, and in a few moments we were out in the open fields again. The landscape was as still and empty as before. I took the left-hand fork when it came up and then passed the burned-out barn and turned into the next lane on the right.

The big man in bib overalls who looked like Kid Slaughter was digging a hole in the ground behind the house. The old woman was sitting in a rickety kitchen chair near him. The large sheet-wrapped object they had brought home in their wagon lay on the ground beside her.

I dismounted unnoticed and tethered Rowena to the front-porch rail. Then I walked around the side of the house. "Good afternoon," I said. "I'm sorry for your trouble."

The man raised his shovel and came at me with pure bloody murder in his glittering eyes.

8

Delights of the Night

As the shovel blade arced toward my head I instinctively stepped backward, and my injured ankle, as limp as cooked pasta, turned under me again. It was the only thing that saved my life. I dropped below the shovel's whistling trajectory and hit the ground with the middle of my back.

The man brought the shovel into position for another swing, and I saw the muscles swell in his great forearms. Hopelessly I tried to shrink into the ground. The blade began its second trip just as the old woman said, in a quiet and unemotional voice, "Anton, no. Put shovel down, Anton."

The man froze, and the shovel stopped in midair a foot from my head. Obediently he dropped his arms and stood staring at me with his eyes wide and his chest heaving. I drew my feet under me and rose carefully, gritting my teeth against the throbbing of my twisted ankle. I hobbled toward the house until I could take some of the weight off my leg by leaning against the wall.

I realized they were waiting for me to speak. I said, "I don't come to cause you any bother. I'm sorry if I interrupted your—your observances. I have a question or two to ask you, and then I'll get myself out of your way.''

The woman waited impassively until I had finished, then said, ''Ask—and then go.''

''In the sheet—is that your son? Is that Anton's brother?''

''It is my son. It is Josef.''

''Josef? Josef Korshak? That was the real name of the fighter who called himself Kid Slaughter?''

She didn't bother to answer again, but sat quietly awaiting my next question. Her son Anton had lowered the shovel blade to the ground, but otherwise had not changed his position since she had halted his attack on me. He was breathing heavily through his mouth.

''How did he get to be a prizefighter?'' I asked. ''Why did he call himself Kid Slaughter?''

The old woman shrugged her narrow shoulders. ''Who knows why men fight? Josef always like to hit with his hands, even hit men who would never hurt him. Anton''—she gestured toward the immobile figure—''Anton would never hurt another, unless to protect someone. But Josef—first it was his wish to fight with his hands, and then he went to fight with guns.''

''To fight with guns?'' I repeated.

''In the war. To ride with the horsemen. To kill and burn and steal, very brave, very handsome!'' Her voice took on the animation of bitterness, and her lips twisted. ''What heroes they were, riding with the schoolteacher under the black flag!''

''He rode with Warren Quarrles. Yes, I knew that. Did he ride in the Cogswell raid?''

Again she didn't bother to answer a question she considered unnecessary. Instead she turned to her son and said gently, ''Dig, Anton.'' The big man immediately buried his shovel in the earth and began to scoop out dirt. The mother turned back to me. ''The schoolteacher—this is what he taught his students. Shooting with pistols, stabbing with swords, taking women by force, burning houses— even in his own town.'' Her pale blue eyes had a milky look as she regarded me from under tired lids. Her folded hands lay lifeless in her lap.

"If Josef was with Quarrles in Cogswell then he must have escaped at Hunter's Creek ford, gotten across the creek and away to Missouri," I said. "What happened then? Did he rejoin the Confederates?" She regarded me in silence. Anton's breathing and the sound of his shovel against dirt continued with mechanical regularity. "When did you hear from him again?" I asked.

"Four, five years after war. He send letter with ten dollars. He say he is a prizefighter now, that his name is Kid Slaughter. He says he will send more money, but he never does."

"Did he ever write you again?"

She shook her head. "No more. We don't hear from him again until last week, when he come by here and give me twenty dollars."

"Did he tell you why he had come back to Cogswell, Mrs. Korshak?"

"I don't ask him, he don't tell. But now I know. He come back to die."

I leaned forward eagerly. "Why do you say that? Was there something wrong with him? Something about his health—some sickness or disease that might have caused his death?"

She repeated dully, "He come back to die. He die. You go now." Anton paused in his digging and stood holding his shovel in both hands, waiting to see if his services would be required in assisting my departure. I raised my hands placatingly.

"I'll be leaving before you know it, but let me ask you one more thing. The Gray Angel, Warren Quarrles—did your son Josef ever see him or hear from him after the

war? Or did he ever find out what happened to him after
he escaped from the army guardhouse?''

Anton took a step toward me. Anna Korshak pushed a
wisp of white hair under her kerchief and made a gesture
of dismissal. ''We did not talk of the schoolteacher in this
house. Now you go and let me bury my son.''

I hobbled backward, one hand steadying myself against
the side of the house. ''I'll not be intruding on your sorrow
any longer,'' I called reassuringly. Anton continued to
come toward me. ''Don't bother about me—I'll just see
myself off!'' I cried as I stumbled around the corner of the
house and untethered Rowena from the porch rail.

Anton didn't appear as I dragged myself into the saddle,
so I proceeded down the Korshak lane at a walk. From the
distance I saw that Anton was digging again, as his mother
sat in her rickety kitchen chair, her hands inert in her lap,
her other son wrapped in his shroud of bedsheeting beside
her.

At the road I turned back toward Cogswell. The landscape ahead appeared to be totally empty. Tall masses of
cloud hung motionless over the horizon, dwarfing the few
visible trees. The only structure in view besides the Korshak house was the burned barn I had used as a landmark,
and it was a quarter of a mile away. To a native of the
urban East like me, it was like being in an open boat in
the mid-Pacific.

Rowena glanced back at me from the corner of her eye,
and I warned her of the fate she could expect if she tried
any shenanigans. We each pursued our own thoughts as we
rocked along the rutted trail. I don't know what hers were,
but mine were concerned with Warren Quarrles, Kid
Slaughter, confidence games, and one hundred and ten
thousand dollars.

Something that sounded like a bee buzzed past my ear,
and a moment later I heard a snap like a dry stick breaking.
I raised my hand automatically to brush the insect away

and then paused as I realized it hadn't sounded *quite* like a bee or *quite* like a stick. Before I could search half the horizon with my eyes I heard the buzzing again. This time it coincided with a slapping sound, and a puff of dust rose from the trail a few feet ahead and to the left. A moment later the stick-snapping sound was repeated.

Rowena's ears cocked forward and I felt a ripple of muscle-tensing through her body. I twisted in the saddle, searching the skyline behind me for the gunman. There was no one to see; except for the Korshak house with two tiny figures beside it, two living and one dead, the landscape was deserted. The sniper lay hidden by a rise of land then, concealed behind the skyline. And I was exposed like a cockroach on a china plate.

The burned-out barn was still a hundred yards away, and the line of trees that marked the creek was another five hundred yards beyond that. I drove my heels into Rowena's flanks and crouched low over the pommel. "If you've never run before, you limb of Lucifer, do it now!" I cried. She started off with a leap and moved through a gallop into a dead run, her small compact body stretched to its maximum. I could hear nothing but her pounding hoofs, both of us breathing, and the creak and groan of leather, but I could imagine the buzzing of bullets around my ears.

I pulled up in the shadow of the barn and swung behind one blackened wall. Rowena, keyed up by the excitement of our dash to safety, snorted and pawed the ground. I gentled her for a few moments, stroking her neck and murmuring endearments in her ear. When she was calmer I dismounted, looped her reins around a charred timber, and attempted to locate my attacker.

Whoever you are out there, I thought as I peered over and around the scorched wallboards, *I'd prefer to think you're not a ghost. It's bad enough being bushwhacked by a living human being—having it done by a supernatural agency would give a man a terrible feeling of hopelessness.*

The full 360-degree circle of skyline was only broken by trees and brush. I could see no betraying glint of metal, no tiny flicker of movement. I inspected my sanctuary. The barn was roofless and doorless, and its walls ranged in height from two feet to ten or twelve. No matter where Rowena and I stood, we would be unprotected from one direction or another. And there was no way to tell from which way the gunman's next shot would come.

I ran my fingers through the mare's mane and tugged gently at the coarse hair. "There's no help for it, Rowena," I said softly. "We've got to wait until the spalpeen shoots again before we can figure out where he's shooting *from*." She shifted her weight and nickered uneasily.

There was the slap of metal against wood two feet from my head, and a moment later the small dry sound of a gunshot in the distance.

The bullet had dug its way two inches into a sturdy timber. I pulled my pencil from my pocket and thrust it into the hole. Its sharpened end pointed toward the horizon, toward a gentle rise no more than three hundred yards away.

"Well, ghost or not, Rowena, we know where's he's hiding now," I said. The mare rolled her eyes and scraped the dirt with one hoof. Keeping care to remain invisible to the sniper, I moved to the end of the barn farthest from the lane. Not more than ten feet from the barn wall was a small draw or gully, hardly more than a fold in the land, running at an angle to the line of sight from the barn to the sniper's hill. Once I was flat on my belly in that shallow furrow I would be concealed from his sight and protected from his fire.

I covered the ten feet in two steps and flung myself face down in the grass.

I began to crawl along the draw, allowing myself to think of nothing but keeping my head, shoulders, and buttocks as close to the ground as humanly possible. The sound of my own scraping movement was so loud in my ears I was afraid it would mark my position for my enemy, and I expected the ground to flatten out and expose me to his sight, but neither of these eventualities occurred. After ten minutes of snakelike wriggling I raised my head until I was able to get a one-eyed view of the surrounding terrain. The burned barn was behind me and the small rise was on my left hand, no more than sixty feet away. A man with a carbine was lying on the ground behind the crest of the rise. As I watched, he brought the rifle to his shoulder, sighted carefully at the barn, fired a shot, levered a new cartridge into the chamber, and slid a few inches down the slope until he was below the crest again.

I ducked and continued to worm my way along the draw. Two or three minutes later I calculated that I was well behind the sniper. I raised my head and saw I was correct; the man now lay with three-quarters of his back facing me. I got to my feet and moved quietly toward him.

Whoever he was, he was obviously no ghost. His broad-brimmed hat lay on the ground beside him, exposing his bald head with its fringe of curly gray hair. Between his ear and his shirt collar I could see a beard of the same color. He was wearing a plaid shirt and dungaree jeans stuffed into the tops of low-heeled boots. As I neared him I could hear his voice as he soliloquized irritably. "No-good fence-climbing, trespassing, hole-digging, cattle-killing sons-of-bitches!" He raised himself to the crest of the rise and fired another shot. "That'll learn you, you claim-jumping, grave-robbing, shovel-pushing, clod-throwing—"

I threw myself on him and twisted the carbine from his hands. We struggled for a moment before I pinned his arms to the ground. "Now will you tell me why you were trying to murder me, old man?" I demanded.

He stared up at me with an expression of incredulity

compounded with righteous indignation. "How'd you get back there to dry-gulch me?" he cried in a high rasping voice. "And what do you mean, trying to murder you? Hell, boy, if I was trying to murder you, you'd be a dead man now!"

I leaned back and eased the pressure on his arms. "All right, why were you shooting at me, then?"

He struggled to raise himself on his elbows. "Because you're one of them no-good, fence-climbing, trespassing, hole-digging, cattle-killing sons-of-bitches! Because you're a claim-jumping, grave-robbing—"

"I heard all that. It doesn't make any sense."

"Make any sense! Make any sense!" he cried shrilly. "You want to see what don't make any sense?" He tore himself loose from my light grip and rose to his feet. "That's what don't make any sense!" He pointed across the grassy prairie.

Two hundred yards away a cow lay on its side next to a freshly dug hole in the ground. The hole was near the base of a solitary tree.

"Last night some of you no-good, hole-digging sons-of-bitches come looking for Quarrles's bank money, and this morning one of my heifers broke her leg in the hole you left! That's the fourth heifer I've lost this year—if they don't break their legs in the holes, they just plain get et! You treasure-hunting dudes from Kansas City, you make it so's a man can't earn a living raising stock no more!"

"Now wait a minute!" I interjected. "I'm not digging for Quarrles's money! I'm a newspaperman from—"

"Lying, fence-jumping, cow-killing sons-of-bitches," the man continued. "Give me back my gun! Goddammit, give me back my gun. I'll give you thirty seconds before I open up on you!"

It took ten minutes to explain to the old stockman that I had no culpability in the digging up of his land, and another five to smooth his ruffled feathers sufficiently so that

I felt I could turn my back on him and resume my ride back to Cogswell. I found Rowena waiting placidly in the barn; her nervousness seemed to have disappeared along with my own. The trip back was uneventful. As we entered the town I tugged my trouser bottoms down to cover my knees and calves, but they were riding high again by the time we reached the livery stable. The same hostler held Rowena's head as I dismounted. His eyes took in my disheveled appearance without surprise. "Have a good ride, mister?" he asked.

"Delightful," I said grimly.

"I reckoned you would. You being the shrewdest judge of horseflesh Cogswell has ever seen, and all." He began leading her to her stall.

"Wait a minute," I said. I dug a fifty-cent piece out of my pocket and handed it to him. "If I ever need a horse again, I want you to get Rowena for me, you hear?" He nodded, pocketed the coin, and led the horse away. Putting as little weight as possible on my ankle, I headed back to the hotel and limped up the stairs.

Jack Farringay was sprawled comfortably across the bed, a glass in his hand and my bottle of Mole's V.S.O.P. open beside him. He smiled as I entered and raised his head an inch from the pillow. "Ah, Bunkie, what a pleasure to see you again. Sit down beside me and pour yourself a drink and tell me the name of your tailor."

"Hello, Jack." I took off my jacket and hung it up, poured the washbasin half full and washed my face and hands. I dried them on a soiled towel and then put two fingers of whiskey into a glass and added water. As I took my first swallow I noticed that my unfinished dispatch to *The Spirit of the Times* was on the bed beside him. I nodded at it. "Keeping abreast of the local news?" I asked.

"You write a gripping story, Moretti, but I sense certain missing elements. Or I should say that *I* sense that *you* sense certain missing elements. Right?"

"I have an unanswered question or two, I'll not deny it. As, for instance, why a nefarious criminal like you is out of jail and drinking my whiskey."

Farringay chuckled. "I didn't mean questions like that—I meant *hard* questions. I'm out because any blown-in-the-glass grifter always has his fall money with him, and for five dollars any jail guard will always get any message to any lawyer, and any lawyer, once he knows there's money in it for him, can persuade any judge to set bail at a reasonable figure."

"So you and Yarnell are out?"

"My dear Moretti—*everybody* is out. Me, Yarnell, Tommy Tompkins, the Bushy-Tailed Kid, and Faro Ed Wheeler—"

"Who?" I interjected.

He waved my question aside and continued. "Tim the Tiger and his handlers, the Kid's handlers, and the shills, they're *all* out. Even those two drunk cowboys are out—the sheriff was so disgusted when the rest of us were sprung he let them go on general principles. That jail is as empty as a politician's promise."

"Then I suppose you'll be on the next train out of town."

He assumed an expression of injured innocence that was belied by his gleaming eyes. "What do you take us for, a bunch of bail-jumpers? Why, that's against the law!" He propped himself up on one elbow, took a drink of whiskey, and winced. "Besides," he added, falling back on the pillow, "the goddamned judge is holding all our money."

"I find it hard to believe you couldn't get as far as Wichita if you wanted to."

His eyebrows rose and his eyes hardened. "Frankly, Bunkie, I don't care a great deal what you find hard to believe. None of us would be marooned in this dismal town today if it wasn't for you. You're the one who arranged for that fat-ass sheriff to raid the store, remember."

"I didn't arrange for Kid Slaughter to fall over dead,

however." I tasted my drink thoughtfully. "Jack, how much do you know about Kid Slaughter?"

"How much is there to know? An over-the-hill canvasback who'd take a dive when the price was right, and the price was always right. Why?"

"Did you know that he came from Cogswell? And that his mother and brother still live here?"

Farringay frowned. "Who gives a damn where he came from?"

"Did you know he was one of Quarrles's guerrillas during the war, and that he was with Quarrles during the Cogswell Raid?" I continued.

Farringay raised his head sufficiently to take a swallow from his glass. Then he asked, "Who were Quarrles's guerrillas, and what was the Cogswell Raid?" in a bored tone.

"You don't know? Never mind. It's ancient history. Look, Jack, during the time you were working the fight store con with Kid Slaughter, did he ever mention anything about Cogswell—about coming home?"

"Not that I remember. Of course, we weren't really working with him. He was working for Tommy Tompkins. Tommy ran the store. Yarnell and I just came whenever we had a mark to play. I don't suppose I ever said more than fifty words to the Kid, if that."

"Tompkins has been here in Cogswell for a year. How much of that time was the Kid here?"

"The last month, maybe. Moretti, you're becoming a bore. Who in the world cares about Kid Slaughter's private life?"

I hesitated a moment before I answered. "Let's say I'm still thinking about claiming that case of Irish whiskey Yarnell offered me."

"No wonder, considering what you've been drinking lately. Ugh!" He set his glass on the bedside table and clasped his hands behind his head. "Now tell me about those people you mentioned—what did you call them?—Quarrles's chimpanzees?''

"Quarrles's guerrillas."

"Chimpanzees, gorillas, they're all in the same family. But what in the world are they doing in Kansas?"

Briefly I told him about the Gray Angel of Death, the Cogswell Massacre, and the Drovers Bank robbery. He listened attentively until I finished, a half-smile on his lips. "And Kid Slaughter was riding at the fiend's elbow, was he? And here he is, dropping dead in Cogswell a quarter of a century later. Small world."

"It's even smaller than that. Tommy Tompkins is also a Cogswell native."

"Yes, I think I'd heard that. That's what brought him back here to open his fight store. What's funny about that?"

"I don't know." I pulled on my lower lip thoughtfully. "Lots of people think the bank money is hidden somewhere close. Every year treasure hunters from Kansas City come here and dig holes all over the place. Cattle fall in them and break their legs. I saw one of the holes today."

Farringay rolled over on his hip and poured himself another drink. "Buried treasure has never excited me. No doubt it's a deficiency. I've always found more than enough challenge and reward in my chosen profession, however—as I'm sure you have too, Moretti. Come to think of it, our professions aren't that much different, are they?"

I looked at him suspiciously. "How do you mean?" I asked.

He shrugged. "I don't know—just a passing thought. What are your plans for the evening, Bunkie?"

"I guess I'll get something to eat downstairs and then take a walk around town. Why?"

"I thought I might pay a visit to the local emporium of wine, women, and song later, and you might want to join me. It's called Moll Sweeney's House of Delights, and I recommend it highly."

"Well, I don't know. I'm not generally one for the carnal vices," I said with limited honesty. "However, if it's companionship you're seeking, I'll not deny you my company."

"You're a brick, Moretti. Pass the bottle."

By the time we descended to the restaurant we were in excellent spirits. Farringay was a delightful raconteur when he chose to be, and he told a succession of stories of swindles and bunco schemes that kept me laughing heartily throughout the meal. Like all confidence men, Farringay had absolutely no conscience about his work. It had never occurred to him, I am sure, to feel a single pang of pity for his victims, and judging from the way he described them it was hard for me to feel any either. "That mope had more larceny in his heart than he had psalms in his hymnbook," he said at one point. "He mortgaged the old family homestead to take his plunge, and I could hardly keep a straight face when we took his roll and blew him off." He excused his callousness by dwelling on the avarice of his victims, and he believed in the old adage "You can't cheat an honest man" as a Christian convert believes in the Sermon on the Mount.

We finished our meal and lingered over our coffee and cigars—very good cigars, supplied by Farringay. He studied the inch-long ash on his *claro* and became philosophical. "*Pues*, my friend, what does it all mean? The hustle and the con, the money boxes and badger games, the bribed policeman and the hanging judge, the moments of triumph and the hours of black despair—when all we really want is three meals a day and a warm place to sleep—"

"—and a Havana to smoke and champagne to drink and a responsive little friend to sleep *with*," I concluded.

He smiled charmingly. "How can I deny it? I have always enjoyed the simple life. But it's the simplicity of vichyssoise rather than the simplicity of potato soup. And talking about responsive little friends, Bunkie, isn't it about time we strolled over to Moll's?''

Moll Sweeney's House of Delights was an opulent whorehouse by any small-town Western standard, and would have compared favorably with many successful New York or Chicago bordellos. We were shown through an entrance hall graced with paintings of the abduction of maidens by satyrs and the rape of the Sabine women, and into a parlor crowded with overstuffed chairs and love seats and gleaming with colored glass and crystal. The walls were covered with old-rose-and-silver paper, except for one wall, which supported an oil painting ten feet long, the subject of which was a creamy-skinned young woman lying in a sylvan glen, clad in a choker necklace and pink satin shoes. Her golden hair was arranged in two braids that clung sinuously to her superb breasts, creating a delightful effect of naive voluptuousness.

As we entered the parlor a woman rose and glided toward us, hand extended. She appeared to be in her late forties or early fifties, and was half again as heavy as she should have been, a condition her strenuous corseting was unable to rectify. Her yellow-gray hair was piled up Marie Antoinette–style on her round head, and the coarseness of her skin was poorly concealed by a heavy layer of rice powder.

''Good evening, gentlemen. I don't believe I've had the pleasure of meeting your friend, Mr. Farringay, so perhaps you will introduce us?'' She spoke in a high, thin voice that was softened by a Deep South accent. Her mouth was small and full and her lips were darkly red, and the combined effect of accent, mouth shape, and mouth color put me in mind of some juicy, overripe fruit.

Jack bowed over her hand. ''Give me a moment to enjoy your company by myself first.'' He kissed the air a half-inch above her knuckles, sighed, and then stepped back as if for a better overall view. "I've never seen you lovelier, Moll. I swear I believe you have some magic potion that causes you to age the other direction from the rest of us, growing younger each day as we grow old."

Moll Sweeney dimpled like a sixteen-year-old. "La, Mr. Farringay, I fear you are a deceiver and a menace to the weaker sex." She turned to me and extended her hand again. "Now you really *must* introduce me to your handsome friend."

I bowed over her small fat fingers, which smelled of gardenia perfume incongruously mixed with the kitchen odors of cabbage and fish. Farringay said, "May I present Mr. Paddy Moretti, the well-known sporting journalist and amateur sleuth, not to mention connoisseur of bottles of spirit and ladies to match. Paddy, the justly celebrated Madame Moll Sweeney."

I said I was delighted to meet her, and she squeezed my hand. "I hope you won't be disappointed in our little establishment, Mr. Moretti," she said coyly. "We offer simple pleasures here, but we like to think we cater them well." She turned to the white-jacketed Negro waiter who had appeared silently at her elbow. "Champagne for the gentlemen, Maurice. From our very best stock." She smiled as broadly at me as her ripe little mouth would allow. "The first bottle is on the house, Mr. Moretti."

Jack and I sat down in two comfortable chairs and waited for our champagne. The large room wasn't crowded, but we were far from its only occupants. Two men in business suits and two women in evening dresses formed a group in one corner, two more women in evening dresses sat in poses of studied negligence on a sofa facing us, a man who looked familiar but wasn't immediately identifiable sat alone with a glass in his hand, and, at the stool of a gleaming black baby grand piano, a man with an embittered face was playing a waltz.

The waiter brought our champagne and filled our glasses.

Farringay sipped from his and said, "I have been less comfortable in my life." I tasted my champagne. It was slightly
sweet, but not too bad for Cogswell, Kansas. As I watched
the bubbles dance upward toward annihilation, I reflected
on Otto Hochmuth's reaction if he were to discover how
The Spirit of the Times's special racing correspondent was
spending his expense money. This caused a qualm of *ma-
laise*, which I sought to banish by reflecting on the enthu-
siastic reaction my dispatch about the Kid Slaughter affair
would no doubt provoke. This reflection was immediately
followed, however, by the realization that my dispatch was
unfinished and perhaps even unfinishable.

I emptied my glass and refilled it from the bottle at my
elbow as I cast about for something more cheerful to think
about. Immediately the memory of a bullet slapping the
burned boards of the barn a few inches from my head thrust
itself into the forefront of my consciousness. *That's the
very devil of a thing for a man to be thinking about when
he's drinking champagne in a whorehouse*, I reflected.

I thought about women, and materialized the lovely face
of Ellen Wyeth, which was immediately joined by the de-
pressing visage of the adenoidal druggist Harold Anspaugh. I groaned and sipped my champagne.

Jack Farringay had been eyeing the two women on the
sofa. He emptied his glass and set it down with a rap.
"Well, Bunkie, has your supper settled enough for an as-
cent to the Delectable Mountains? Which is to say, want
to get your short rib fricasseed?"

I said I thought I would wait a while. He crossed to the
sofa, sat down between the two women, and began an animated conversation. At this signal the waiter brought the
three of them champagne, and they had a glass together
before rising and moving to the curved stairway in the hall.
Jack went up the stairs with an arm around each woman,
the champagne bottle in one hand and three glasses in the
other.

I looked around the room again. The solitary man I had noticed before was still sitting in the corner. This time I placed him; he was the shabby man who had pronounced Kid Slaughter dead in Eakins's barn, and whom I had later seen briefly in Sheriff Bybee's office—Doc Bennigsen. Our eyes met, and prompted by a desire to escape my own thoughts, I carried my bottle and glass across the room and sat down beside him.

"Hurt your ankle?" he asked in his whiskey voice. He regarded me with interest from wide eyes, which were somehow childlike in spite of their networks of red capillaries.

"Turned it today, but I'd almost forgotten about it. My name is Paddy Moretti, Doc—do you mind if I call you Doc?" He raised his eyebrows slightly, as if to question what else I would call him. "Taking time off from your professional duties, are you, Doc?" I asked.

"This *is* my professional duty—part of it, anyway." He held out his empty glass and I filled it from my bottle. "I check the whores over so studs like you don't have to worry about clap or syph. Moll and I have a deal. Twice a week I come and look the girls over—look but don't touch, you understand—and if any of them are sick she takes them out of service. Then I come downstairs for two free drinks." He drank and wiped his lips with the back of his hand. "Cheap at twice the price, right, Moretti?"

"It's wonderful work being a healer," I said neutrally. "Another part of your professional duties is doctoring for Tommy Tompkins's fight store, isn't it?"

"*Was—was* one of my professional duties. No more fight store in Cogswell, not after Alf Bybee decided to stick his nose in, finally." He belched and drank again. "Stuff's weak as rainwater—no offense, Moretti. Never look a gift horse in the mouth."

"What exactly killed Kid Slaughter, Doc?"

"Hell, you were there. You saw it, didn't you? His heart stopped."

"What I mean to say is, *why* did his heart stop?"

He hesitated a moment before he answered, "A good wallop can do that. I've seen it happen before."

"Are you sure the wallop did it?"

"Hmmm?" He looked at me owlishly. "What do you mean? What else could have done it?"

"I was thinking there might have been something wrong with him already—something that was aggravated enough by the blow on the chest to cause death. He could have had a bad heart to begin with, or—" I paused as I tried to think of another potential cause of the Kid's demise.

"Never saw a fighter with a weak heart," Doc Bennigsen said. "Fighter with a weak heart would be dead before he started. Foolish idea, Moretti. Any more of that rainwater in the bottle there? Don't want to order my other drink before I have to."

I filled his glass, which emptied the bottle. I signaled the waiter to bring another, which he did. "That will be five dollars, sir," he said. I paid him, resolutely refusing to admit the specter of Otto Hochmuth into my thoughts.

I changed the subject. "How long have you lived in Cogswell, Doc?"

"More than a lifetime," he said indistinctly. "Longer than I can remember. More years than I can count."

"Since the War Between the States? Were you here for the Cogswell Massacre?"

Doc didn't seem to hear me. His head had sunk on his chest. "More years than I can count," he repeated. His arm dropped to the armrest of his chair, and the glass in his hand slopped champagne on the rug. I grabbed the glass before it dropped from his fingers and set it safely aside. He sighed heavily, and his loose lips vibrated.

"Now there's a sweet picture—the squealer and the souse getting liquored up together in a notch house," said a voice

I had heard before. I turned to face two men I had last seen
in the holding cell of Sheriff Bybee's jail—the black-haired
man called Wheeler, who had accompanied the mark Magruder, and another man with a chubby face, a snub nose,
and a lower lip that stuck out like the cowcatcher on a
locomotive; he looked like a middle-aged six-year-old.
Wheeler went on, "My God, Moll don't care who she lets
in! I've got half a mind to throw you out on your ass,
Moretti. What do you think, Bushy?"

"That you ought to use the other half of your mind,"
the chubby-faced man answered. "I didn't come here to
get into a free-for-all." He looked at me through eyes that
appeared to be perfectly round, with a quarter of an inch
of white circling each shiny brown iris. "Although under
other circumstances it might not be a bad idea."

I stood up, uncertain whether to heed the commanding
voice of honor or the cajoling voice of expediency, and
therefore doing both. "If it's a broken head you're looking
for, or the peacemaker's glass of wine that says 'Let bygones be bygones,' you've come to the right place for it.
Accommodation is our middle name, right, Doc?" I
thought it wise to include Doc Bennigsen in the conversation under the theory that a weak ally is better than no ally
at all. One look at Doc, however, placed that theory in
doubt. He had shrunk back into his chair as if trying to
crawl under the cushions.

"No trouble," he said hoarsely. "We wouldn't want
trouble here. Might go back to jail."

The man called Bushy—which was short for the Bushy-
Tailed Kid, as I later learned—gave a bark of laughter.
"Don't worry, Doc, we're not going to have any trouble.
That peacemaker's glass of wine sounds good, Mr. Ac-
commodation Moretti. Eh, Ed?"

Wheeler gave a sullen nod. I signaled the waiter to bring
two more glasses and another bottle of champagne. The
Bushy-Tailed Kid and Faro Ed Wheeler joined Doc and me

in a drink, and almost immediately the atmosphere became easier. Wheeler addressed his glass in silence, but the Bushy-Tailed Kid became garrulous. "Well, easy come, easy go is my motto, boys. I mean to say, nothing lasts forever. We've had us a good store for a long time. I guess it won't hurt us to go back to playing the marks against the wall for a while. Right, Ed?" Faro Ed grunted noncommittally and the Bushy-Tailed Kid went on. "You know, Moretti, the great thing about the Profession is that any time you really need a stake, any time you're really up agin it, then, just like clockwork, along comes Mr. Bates!"

"Mr. Bates is another name for the mark?" I asked.

"Mr. Bates is the eternal mooey-cow, from whose tits all blessings flow. Mr. Bates can nourish the world!" He contemplated a Tiffany lamp through his champagne glass, thrusting out his lower lip thoughtfully. "The human race is divided into three classes of people, Moretti. First, there are the Good People. That includes all of us in the Profession, as well as many folks in allied endeavors. Second, there is Mr. Bates, who is provided by God to keep us alive and well. Third, there is everybody else, which means you and all the other millions of clams like you, who do whatever it is you do and don't matter a damn bit in the eternal scheme of things."

"Moretti mattered enough to bring the town clown out to the store to curdle the play," Faro Ed growled.

"Bygones, bygones, Ed," the Bushy-Tailed Kid admonished. "Anyway, I was speaking in a philosophical sense. Philosophically, all that matters is the Great Game of Life, and it is a game for two players, Us and Mr. Bates. We win, Mr. Bates loses. That's the way the game is supposed to be played; the rest is sideshow." He was silent a moment, then he raised his glass. "Here's to that unfortunate chamois-pusher in Cell Ninety-nine," he said.

I raised my glass also as I asked, "Chamois-pusher? Cell Ninety-nine?"

"The boxer, Kid Slaughter," Bushy explained. "Cell Ninety-nine means he's cold meat." We all drank and refilled our glasses. This emptied the bottle; in deference to my expense report I ordered an individual Irish whiskey and let the others fend for themselves. The drink I received was certainly not Irish whiskey, but it was a cut above the wares Mole had been foisting off on me.

Just then I caught sight of another familiar face. Hamp Wyeth had just entered the parlor. I waved him over and introduced him to the others. He shook hands all around and then ordered himself a drink. "You didn't waste any time getting here, I see, Moretti," he said.

"I happened to be in the neighborhood," I answered. "Just stopped in for a drink and a little conversation."

"Of course you did," Wyeth replied sympathetically. "These gentlemen are some of Tommy Tompkins's friends, I gather. They didn't stay in jail very long." I told him that everyone who had been arrested at Eakins's barn was now free. He grunted. "It should be a hell of a night here at Moll's," he said.

His drink came and we sipped sociably together. "Oh, by the way," I said, "I was thinking about that girl you mentioned to me at the newspaper office—Billie Mae, wasn't it?" I reminded him of the unusual physical endowments and abilities that he had attributed to her. "But I guess you were just joshing me—I don't suppose any of that's true. Is it?"

He looked at me owlishly. "It's gospel, son. You have to see it to believe it."

"Ah," I said. I swallowed a mouthful of whiskey and glanced around the parlor, which now contained a half-dozen young ladies in various attitudes of casual relaxation. "Would she happen to be here now?"

He surveyed the room. "As a matter of fact, she's there on the couch by the piano. The girl with all the hair, in the blue dress."

As I stared at her she raised her head and gave me a level look. She had dark, slightly slanting eyes, high cheekbones, and a broad, rather low forehead. Her mouth was full and cruel, and her face was framed by an incredible amount of curly bronze-colored hair. I swallowed and smiled.

Then C. Hamilton Yarnell and Tommy Tompkins came into the room. Spying us, Yarnell waved his hand in salutation, and they came to join us. "Greetings, colleagues, Doctor, Moretti," Yarnell said. I introduced him to Hamp Wyeth, and they shook hands. Yarnell turned to me. "I see you like to combine your drinking with, ah, calisthenics; no doubt it's healthier that way. Have you by chance seen my young friend Farringay?"

I told him Jack was upstairs, where I had every intention of being myself, immediately. "Unless," I said politely to Wyeth, "your intentions include Miss Billie Mae—"

He waved a brown-spotted hand in refusal. "No, no. I'm *really* here for what you said you were here for—a drink and some conversation."

"Nonsense, Moretti," Yarnell said authoritatively. "There's plenty of time for a slap and a tickle later. It's a long night, and what's there to do afterward in this benighted town? Stay and have a drink with me."

Nothing would do the old scoundrel but a bit of chitchat over a glass, so I threw what I hoped was a significant glance across the room to Billie Mae, and settled back with a fresh whiskey.

Yarnell reminded me of his offer in the jail. "Have you had any luck in getting us off the hook over Kid Slaughter?" he asked.

I told him about my visit to the Kid's mother and brother, and about my eventful ride back. Yarnell and Wyeth listened intently. When I finished, Wyeth said, "That was Shep Fothergill taking potshots at you. Can't say as I blame him. Those digging fools have got his land looking like the third day at Gettysburg.''

"Ellen told me you get a lot of them every year," I said, and then felt a flush of embarrassment at mentioning her name in a house of ill repute.

Hamp Wyeth took no offense. "You bet we do. Thank God for Quarrles's curse. If it wasn't for that, they'd be digging the ground out from under our feet.''

"When you were out at the Korshak place," Yarnell said, "did the old woman say anything that might suggest a reason why the Kid keeled over in the ring?''

I shook my head. "Not a thing." Across the room a fat man in a blue serge suit was talking to Billie Mae and her companions on the couch. I threw her another significant glance around the fat man's back, raising and lowering my eyebrows furiously.

Yarnell said, "Well, keep sniffing around, Moretti. You may earn that case of Irish whiskey yet.''

Another man was entering the parlor. It was Elwood Flocker, carrying his tall, narrow-shouldered body in a way that suggested both diffidence and defiance. He stopped just inside the archway of the entrance door and looked around the room. As his face turned toward me I raised my hand in a salute. His expression hardened and he swept his eyes past me without hesitation. Moll Sweeney tripped up to him, and they walked together toward the card room, which opened off the parlor.

"Look at that! Moneybags Flocker's getting his ashes hauled!" Hamp Wyeth said. "I haven't seen him here in five years!''

"Whorehouses are one of our most democratic institutions," Yarnell said. "They put all men on one common horizontal level of equality.''

The fat man in the blue serge suit was still talking to Billie Mae and her companions. The thought occurred to me that it wouldn't be a bad idea to ask Tommy Tompkins a question or two while he was in the vicinity. He was standing a foot away. I tugged on his coattail. "Tell me something, Mr. Tompkins. Why did you decide to open a fight store in Cogswell?"

He looked at me with an expression of distaste on his heavy florid face. "I don't believe in talking to marks about the business, Moretti, and particularly not to you. Go peddle your papers."

"Did you know Warren Quarrles before the war?" I asked.

His eyes widened momentarily and then narrowed. "I don't know what you're talking about," he said flatly as he moved away from my chair.

Across the room the fat man in the blue serge suit had apparently chosen one of Billie Mae's companions. Billie Mae looked at me for a moment and then studied her fingernails. I put my hands on the arms of my chair and prepared to rise. "Well, gentlemen, it's been pleasant talking to you all, but if you'll excuse me—"

From behind me a hand closed on my shoulder. A voice grated in my ear. "Sit down, Moretti. I want to talk to you."

9

Delights of the Night
(Continued)

I turned to look into the face of the man called Magruder, whom I had last seen in Sheriff Bybee's office, where he had made an impolite remark about "fatheads" as he was leaving. I struggled to rise, but the pressure of his hand defeated my efforts, and I sank back in my chair. "Well, I don't want to talk to *you*," I said, and then added "God-dammit!" for emphasis.

"Well, you're going to," he said truculently. "There's a couple of things you and I have to get straight." His face, which I had thought looked dignified and aloof when I had seen him at the restaurant and in Eakins's barn, seemed brutal now, with small, cold eyes and a loose, heavy mouth. His mutton-chop whiskers looked inappro-priate; not fake, but as if they should have belonged to another man. "We're after different things, but that doesn't mean we can't help each other," he added.

"What I'm after now is something you can't be a bit of help on," I retorted. Across the room Billie Mae got to her feet and walked languidly around her sofa. The sinuous fluidity of her movements made it seem impossible they were generated by anything so mechanical as bones and muscles. I started to rise again. Again Magruder pushed me back.

"Listen, one hand washes the other," he whispered hoarsely. "You help me get what I'm after, and I'll see you're taken care of. You want a story for your newspaper? I'll give you a story. You just have to play along, that's all."

"Mr. Magruder, if that's your name," I said firmly, "I have no intention of talking to you now. I have, as they say, other fishes to fry. Whether I talk to you later depends to a large extent on how persish—per*sist*ently you continue to annoy me. Do I make myself clear?"

"That's telling him, Moretti," Hamp Wyeth said approvingly.

Magruder changed his tone. "Listen, I have to talk to you. It's as important to you as it is to me. Promise me you'll talk to me tonight."

"Let the poor fellow alone, can't you?" said Hamilton Yarnell, forgetting that less than five minutes before he had been pressing me to stay and talk to *him*. Magruder hesitated a moment, and then drifted away toward a poker game in progress in the adjoining card room.

I started to rise again and then noticed that a man in a satin waistcoat and Mexican boots was talking to Billie Mae. I sank back in my chair. Yarnell laughed and signaled the waiter. He offered to buy another round, and it seemed gauche to refuse.

The four confidence men, Yarnell, Tompkins, Bushy, and Faro Ed, struck up a conversation so full of the specialized vocabulary of their profession that it was incomprehensible to me. Hamp Wyeth applied himself to his drinking with single-minded attention. Doc Bennigsen sat slumped in his chair, apparently asleep, his glass held between his hands on his lap. I noticed with surprise that my drink was gone, and, since Billie Mae and Mexican Boots were still talking, ordered another one.

Harve Kilpatrick came in and looked over the now crowded parlor. Our eyes met and he nodded curtly, then headed into the card room. Tim the Tiger O'Meara appeared, muscles bulging under his double-breasted, waspwaisted suit, and caused a ripple of interest among the women in the room. He was greeted exuberantly by our group and joined us. The Bushy-Tailed Kid excused himself and went upstairs. Two women came over and attached themselves to the Tiger's arms. I observed that Billie Mae was still in conversation with Mexican Boots, and ordered another drink. Faro Ed went upstairs.

Finally Mexican Boots went away. Billie Mae turned to look at me again, and I was surprised to see two of her. I rose and carefully navigated the room toward her. As she saw me approach she put her two faces back together again and patted the cushion beside her invitingly. Her *décolletage* was as coolly inviting as the snow-covered slopes of Mont Blanc, and her bronze curls seemed to bob an affirmative answer to every unasked question. I stopped before her and opened my mouth to speak.

"Well, pepper my ass and carve me for a greaser stew," roared a voice in my ear, "if it ain't Ned Buntline's friend from New York! You come have a drink, pard! We got things to talk about!"

I was immobilized by an arm like a wrestler's thigh around my shoulders. At the other end of the arm was Sidewinder Sam Sallee. His hair was slicked down wetly on his pumpkin-shaped head, and he was wearing a swallowtail coat over his dirt-glazed shirt and faded jeans. The coat was at least four sizes too small, and his belly ballooned beneath it impressively. The composite smell that emanated from him seemed to have acquired two new constituents—mothballs and gardenia toilet water.

Barely visible beyond him, searching for a flexible spot in his bandanna, was Charlie Moon. He blew his nose loudly and said, "Didn't come here for no goddamn talking."

"Now hold your horses, Charlie," Sidewinder Sam said reasonably. "We got us a long night here, and there ain't no reason we can't spend some of it making ourselves famous from coast to coast. We'll cover us a couple of heifers later." His massive arm drew me back across the room away from Billie Mae. I watched her helplessly as she diminished in size and became double again.

Sidewinder Sam pressed me down on a couch, gestured Charlie Moon to sit on one side of me, and dropped his own seventh of a ton on the other side. He signaled for drinks. "Now you just sit there and wet your whistle, Mr. Moretti, while I tell you the full and truthful account of the Sawdust Stable Shootout." He cleared his throat commandingly and began, "There I was, with a hogleg Colt and a fifty-caliber carbine, both of them so hot they was scorching the skin off'n my hands—"

I leaned back and closed my eyes and felt the room begin to spin gently. Something cold and wet was placed in my hand; I realized it was another whiskey and water. *The Unforgivable Sins are Presumption and Despair,* I thought helplessly, *and surely I'm being punished for a bit of the former with a murrain of the latter.* I took a swallow from my glass because there seemed no reason not to. Sidewinder Sam's voice rose and fell in my ear, telling some unfathomable tale of people named the Maxey Brothers and Jimmy Mattoon and the Poncho Kid. Other voices from around the room blended in meaningless counterpoint.

Then the spectral figure of Otto Hochmuth appeared in my mind's eye, one bony finger pointed at my heart and a terrible smile on his thin, purplish lips. *This is the day, Moretti! The final day, the red-letter day, the day of reckoning! Der Tag, Moretti! The day we end the pretense that you are an employed journalist exchanging professional skill for pecuniary gain!* The horrid apparition began to caper to the rhythm of music, and it took a few moments for me to realize the music was really there and Hochmuth wasn't.

At least three men's voices were joined together in song:

> *Sitting by the roadside on a summer's day*
> *Chatting with my mess-mates, passing time away,*
> *Lying in the shadow underneath the trees,*
> *Goodness, how delicious! eating goober peas!*

I opened my eyes and looked in the direction of the singers. My gaze encountered only the enormous, out-of-focus visage of Sidewinder Sam Sallee, who was saying, "—being as I had three slugs in me, they figured I was plumb harmless. So they starts a-sneaking out from behind them bales like a couple of coyotes heading for a hen-house—" Behind him the singing went on:

> *Peas! Peas! Peas! Peas!*
> *Goodness, how delicious! eating goober peas!*

For a moment it seemed important to me to identify the singers. I craned my neck to see beyond Sidewinder Sam's bulk, but he moved right along with me, keeping us eyeball-to-blurred-eyeball on the couch. "Clayton Moxey spins around like a toe dancer when my bullets hit him. I can see he realizes who puts the lead to him—just for a moment before he dies he thinks, 'Oh, God, why did I ever cross Sidewinder Sam Sallee?' and then he flops down all perforated clean through and dead as a doornail—"

The singers started another verse:

> *Just before the battle the Gen'ral hears a row,*
> *And says, 'The enemy's a-coming, I can hear their*
> *rifles now—*

I decided the problem of seeing around Sallee was unsolvable, and sank back on the couch. A feeling of undeserved tragedy overcame me. I would never make the acquaintance of the uniquely desirable Billie Mae. I would sit in the parlor of a whorehouse for days on end, listening to the repetitious lies of a malodorous saddle-tramp. Periodically a waiter would press a fresh glass into my hand, which I should ultimately have to pay for with money provided by an unsympathetic Owner, who would charge me with misappropriation of funds, and would direct his editor Hochmuth to enshrine my name on the blacklist of journalistic untouchables.

Some time must have passed during these reflections, because when I became aware of my surroundings again the singing had ceased and an altercation had taken its place. There seemed to be three or four men involved; the voices seemed familiar, but I couldn't pin them to specific individuals.

"—own goddamn fault," one voice said loudly. "Booking two turns the same damn day—no wonder it curdled."

"That's not the point," another voice answered. "Okay, maybe it was a slip, but just the same there wasn't no bobble. Neither chump was wise. Everything was coming off all right till the Kid caught a chill."

"You say! You say! What do you mean, neither chump was wise? They were *both* wise, for Christ's sake!" the first voice cried. "If you'd had your mind on your job instead of worrying about that heist twenty-five years ago—"

"Shut up!" barked a third voice. "You want every mark in Kansas to known the skinny? I swear, every time you open your mouths, half your brains fall out!"

Beside me, Sidewinder Sam had interrupted his interminable monologue and turned his huge head toward the disputants. Now he boomed, "Hush up, you galoots! Ain't you never been in a first-class whorehouse before? Show some respect, now!"

"Ah, stuff it up your keister, trail-bum!" snarled the first voice.

"I don't think that's very respectful," Sallee said thoughtfully. "Do you think that's very respectful, Charlie?"

From the other side of me Charlie Moon replied he sure as hell didn't. Sidewinder Sam nodded in agreement and rose to his feet. "Excuse us a minute, Mr. Moretti. You just suck on that drink. We'll be back directly."

I watched the massive cowboy and his tubular sidekick cross the parlor with a feeling of utter fatalism. *Que será, será*, I thought numbly. Sidewinder Sam approached the three men standing by the piano. I saw they were Hamilton Yarnell, Tommy Tompkins, and Tim the Tiger O'Meara. A hush fell over the parlor. The card players in the adjoining room stopped their game to watch the impending confrontation; Elwood Flocker and Harve Kilpatrick turned in their chairs for a better look, and Magruder's head appeared around the door frame. Moll Sweeney entered swiftly, gesturing to her girls to join her, and approached the piano. "How about some more music, Professor?" she asked sweetly. "And, Maurice, another bottle from my own stock. It's like a wake in here, gentlemen!"

Sidewinder Sam hit Tim the Tiger with a looping left that would have lifted most men clear over the piano, but the boxer caught it on his shoulder and returned a piledriver jab to Sallee's belly. His fist appeared to sink in at least six inches, but Sallee didn't as much as exhale. Instead, he launched another haymaker that caught the Tiger off balance and bent him backward like a strung bow.

A moment after his partner began the fight Charlie Moon kicked Tommy Tompkins on the kneecap and poked two fingers at Hamilton Yarnell's eyes. Tompkins sat on the floor. Yarnell narrowly avoided the fingers and hit Charlie Moon on the cheekbone, sending him careening into Moll Sweeney. Moll swore and backhanded the little cowboy back to Yarnell. Yarnell hit him again and sent him flying into one of Moll's whores, who collapsed under him, squealing like a shoat. Charlie Moon disentangled himself from her skirts and started to rise again. Moll Sweeney yelled, "Miserable little son-of-a-bitch!" and launched a kick at his head, which he avoided. Moll sat down heavily on the floor.

Sidewinder Sam and the Tiger had their arms around each other, apparently trying to crush each other's ribs. Tommy Tompkins, having regained his feet, swung a champagne bottle at Sidewinder Sam's head, but by the time it landed Sam had waltzed the Tiger under it. It exploded in a brilliant halo around his head, and he slid bonelessly from Sallee's arms to a recumbent position beneath the piano.

The sound of thudding fists and screaming women accomplished its usual inciting effect, and men began to stream from the card room to join in the mêlée. Magruder ran past me and threw himself on Tommy Tompkins and immediately disappeared under another new arrival who threw himself on Magruder. Harve Kilpatrick arrived a moment later and dived into the welter of bodies. Sidewinder Sam appeared like a whale rising to the surface to spout, with one man on each arm and another hanging around his neck. Charlie Moon flew through the air, caught at a crystal chandelier, and brought it crashing to the floor with him.

Alone among the women in the parlor, Billie Mae had kept her seat on the couch. She watched the mayhem around her as though it were mildly diverting but of no consequence, her dark brows raised, her eyes wide, and one finger touching the corner of her sensuous mouth. The snowy flesh that showed above her dress and the firm globes that molded its bodice rose and fell with her unhurried breathing, and one of her pointed shoes tapped the floor idly. I found myself wondering if it could really be true, what Wyeth said about her. It didn't seem possible.

A mirror crashed to the floor and shattered. A lamp went out, and then another. Men swore, women shrieked, bodies struggled in the half light. Then the last light in the parlor went out, followed immediately by the light in the card room. We were all plunged into darkness, relieved only by a panel of yellow light that fell across the floor by the hallway entrance.

Except for the sound of shifting bodies and labored breathing, silence fell in the parlor. Then Moll's voice rose like a sea gull's: "Christ on a crutch, can't somebody get some light in here? Irene—Pearl—anybody upstairs! Get off your ass and bring a light down!"

It took all of one minute for a light to appear, and during that time there was continuous movement around me. There was no longer any spirit of belligerence in the air, but rather a curious and even amused interest in what had happened and what would happen next. Hands touched my face and body as men and women moved around in the dark; there were chuckles and comments and rueful complaints:

MOLL'S VOICE: Somebody's going to pay for this!

YARNELL: Cheer up, Moll. Call it an exhibition and list it under operating expenses.

A MAN: My God, I've lost two teeth!

SIDEWINDER SAM: Well, hello, honey! Hey, there shore is a lot of you!

MOLL: Get your goddamned hands off me, you ape! (*Guffaws and titters*)

TOMPKINS: Anybody got a drink in this place?

KILPATRICK: Let's get some light first. Lights, anybody! Lights!

TIM THE TIGER O'MEARA: Wha' happened? What— MY GOD, I'M BLIND!

YARNELL: Didn't I warn you about that rotgut whiskey, Tim? (*More guffaws and titters*)

This sort of thing went on until a light appeared at the doorway, and we watched one another take shape as the darkness ebbed away. I saw that most of the people in the parlor
had found seats; only Moll Sweeney, Sidewinder Sam, Tim
the Tiger, and Magruder were still on the floor. Moll, her
Marie Antoinette coiffure sadly disheveled, sat with her
back against an armchair, rearranging her bulky torso within
her corsets with pats, prods, and pushes. Sidewinder Sam
sprawled beside her, his weight resting on one elbow and
his eyes fixed on her bosom. Tim the Tiger, still under the
piano, started to sit up and rapped his head smartly on the
underside of the instrument. Magruder lay on his back con-
templating the ceiling.

With a gallant bow Yarnell helped Moll Sweeney to her
feet, and Sidewinder Sam followed her. He looked around
the room until he located Charlie Moon, stretched out on
a sofa with his head in a young woman's lap, and me, still
on the couch where he had seated me to listen to his rem-
iniscences. "Charlie, sit up there, pard," he called vexedly.
"I told you there'd be time enough for that stuff later. We
ain't finished telling Mr. Moretti about the Sawdust Stable
Shootout."

Tim the Tiger O'Meara raised his head more carefully
and crawled out from beneath the piano. Moll Sweeney
appeared to weigh the options open to her and decided to
resume the role of ante-bellum Southern hostess. She patted her mountain of yellow-gray hair coquettishly and
formed her ripe little mouth into a moue. "I declare,
gentlemen *will* be gentlemen, and there's nothing in the
world a frail vessel of a woman can do to prevent it." She
raised her voice. "Maurice! Maurice! La, where is that
worthless darky? MAURICE, YOU GET OUT HERE
NOW!" The waiter appeared at the door and paused as his

eyes moved cautiously around the parlor and the card room. "Maurice, bring everybody some champagne and then pick up this mess, you hear? And, Professor, may we have some music?" She gestured expansively to everyone. "Ladies, gentlemen—socialize!"

Maurice disappeared into the rear of the house, the pianist began to play "Long Lives the Merry, Merry Heart/ That Laughs by Night and Day," and a hum of conversation and laughter arose. Elwood Flocker, standing near the piano, tugged his waistcoat down to cover his soft belly and announced that it was time for the card players to return to their unfinished game of chance. He led the way back to the card room, followed by Harve Kilpatrick and three or four other men.

Tommy Tompkins bent over the recumbent Magruder. "Up and at 'em, Mr. Bates. Time to stop blocking traffic and go lose your money like a man." Magruder didn't move. Tompkins leaned closer and tapped Magruder's cheek. Magruder's head rolled to one side. Tompkins looked around the room, his face grave. He discovered Doc Bennigsen, still slumped in his chair, his head on his breast, his black bag by one shoe, and an empty glass by the other. "Wake up, Doc," Tompkins ordered the room in general, "give him a drink, and tell him he's got some work to do."

"Lord God, what's happened now?" Moll Sweeney wailed.

"Unless I miss my guess, you've got yourself a load of cold meat here," Tompkins answered.

10

Pillow Talk at 3:00 A.M.

Magruder was, indeed, cold meat, as a shaken Doc Bennigsen confirmed two minutes later. He had been stabbed to death; the blade had entered his back below the left shoulder blade and penetrated the heart. He must have died instantly. The knife was nowhere to be seen.

Among the patrons of Moll Sweeney's House of Delights there was a natural and predictable impulse to bolt, but wiser heads prevailed. As Tommy Tompkins told some of the married men present, a man had gotten himself murdered and everyone who had been at the scene would be questioned. It was up to them to decide if they preferred to be questioned here, or in front of their wives and children at home.

By the time Sheriff Bybee arrived all the patrons and their erstwhile partners who had been upstairs during the fight had joined the rest of us in the parlor. There must have been close to thirty people in the room when the sheriff and his deputy pushed their way in from the front hall. Doc Bennigsen met them. "The body's over here, Sheriff," he said.

"How'd the son-of-a-bitch find enough room to lay down

in?'' Bybee grumbled as he elbowed through the crowd. "Pardon me, ma'am.''

After he inspected the body, the sheriff took all our names and then settled down to talk to each of us individually. I sat down by myself, hoping to get my thoughts in some semblance of order. A moment later Sidewinder Sam Sallee crashed down on a chair beside me.

"Now, let's see, Mr. Moretti, where was I?'' he boomed.

"Oh, no!'' I cried. "A man's lying fresh-killed in his own blood, and you want to give me two more hours of the Sundown Stable Slaughter?''

"The Sawdust Stable Shootout,'' he corrected. "Why, it ain't my fault somebody went and punctured that feller there—*I* shore as hell didn't do it. You ain't going to let it interfere with getting the story of a lifetime, are you?''

"Let me put it this way. I think maybe some other time I might give it more of the attention it deserves.''

Sidewinder Sam gave a reproachful snort and lifted himself out of his chair. "Well, I reckon I might as well get me a heifer to cover, then.''

I stared at him incredulously. "You're not thinking of taking a girl upstairs *now*, are you? My God, man, the sheriff's not twenty feet away!''

"He'd be farther away if I was upstairs,'' Sidewinder Sam replied logically. He looked the room over. "I wonder if old Moll's in the mood.''

I sat for half an hour before Sheriff Bybee summoned me. He was sitting at the card table in the alcove and laboriously making notes on a sheet of paper. He looked up as I entered, put his pencil down, and pulled on his nicotine-stained mustache. "Grab a chair, Mr. Moretti, and let's us palaver,'' he said.

I sat. "Sheriff,'' I asked quickly, before he could begin, "just who was this man Magruder, really?''

"I got you here to answer questions, not ask them,'' he

grumbled. "All right—Magruder was one of them private inquiry agents, worked out of an office in Kansas City."

"A Pinkerton man?"

"No, it warn't Pinkerton's. A smaller outfit, name of Shield's Confidential Services. He checked with me when he come to town—said he was after a couple of confidence men who were wanted back East."

"Yarnell and Farringay?" I asked in surprise.

"No, the ones he said he was after was them two they call Faro Ed and the Bushy-Tailed Kid."

"Was there a flyer out on them? Was there a reward?"

He shook his head. "Not that I know of. If there was, he didn't let me in on it. I think it was something more personal-like. I told him to go ahead, like I told you."

"When was this, Sheriff?"

"The day before you come to see me, and we set up the raid out of Eakins's barn."

"So he didn't know about the raid till it happened?"

"Not from me he didn't. I didn't figure I owed him anything." He rubbed his globular red nose and then slapped the table with his hand. "Now I want you to tell me everything you know about what happened here to-night."

I began with Jack Farringay's and my arrival, mentioned that I had talked to Moll and then Doc Bennigsen while Jack went upstairs, and that Faro Ed and the Bushy-Tailed Kid had joined us. "And to tell you the truth, Sheriff, I don't remember much after that with crystalline clarity."

"Well, do the best you can. You say this Farringay fellow went upstairs." He looked at the list of names on the table before him, running his finger down it in time to his moving lips. "I don't see his name here. When did he leave?"

"Why, I'm not sure," I answered. "Sometime before the fight, I imagine. I tell you, Sheriff, there's a lot I don't remember."

He grunted. "All right, get on with it. What's next?"

"I think Yarnell and Tommy Tompkins came in next—that's right, first it was Yarnell and Tompkins, then Hamp Wyeth. I told them about the old farmer shooting at me—"

Bybee interrupted to demand details, and I told him about riding out to the Korshak house and being waylaid on my return. "Hamp Wyeth says the man's name was Shep Fothergill. Apparently he was angry about people digging up his land and leaving holes his cattle fall into. You should have heard those bullets whizzing by, Sheriff. I thought I was a goner for sure."

Bybee regarded me with amusement. "The ones you hear whizzing by ain't going to do you a speck of harm, Moretti. It's the ones you don't hear that ventilate you." He scratched himself under one arm. "Well, I don't blame Shep for being a touch put out, but I reckon I better tell him to hold off scaring folks from back East. We got a bad enough name as it is, what with confidence games and Quarrles's curse and all."

"I've been doing some thinking about Quarrles's curse, Sheriff."

"You have, have you?"

I lowered my voice and leaned closer to him. "I suppose you know that Kid Slaughter rode with Quarrles's guerrillas during the War of the Rebellion?"

He regarded me unwinkingly from his tiny eyes. "A lot of people from around here rode with Quarrles during the *War for the Confederacy*," he said.

"Oops," I said. "Well, whatever you call it, Kid Slaughter rode with Quarrles in it. He was with him during the Cogswell Massacre, did you know that?" Bybee didn't answer, so I continued. "Sheriff, Quarrles rode out of town with a hundred and ten thousand dollars, and none of it has ever been seen since. Where is it?"

"The people digging holes on Shep Fothergill's place think it's hid somewhere near Cogswell."

"What if Kid Slaughter knew where it was? What if he had come back for it?"

"Kid Slaughter got killed accidentally box-fighting," Bybee said flatly.

"Do you believe in Quarrles's curse, Sheriff?"

"What are you getting at?" Bybee said, frowning.

"Just that if the Kid was thinking about finding the money and making off with it, he'd be a prime candidate for the curse, wouldn't he?" I began to speak with animation as the story possibilities unfolded in my mind. "Look, Sheriff, assume that there really is something to this curse story, some strange and ancient evil unknown to modern science—"

"Now hush up, Moretti, goddammit!" Bybee barked. "If there's one damn thing I don't need right now it's a damn curse!" He shook his head like a wet Labrador retriever and took two deep breaths. "All right, you were telling Wyeth and the confidence men about Shep Fothergill. Then what happened?"

"Well, I think it was about then that Magruder said he wanted to talk to me."

"Oh, he did, did he?"

"Yes, sir, he did. He said something about one hand washing the other. He said that if I was after a story he could help me get it."

"Did he say what the story was?"

I shook my head. "No, he didn't. I wouldn't talk to him, and he came in here to the poker table, I think."

Bybee nodded. "All right, go on."

I spread my hands helplessly. "After that people just kept coming and going. I remember Harve Kilpatrick came in about that time—also Elwood Flocker. Tim O'Meara came in. The Bushy-Tailed Kid and Faro Ed went upstairs, I think Bushy went first."

"They come down again before the fight?"

"I don't know. They could have. I just don't remember,

Sheriff. By that time Sidewinder Sam was feeding me drinks and telling me the story of his life. A Saint Patrick's Day parade could have come through the parlor and I wouldn't have seen it."

"And then the fight started," Bybee said thoughtfully. "Your friend Sidewinder Sam goes over to pick over a couple of bones with your friends the confidence men, and when it's all over your friend Magruder is dead on the floor. That's about the lay of it, ain't it?"

I explained that none of the persons he had just mentioned could, by the farthest stretch of his imagination, be called my friends.

He didn't choose to comment on that. He made a note or two on the sheet of paper before him and then looked up at me. "All right, Mr. Moretti, I guess that's all for now. You ain't the most eagle-eyed witness in the world, but from the amount of firewater you been putting away it's lucky you seen anything at all. You go on back to your hotel now." As I rose to go he added, "By the way, you wouldn't happen to have a knife on you, would you?"

"I never carry one. You can search me if you want, Sheriff." He waved one hand in negation and said it wouldn't prove anything if I did—half the men in Moll Sweeney's had knives in their pockets. I hesitated a moment. "What about that knife wound?" I asked. "It was in Magruder's back, but Magruder was lying on his back."

"I reckon whoever killed him identified him from the front, and then reached under his arm and drove the knife in from behind."

"Identified him how? It was pitch dark where he was."

"Easy. He was the only man in the room with muttonchop split whiskers. You feel a clean-shaven chin and hairy cheeks, and you know you got your man."

I left the alcove and headed for the front door. Behind me I heard the sheriff call for Sidewinder Sam Sallee. After he had called twice the deputy approached him and spoke softly into his ear. Sheriff Bybee slapped the table in front of him with both hands. "Well, goddammit, drag him off and get him down here!" he roared.

Back in my room at the Barnard Hotel I decided I was tired enough to sleep without the insurance provided by a glass of Old Mole. I hung up my suit, put on my nightshirt, and climbed between the sheets, thankful that for the time being I had the bed to myself. I fell asleep almost instantly.

The next thing I knew was the glow of gaslight through my closed lids. I opened my eyes to see Jack Farringay hanging up his jacket. "Greetings, Bunkie," he said cheerfully. "I see you survived your evening of carnality."

"What time is it?" I mumbled.

"A bit short of three A.M. No longer the shank, I'm afraid." He took off his vest and trousers and hung them with his jacket, peeled off his shirt, collar, and tie and tossed them casually on the dresser. Then, clad only in his ribbed cotton union suit, he lit a cigar and dropped into the room's single armchair. "Ahh, tobacco," he puffed, "where would we poor sinners be without you?"

I coughed, groaned, and sat up in bed. I had been asleep long enough to develop the beginning of an impressive hangover. "Where have you been till three in the morning?" I asked.

"I'm afraid I fell asleep in the arms of Aphrodite," he answered blandly. "From an excess of masculine exuberance, no doubt." He yawned and patted his mouth. "I only woke up half an hour ago. It cost me an arm and a leg, I'll tell you."

"You've been upstairs at Moll's all night long?" I asked.

"Guilty as charged, your honor." He blew a smoke ring. "Did you ever get your nose out of your glass and find your way up Jacob's Ladder?"

"I had myself one of the most interesting nights of my life," I replied.

"Ah, that's good. I'm delighted to hear it." He offered me a cigar, which I declined. Instead I drank a glass of water. It helped, but not enough. I refilled the glass and added a finger and a half of Old Mole to deaden the pain. "Cheers," I said thoughtfully.

Farringay didn't want to go to bed, so we talked for half an hour. Or rather he talked and I listened. He was in an anecdotal mood, spinning one tale after another about successful cons and cons that failed spectacularly; about Still Hands and Ribbing Hands and Big Mitts and Tin Mittens, and about the games con men play on each other. He described how a group of grifters working the resorts in Hot Springs, Arkansas, once decided that Hamilton Yarnell was getting too big for his britches and deserved to experience the chastising effect of the Engineer's Daughter. Another grifter's lady friend was pointed out to Yarnell as a veritable cup from whence all amatory blessings flow, and Yarnell leaped for the bait. Three days, two carriage rides, two tea dances, and an *intime* champagne supper later, just as the enraptured Lothario was maneuvering his inamorata toward her canopied bed, the door burst open and the girl's lover rushed in, dressed in engineer's overalls and brandishing a revolver. "Fornicator!" he cried through his false whiskers, "Defiler of innocent virgins, I'll kill you for this!" "Quick, for your life!" the girl urged Yarnell, seizing his hand and drawing him quickly through a door to another room with a window opening on a fire escape. Pushing the almost nude confidence man through the window, she hissed, "Save yourself! I'll keep Father from shooting you!" Yarnell swarmed down the metal ladder like a hairless monkey—and was met in the alley by every grifter from Texarkana to Little Rock, all ringing bells, beating pans, and twirling sparklers.

"You've got to hand it to old Hamilton, though," Farringay said. "He didn't turn a hair—just bowed and said,

'Welcome, gentlemen. I'd buy you all a drink, but I seem to have left my money in my pants.' ''

"I guess that's what they call *savoir-faire*," I said.

He nodded. "The *sine qua non* of the profession, Bunkie."

I glanced at the graying sky outside the window. "Would you please put out that stogie and turn down the light? Another half hour and it'll be broad daylight."

Farringay acquiesced without argument, and a few moments later we were lying side by side on the lumpy mattress. I closed my eyes and covered my ears with my pillow against my bedfellow's expected snores, but sleep refused to come. I felt edgy and jejune, my head ached and my throat was constricted, and my thoughts moved restlessly from Kid Slaughter's death in the ring to Magruder's death in the bordello, from Otto Hochmuth to Sheriff Bybee, from Ellen Wyeth to Billie Mae.

I remembered the bee-buzz of bullets passing my head, and imagined the crashing charge of Quarrles's guerrillas into the center of Cogswell. I thought about the two saddlebags of bank money, and the curse the Gray Angel had placed on anyone trying to disturb them. Had Quarrles really expected to rejoin his command at Hunter's Creek ford that day? Or had he perhaps staked them out like a goat for a tiger, while he disappeared with the money?

I thought about the fact that Jack Farringay had lied about spending the evening at Moll Sweeney's.

I thought that there were a lot of confidence men around Cogswell with no apparent means of support, now that Tommy Tompkins's fight store was finished.

I came back to the Drovers State Bank money. Did it still exist? Was it hidden somewhere in or near Cogswell? Did anyone know where? Had Kid Slaughter known? Or Magruder? What had Magruder meant when he said one hand washes the other?

My head began to whirl with unanswerable questions. I

took a grasp on my thoughts. Very well. I would assume Quarrles had hidden the money somewhere nearby, intending to return for it at a later date. Where? The answer must lie in the history of the man himself—the places he lived and visited and worked, the people he knew and loved or hated, the habits that drew him to a certain stream for fishing, a certain woods for hunting, a certain trysting place for loving.

If the whole thing isn't just one big confidence game, I thought. But how could it be? The money *had* been stolen, *had* disappeared—that was historical fact.

"Quarrles," I muttered aloud. "God damn you, Quarrles, what did you do with it?"

I felt Jack Farringay shift in the bed beside me. "You still awake, Moretti?" he whispered. I said I was. "I can't sleep either," he said. I didn't answer. For a few minutes we lay side by side, silent except for our breathing. Then he said thoughtfully, "Paddy Moretti. Moretti's Italian, obviously. But where did Paddy come from? A nickname?"

I told him that my mother's maiden name was Sheila O'Kelly, and that I had been named for her younger brother, who was and probably still is a resident of County Clare.

"And your father was Italian? Didn't that make for a rather peculiar home life?"

"I don't know—I never thought about it," I answered honestly. "It was just the way things were. Mama had red hair and a brogue you could grow shamrocks on, and Papa was short and swarthy and had a big black mustache and sang Verdi arias when he was happy just like Italians are supposed to. They were both Catholics, of course, although Mama worried more about it than Papa. And I guess they loved each other."

"What did your father do for a living?"

"He ran a store. In Corbo County, Ohio. I've never

been exactly sure how he got there.'' I stared at the ceiling, just beginning to become visible in the waxing gray light, and remembered the man who had inspired more love and more trepidation in me than anyone I had ever known. ''When he was a young man in Italy he fought with Garibaldi for the Roman Republic. He was in the great retreat in 'forty-nine, and after that he had to get out of the country, so he came to America. He had relatives in New York City, and they got him a job working in the market. He stayed there a year, but he hated the Lower East Side, so when he got the chance to come West he took it. He tried Pittsburgh for a while, decided it was too big, and moved to Columbus, Ohio. That's where he met Mama.''

''In the Catholic Church?'' Farringay sounded amused.

''Where else? I don't think the O'Kellys liked the idea much, but they got married. Then Papa decided Columbus was still too big and started looking for a smaller town to settle in. After a couple of false starts he found Goshen, the second largest town in Corbo County.'' I turned my face toward the dim shape of Jack Farringay. ''Will you tell me why we're lying here at five o'clock in the morning talking about the history of the Morettis?''

''You loved your father, didn't you?'' he asked broodingly. ''I don't think I ever loved mine.'' He paused as if to put his evidence in order, and then went on. ''He was wounded in the war, and had one leg cut off above the knee. Wouldn't wear an artificial leg, said it hurt him. Instead he pinned his pants leg up over the stump and used a crutch. I don't think it hurt him a damn bit—I think he just wanted to be sure everybody remembered all the time that he was a cripple.

''He was with Burnside at Fredericksburg when he was shot. He used to tell about how their officers sent them up the hill, wave after wave of them, right into Stonewall Jackson's guns. He said it was plain murder, and they all knew it, and nobody did anything to stop it. He said it was easier for an officer to get his platoon or company blown to pieces than to argue with a higher-up and get a black mark on his record.

"Anyway, he got himself a minié ball in the leg, and it infected, and they had to take his leg off. I guess that was the most useful thing that ever happened to Daddy in his life, because from then on he had an excuse for everything that ever went wrong—with his job, with his marriage, with his children, everything."

I looked at Farringay again. He was staring straight up at the ceiling, and his profile was lumpy, as if the muscles around his mouth and chin were clenched. I said awkwardly, "It's not easy to judge people sometimes."

He laughed shortly. "It's easy to judge Daddy, because all the evidence is on one side. He was ignorant and mean and selfish, he was untalented, and he was a whiner and a bully. Because of him I left home when I was twelve years old. If I'd stayed another year I would have killed him."

Outside the sky had lightened enough so that gray clouds were visible, placidly awaiting the sun like sheep awaiting their collie. I couldn't think of anything to say, so I watched the clouds browse. After a few minutes Farringay said, in his usual flippant tone, "Well, I don't know about you, Bunkie, but after my evening's exertions I need my beauty sleep. Nighty-night." He turned on his side with his back to me, and after a minute or two his deep, regular breathing became edged with nasal resonance.

The ceiling was now so light I could make out the network of cracks in the plaster. I gave an unspoken groan. *It's broad daylight, and not one wink of sleep have I gotten this night*, I thought slightly inaccurately. *I might as well try to sort out this unholy mess I'm in.*

Whereupon I immediately fell asleep.

11

The Tempter Hath
a Snare for All

When I awoke the browsing clouds were gone; the sky was a leaden gray and thunder rumbled in the distance. Farringay lay on his side facing me, his head resting on his bent arm, his eyes closed. He was snoring gently. In sleep his face had an appealing innocence about it, like that of a small boy who has been tempted by mischievousness but has yet to succumb to it.

I sat on the edge of the bed and inventoried myself. My head throbbed and my throat was dry, but not as much as I deserved; my ankle was slightly swollen and sensitive to pressure, but certainly presented no impediment to movement. I washed, put on a clean shirt, and opened the closet door to get my suit.

Jack Farringay's shoes were sitting on the floor beside my own. As I glanced at the two pairs I was struck by the difference between them. His were well shined and mine were scuffed and dull; his heels were crisply right-angled while mine merged side and bottom in one flowing line; his soles—I bent over in surprise and picked up one of his shoes for a closer look—his soles were edged with reddish mud.

Making sure that my back blocked the view from the bed, I picked up one of my shoes for comparison. There was no reddish mud on my shoe.

I replaced Farringay's shoe beside its mate on the floor, picked up my other shoe, and set both of them on the floor by the chair. Then I continued with my dressing.

As I closed the door quietly behind me, I saw that Farringay's eyes were still closed, the expression of innocent mischievousness still on his face.

In the lobby the desk clerk called, "Hey, Mr. Moretti, you got another telegram. Come about an hour ago." He handed it to me. As I took it I became aware that my head was throbbing more forcefully, my mouth was considerably dryer, and my ankle hurt like hell.

PADDY MORETTI, BARNARD HOTEL, COGSWELL, KANSAS

REPORTER MCANLY WILL ARRIVE COGSWELL WITHIN FORTY EIGHT HOURS STOP PROVIDE HIM WITH YOUR NOTES AND RETURN HERE WITH ALL FUNDS SENT YOU STOP YOU ARE AT END OF YOUR TETHER MORETTI

HOCHMUTH

I folded the paper and stuffed it into my pocket as the world reeled around me. I sank into a frayed armchair and rested my head in one hand. There was a spittoon on the floor near my foot; two soggy cigars butts floated in it like dead rats in a cistern. The rug around it was dark with near misses. It was a symbol of my life.

He's done it to me finally, the spalpeen, I thought numbly. *After all my years of dedicated loyalty. After the glorious stories I've written. After the uncomplaining diligence with which I've pursued my assignments under impossible conditions. And Mother of Mercy! he twists the knife with Bert the Barnacle!*

Bert the Barnacle was the name by which most of the
staff of *The Spirit of the Times* referred to Bertram Mc-
Anly. Partly the name was due to his job as a reporter on
the aquatic sports staff, and partly it was due to a general
aversion to his personality, which was by turns condescending and obsequious, depending on his self-interest.
He and I worked side by side in the editorial office, and I
detested him as much as he detested me. And of course
Hochmuth knew exactly how we felt about each other.

So I was to give my notes to Bert the Barnacle! My story
would appear, if it appeared at all, under his byline! Truly,
Hochmuth had ended our relationship with a terrible stroke
indeed.

I sat with my head in my hands, my eyes closed against
the sight of the spittoon by my feet. After a minute or two
the beginnings of coherent thought entered my dazed brain.
I lowered my hands and sat up straighter and looked directly in the eye of the corset drummer who was staring at
me from across the room.

McAnly was due to arrive in forty-eight hours, Hochmuth had said. Well, by the ballocks of Brian Boru, a lot
could happen in forty-eight hours! I squared my shoulders
and glared fiercely at the corset drummer, who looked
away. *You're the Moretti, remember,* I told myself. *And
the fight isn't over till they carry you from the ring.*

I decided I needed food for my brain to work on, and
went into the restaurant. The waitress brought me black
coffee and I ordered flapjacks and a small beefsteak. While
I waited for the food I tried to make sense out of the three
new elements in the case—Magruder's murder, Farringay's
absence from Moll's, and the red mud I had discovered on
his shoes.

I hadn't succeeded in putting them into any logical pattern when the voice of Ellen Wyeth said behind me, "Mr.
Moretti—Paddy—I'm so glad you're here! May I join
you?"

I jumped to my feet and pulled out a chair for her. She sat down and folded her hands in front of her like a school-girl at her desk. As a matter of fact, I thought, she almost looked like a schoolgirl. Her hair was braided and the braids were wrapped around her head, and she was wearing a starched white shirtwaist with a high, frilly collar. I asked her if she would eat with me, and she agreed to have a cup of coffee.

"I want to talk to you about the story," she said as she stirred cream into her cup. "About what happened at Moll Sweeney's last night, and how it fits in with the other things."

"What other things?" I asked as I leaned back to allow the waitress to place a mighty stack of pancakes in front of me.

She frowned impatiently. "You know what other things. The confidence men and their swindle, and the boxer who was killed, and you asking questions about Warren Quarrles. Please don't treat me like a simpleton, Paddy. I told you that I work on stories for the *Free American*. Well, that's what I'm doing now. I'm a reporter just like you are, and I want you to treat me that way."

"Reportering can be a grubby business for a pretty young lady. You can see an awful lot of the beastliness in human nature, particularly when you're dealing with the criminal element." I spread butter on my flapjacks and poured syrup over them and cut a bite of beefsteak. "I'm not sure but what you'd be happier reporting weddings and church socials."

"Now listen to me," she said intensely, clenching her small hands into fists. "My father has a drinking prob-lem—I told you that. During the last couple of years he's paid more and more attention to the bottle and less and less attention to putting out a newspaper. The results have started to show up in the circulation figures. During the last six months we've lost thirty percent of our readers.

We're down lower now than we were when Daddy bought the paper in eighteen-seventy.''

I listened and continued to eat my breakfast.

''If it keeps going the way it's been going, we'll be out of business in another year,'' she went on. ''And that would just kill Daddy. It wouldn't be so bad for me, because I have—other plans. But for Daddy, why, there just wouldn't be any reason to go on living if he didn't have the paper. Can you understand that?''

I said I could. I watched her face as her emotion caused the blood to rise to her cheeks. ''Then you have to help me!'' she cried. ''If I can get a story, a *big* story, the kind that newspapers back East will copy, it can turn our circulation figures around! People will think about us the way we used to be! We'll be important in Cogswell again!''

''And you want me to share whatever information I get with you? It's a laudable idea, and you're a lovely colleen who would delight any father's heart, but it's a trifle unrealistic, wouldn't you say?''

''Why is it? You work for a sporting newspaper—any story you wrote would emphasize the sporting aspect. But my story would lean more on the local things, the Quarrles angle if that proves to be important, and that business at Moll's last night. They would be two different stories, really.''

I impaled two bites of flapjack and a chunk of steak on my fork and wiped them through a pool of syrup. ''And just what would happen to me if I allowed myself to be scooped on a story my employer has already spent a small fortune on?''

''But you wouldn't be scooped!'' she insisted. ''I guarantee I wouldn't let my story run until after your deadline. It couldn't possibly be picked up by any big-city paper until after your story has been printed and distributed. I promise! Cross my heart and hope to die!''

I wiped up the last of the syrup with the last of the

pancakes. "All right, we'll pass that question. But tell me this: I hate to use the cold language of commerce in a conversation with a lady—but what's in it for me? What I mean to say is, an agreement should be a two-way street. I know what I'd be giving you, but what would you be giving me?"

She sat up straight in her chair and tilted her chin out at me. "Information you don't have," she answered.

"Such as?"

"If I tell you, will you agree to our working together?"

"If I think the information is worth it," I said. Her expression hardened, and I went on. "I'm sorry, Ellen, but that's the way it has to be. Otherwise I couldn't possibly justify letting another reporter in on one of my stories, either to myself or my editors, who would certainly find out about it if your story was picked up by any major papers. You must see that."

She relaxed slightly and said, "I suppose so."

"Then tell me what you've got."

She leaned toward me and her eyes widened. "Warren Quarrles is in Cogswell," she whispered, "or at least I think he is."

"Oh?" I struggled to keep the excitement out of my voice. "What makes you think so?"

"I've heard it from three different people in the last twenty-four hours."

I took a sip of coffee, spilling a fair amount into my saucer. "And they said they saw him?"

"No, none of them actually saw him—that's why I said I *think* he's in Cogswell. Each of them heard it from somebody who heard it from somebody else who heard it from somebody he can't remember. So I don't really have any eyewitness evidence. But all three of the people are good, honest, dependable folks. I'm sure none of them would lie or deliberately pass on a lie."

"Where do they say he is?"

"They don't say. Just that he's been seen, riding along the roads outside of town. Late in the afternoon, they say, right around sundown. And Paddy—they say he was wearing a Confederate uniform."

A chill ran down my spine. "A uniform that's twenty-five years old," I said lightly. "They must have made them to last in those days. Tell me, Ellen, do you think there's any chance you could track one of these stories back to an eyewitness?"

"I can certainly try." She crossed her arms and regarded me anxiously. "Is that good enough? Are we partners?"

"When the Almighty in his infinite wisdom decreed that I should break the habits of a lifetime and take on a partner, I can only be grateful that he decided the partner would be the loveliest lady in the state of Kansas."

Her cornflower blue eyes sparkled and a pink flush rose to her cheeks. Impulsively she put her hand on mine. "Oh, thank you, Paddy! I think you're the nicest man I ever met!" She took her hand away and continued. "Now tell me what you've found out!"

Half an hour and four cups of coffee later I had told her everything I knew about what I referred to as "the Cogswell business." She sat silently for a few moments, digesting my information. "So far it doesn't add up to much, does it?" she asked at length.

I shrugged. "It better. Or in forty-seven hours or less I will be an ex-employee of *The Spirit of the Times*." I told her about the approach of Bert the Barnacle and its predictable result unless I could put a coherent story together before his arrival.

She listened with a expression of indignation, and when I had finished she clapped her hands together and said, "That's just terrible! But don't you worry. We'll have the whole story before that Barnacle person gets here, and we'll just tell him to get back on that train and go back to New York!"

"Ah, you're a tonic to me confidence."

She rose purposefully from the table. "Well, I don't have any time to lose if I'm going to track down those eyewitnesses," she said briskly. "I'll see you this afternoon if I find out anything—partner."

I watched her, along with all the other men in the restaurant, as she made her way between the tables and out the door. She was certainly someone worth watching. *The best thing about our partnership,* I thought, *is that it's purely journalistic. No pharmacists need apply.*

I sipped my coffee slowly and listened to the thunderstorm move into town and break into a million thudding raindrops that darkened the sky almost to night again. Lightning flared in jagged lines that silhouetted buildings like paper cut-outs. The thunder boomed, and the dust in the streets turned to black, shiny mud, and wide puddles suddenly appeared, reflecting the lightning in their drop-spattered surfaces.

I sat by a window and watched until the rain slackened, the thunder rumbled away into the distance, and the flat sky became three-dimensional again. Then I paid my bill and went out into the street.

I drew a deep breath and stopped in surprise. The air had a fresh sweetness to it, a May wine fragrance that blended evergreens and wildflowers and cool running water. It was the kind of smell Nature sometimes lets us experience when we've begun to believe that the world is all dreariness and despair. Gloomily we slog around a corner, and suddenly it hits us, the aroma of fresh-turned earth and dewy grass—the smell of renascence, the promise of new growth. (This is the kind of paragraph Otto Hochmuth would never allow in *The Spirit of the Times*, but Otto Hochmuth is not editing this narrative.)

Dodging puddles, I made my way along the street to the county courthouse. I climbed the wide front steps and entered the building. The first door I came to was labeled

County Clerk. I pushed it open. "Can you tell me where I can find land title information?" I asked. It took me more than two hours to find what I needed to find. I found it in the dusty ledgers that listed land title transfers.

On November 23, 1855, title to a 44-acre farm four miles south of Cogswell had passed into the hands of Agnes Kilpatrick, wife of Thomas Kilpatrick. The previous owner was listed—almost unreadably, under a blob of brown discoloration—as Charles Montfort Farringay.

I stared at the name for a long moment before I copied the entry into my notebook.

"Find out what you wanted?" asked the clerk, an old man with a jaundiced complexion and very few teeth.

"I wouldn't say it's what I want," I answered, "but maybe it's what I need. Could I have the next year's records, please?"

The next reference to that particular parcel of land came in 1857, when Thomas and Agnes Kilpatrick sold off 16 acres to Stefan Korshak. The third reference, which was the last I found, came in 1859, when Thomas and Agnes Kilpatrick sold the balance of their holding, 28 acres, to J. Frederick Roper. According to the clerk, the farm was still owned by the Roper family.

I left the courthouse and walked toward the *Free American* office. I hadn't gone ten feet when a voice halted me. "Ah, Bunkie! I was just asking myself what my erstwhile companion in dissipation was doing today, and here you are trotting along as purposefully as a beagle after a rabbit." Farringay hooked an arm through mine chummily. "Where have you been and where are you headed?"

"Oh, hither and yon, around and about," I answered. "Searching for inspiration, you might say. Blowing idly as a leaf in the breeze."

"I would have thought there was more purpose in that elastic stride of yours." He matched his steps to mine.

"Don't tell me: you're hot on the trail of the man who murdered Magruder last night. Am I right?"

"Oh, you know about that now," I said.

He laughed delightedly. "You're wondering why I told you I spent the whole night at Moll's, when I obviously couldn't have because I was unaware that Magruder was murdered while I was supposedly upstairs *in flagrante delicto*. You harbored dark thoughts about your roomie, and yet you never let on to me." He shook his head admiringly. "Oh, what a dissimulator you are! You missed a great career in the confidence profession!"

"All right, I give up. Why did you tell me you spent the whole night at Moll's?"

"Can't you guess? I had a midnight rendezvous with a young lady, and delicacy forbade my mentioning it to you." He inspected his fingernails.

"After disporting yourself with two of Moll's girls at nine o'clock you had a rendezvous with another woman at midnight?"

"Once my appetite is aroused, I tend to become insatiable," he said simply.

"What do you mean about delicacy forbidding you to mention it?"

"Well, I'm not a total cad, Bunkie. And since I knew you have some regard for the young woman in question—" His voice trailed off, and he looked away from me with a sad smile on his face. After a moment he coughed apologetically and changed the subject. "Didn't I see you coming out of the courthouse just now?"

A cold anger swept through me, and I delayed my answer a moment until my voice was under control. "The courthouse? Oh, the *court*house," I said, as if the pronunciation of the word made a difference. "Oh, yes. I needed a few facts about Cogswell for my story, you see. Historical data—who founded the town, and when, and a bit about its early history. That sort of thing."

He squeezed my arm. "A reporter can't do too much research, can he? It's a solemn responsibility, being a journalist." He leaned closer to me. "How goes the story? Who killed this Magruder fellow? Have you found out anything about the Kid's death that might help us? Our offer of a case of Irish whiskey still goes, you know. And what about What's-his-name, the fellow with the gorillas? Do you know where he hid the buried treasure?"

"Warren Quarrles. No," I sighed, "I can't seem to work anything into a pattern. And about Quarrles, I haven't found out a single thing about the man. A total enigma is what he is, a man without a history, as far as I can tell. He could have sprung up out of the ground."

"Like the soldiers who grew out of the dragon's teeth that Cadmus sowed?" Farringay asked with a quizzical expression. "Oh, surely you've learned one or two things. That he was a native of this benighted town—that he came back and stole all the money in the bank and behaved abominably in general—that he stashed the loot and disappeared into thin air. I wouldn't say he was a total enigma to you at all."

"What I meant was, I haven't learned any more about him than that."

"But you're still looking, aren't you? The bloodhound of the press, hot on the heels of the breaking story. Ah, I envy you, Bunkie, I surely do. What an exciting life you lead!"

We walked arm in arm along the sidewalk as matey as two sailors on shore leaving heading for a saloon. Behind me I heard the clock in the courthouse chime one o'clock. Farringay said, "Have you eaten yet? I haven't. There's still time to break a loaf at the hotel restaurant."

"I ate an hour ago," I lied. "But you go on, Jack. I still have some dull, boring files to go through. I'll see you back at the room, and we can have supper together." I unhooked my arm from his and walked swiftly away from him. I sensed his eyes on my back as I hurried toward the newspaper office, but he didn't follow me.

I was out of breath as I reached the top of the stair and entered the untidy city room/press room/warehouse of the *Free American*. I didn't have to step over a sleeping Oscar, because he was up and setting type from a job case. Hamp Wyeth was sitting at his desk reading a copy of the *Chicago Inter-Ocean*. He put it down as I came in. "Moretti! Come to exchange recollections of the festivities at Moll Sweeney's last night? How about a drink?"

Remembering his temperance lecture the last time I had visited the newspaper office, I answered firmly, "No, thanks. It's too early for me."

"Too bad." He put a hand into one of the pigeonholes in his desk and withdrew, not a jar of peppermint candies, but a pint bottle of whiskey. "Twelve-year-old Kentucky bourbon—mellowness with authority." He uncorked it and took a deep swallow, then replaced it in his desk. "That's right, you prefer peppermint drops in the daytime, don't you?" He dug out the candy jar from another hole, and I popped a candy into my mouth philosophically.

We talked a few minutes about Magruder's murder. Wyeth hadn't met the man, and knew nothing about him other than that he had been a private detective. As we talked he took two more drinks from his bottle. Finally he decided we had exhausted the subject and took up his newspaper again. He read for a moment and then said, "What do you think, Moretti? They ever going to get a canal dug across the Isthmus of Panama?"

"To tell you the truth, I haven't thought about it much lately."

He frowned judicially and pulled on his lantern jaw. "It seems to me that if God had wanted North and South America separated from each other, he wouldn't have hooked them together in the first place, Ferdinand de Lesseps and James G. Blaine notwithstanding."

"A well-taken point, surely. Where do you keep your back issues?"

Wyeth gestured to an unstable column of bound volumes in one corner of the room. "Help yourself." He returned to the question of the Isthmus. "Did it ever occur to you that the North American continent might be holding up the South American continent, or vice versa? And if we go ahead and hack them apart, one or the other of us is going to sink into the ocean like a stone?"

There was no doubt about it: Hamp Wyeth was well into his twelve-year-old bourbon.

As I began to inspect the bound volumes I hesitated, and then turned back to Wyeth. "I wonder if you could answer me one more question," I said.

"Sure. Shoot."

"When I was here before you told me you couldn't keep any whiskey in the office"—I lowered my voice tactfully so it wouldn't carry to the printer's ears—"because Oscar would find it and drink himself to death. Today you whip out a pint of bourbon from a pigeonhole in your desk. Why?"

"Yesterday a very important event took place here. My daughter Ellen persuaded Oscar to take the pledge."

"I see. Well, if I remember correctly, you also said that not drinking during the day was important because it separated the productive citizen from the souse."

"Did I say that?" Wyeth asked in surprise. "Well, remember what Emerson says, Moretti—a foolish consistency is the hobgoblin of little minds." He returned to the perusal of his newspaper.

The earliest of the bound volumes was marked "1854–1855." I took it down and started leafing through the early issues of the *Free American*. The first appearance of the name Farringay was in November, 1854, in a brief story that announced the arrival in Cogswell of Charles Montfort Farringay, together with his son-in-law and daughter,

Thomas and Agnes Kilpatrick, and his grandchildren Sally and Harvey Kilpatrick. According to the story Farringay and the Kilpatricks had formerly resided in Quincy, Massachusetts, where the family had been active in the Antislavery Society, and where Farringay had served as a deacon in the Congregational Church. The family would take up residence on the farm recently acquired by Mr. Farringay four miles south of town. "Cogswell welcomes this freedom-loving Christian family, and congratulates it on its decision to share in the glorious destiny of a free Kansas," the article concluded.

Behind me I heard the clink of glass and a swallowing sound. Hamp Wyeth said, "How about you, Moretti? Another peppermint drop."

"Thank you, no, Mr. Wyeth," I said. "One's my limit. I have a lot of back copies to go through."

During the next year, 1855, Warren Quarrles made his first appearance in the paper, as a guest at a birthday celebration for a Miss Eliza Watrous. A month or so later there was news first of Charles M. Farringay's illness, and then of his death; the author of the obituary expressed the community's deep sympathy for this distinguished citizen's grief-stricken daughter and son-in-law and their two fine children.

In early 1856 Warren Quarrles was appointed schoolteacher, replacing a Mr. Sobel who was returning East. A month later came the report of John Brown's Pottawatomie massacre, followed by an account of his bloody defense of Ossawatomie in August. The border was in flames, but life continued its even tenor in Cogswell: during the fall and winter Warren Quarrles's name appeared on many guest lists for socials and dances and picnics, often together with the names of Carrie Heckman, Sally Kilpatrick, and Elwood Flocker.

In February, 1857, Warren Quarrles and Carrie Heckman announced their engagement.

"Goddammit, Moretti, I don't mind if you whistle, but do you have to whistle Rebel songs?" Wyeth complained behind me.

I hadn't been aware that I was whistling, and it took me a moment to reconstruct the tune. I said, "Oh, I didn't know 'Goober Peas' was a Rebel song—I thought both sides sang it."

Wyeth snorted. "Hell, goober peas are peanuts. How many Union soldiers ever got a taste of peanuts during the war? No, it was purely a Reb song, a Reb cavalry song, as a matter of fact. Private property of the Cavaliers of the Confederacy."

"The kind of song they'd likely sing in Quarrles's command?" I asked.

Before he could answer, Ellen's clear soprano voice cried from the door, "Oh, Daddy, it's hardly even afternoon, and you're drinking! Aren't you ashamed? And just when I've persuaded Oscar to take the pledge!" She stood in the open doorway, and the sunny light behind her edged her blond hair with a halo and outlined her figure with a golden line. Her hands were on her hips in a posture of vexation.

"Good Lord, child, that's why I have to do it!" Hamp Wyeth retorted. "The honor of the profession requires it. Did you ever hear of a newspaper without a drinking man on the staff? It's a contradiction in terms—a veritable oxymoron. Ain't it, Moretti?"

"I'm not sure what an oxymoron is, Miss Ellen, but I'm not the man to argue with your father about it," I said, and then added virtuously, "Of course, I'm not drinking myself."

Her blue eyes rested on me approvingly a moment before they returned to her father. "See, Daddy? Mr. Moretti is a successful New York journalist, and he doesn't drink on the job!" She clasped her hands together in front of her tiny waist. "Don't you remember what Mother used to say? 'To think that a man would put into his mouth that which will steal away his brain.' Don't you remember that, Daddy?''

Hamp Wyeth groaned. "Oh, do I not! It's one of the things about your mother that's engraved in my memory. Perhaps I mean enshrined. Ah, well." He put his pint bottle of whiskey into the bottom drawer. "I reckon you're right just like she was. Now, what can I do for you, child?"

She gave me a significant glance and shook her head slightly, then looked back at her father. "Oh, Daddy, there's a new shipment in at Tuttle's—perfectly divine things like tulle and moiré and velvet, and Spanish combs, and ivory buttons shaped like little elephants—"

"With careful management," Wyeth sighed, "how much?"

"Five dollars," Ellen answered quickly. Her father handed her the money. She turned to go, then said over her shoulder, "Goodbye, Paddy. I hope you're having a more rewarding day than I'm having."

"I'd call five dollars in thirty seconds pretty damn rewarding, if I was you!" Wyeth shouted after her as she left.

He returned to his *Inter-Ocean* and I resumed my study of *Free American* back issues. In the summer of 1857 I encountered the name of Tommy Tompkins for the first time: he was found guilty of drunk and disorderly behavior, and was fined two dollars and sentenced to two days in jail.

I didn't expect to see any mention of the Warren Quarrles–Sally Kilpatrick scandal, of course, and there was none in the news columns. But there was an oblique reference to it in an editorial titled "Cogswell's own Ichabod," in which Whittier's lines, originally applied to Daniel Webster, were quoted:

> *Revile him not, the Tempter hath*
> *A snare for all;*

And pitying tears, not scorn and wrath,
Befit his fall!
Oh, dumb be passion's stormy rage,
When he who might
Have lighted up and led his age,
Falls back in night.

As I read the bitter and disillusioned words I realized how much Warren Quarrles, in the short time he had lived in Cogswell, had made himself a valued member of the community. Perhaps, as Carrie Heckman had dreamed, he might have pursued his destiny to Washington had circumstances willed it.

The next item I jotted down in my notebook was the sale of sixteen acres of farmland by Thomas and Agnes Kilpatrick to Stefan Korshak.

In 1859 the name of Warren Quarrles began to appear in accounts of guerrilla raids. In one story it was suggested that a number of young ne'er-do-wells from Cogswell had joined his band of border ruffians.

A sympathetic note during the summer mentioned that the Kilpatricks' barn had burned. "Their many friends in Cogswell hope this marks the end of their run of bad luck," the writer editorialized. But it did not, for less than a year later the Kilpatricks sold off their remaining acreage and moved into town.

As the 1860s began the paper became more involved with questions of war and peace, and less space was given to the personal affairs of Cogswellites. Aside from reports of Quarrles's activities, the only items I recorded were Harvey Kilpatrick's enlistment in the Third Kansas Infantry and Elwood Flocker's appointment as cashier of the Drovers State Bank.

Then I came to the account of the Cogswell Massacre.

As I read the description of Quarrles's savage incursion I could almost hear the rattle of gunfire, the groans of dying men, and the screams of terrified women; could almost smell the stink of black powder, horse sweat, whiskey, and blood; could almost see the flickering flames that turned homes into funeral pyres. I offered silent congratulations to the writer, whoever he might have been. Through his words I watched the Gray Angel of Death sweep up before the bank, dismount and enter with his uniformed accomplices, and emerge minutes later with two hostages and a sack stuffed with greenbacks. I saw the man I had first seen in the framed illustration in Carrie Heckman's room—oriental eyes, hollow cheeks, drooping mustache, pointed chin, a man short in height but well-muscled and vigorous—as he strode from the bank, filled his saddlebags, and swung into the saddle, barking orders as he reassembled his command and led them along the road to Hunter's Creek ford. I saw his men kill an old man and a boy, ride another man down in the street, and shoot a woman for cursing them.

I closed the bound volume for 1863 and returned it to the unstable pile. Hamp Wyeth was asleep at his desk, his face buried in the *Chicago Inter-Ocean*. Sunlight, dense with dust motes, slanted obliquely through the windows. I realized it must be late afternoon. I stretched my body and felt sudden aches from my neck to my calf muscles.

I started to awaken Wyeth to thank him, but decided I could thank him better by letting him sleep. Oscar was still setting type; I waved to him as I left the *Free American* office and headed for the hotel. I hadn't covered more than fifty feet when a hand grasped my arm and a voice boomed in my ear, "Where you been hiding out, Mr. Moretti? We got us some work to do!"

Four of my five sensory organs confirmed that Sidewinder Sam Sallee was standing beside me—I didn't notice that my sense of taste was affected. Charlie Moon was with him, a rigid red bandanna in one hand.

With Bert the Barnacle en route to Cogswell, the thing in the world I had the least time for was the Sawdust Stable

Shootout. I explained that I was on my way back to my
hotel to finish a newspaper article that was already overdue
in New York. Sidewinder Sam argued that the story he
would give me was incomparably more interesting than any
story I might be working on. "Why, just look at it from
the cold meat angle, Mr. Moretti," he said earnestly.
"You're worrying about the mortal remains of two people,
an over-the-hill box-fighter and a shifty private lawman.
Hell, that ain't a patch on the Sawdust Stable Shootout!
There was *twelve* dead there, not counting them as was
crippled, deformed, mutilated, and maimed for life!"

By swearing on my sainted mother's virtue that I would
listen to a full account before I left Cogswell, I finally
escaped them. I walked quickly to the hotel. The clerk
called me to the desk. "Note in your box, Mr. Moretti,"
he said, handing it to me.

I unfolded it with a tremor of anticipation. The message
was written in a formal, flowing script, a schoolteacher's
script, one might say.

Dear Mr. Moretti,

*It is time we met. I will be at Eakins's barn between
five and seven o'clock today. Tell no one of this appointment.*

W.Q.

12

Digging Up Some of the Facts

It was after 5:30 when I tied Rowena outside Eakins's barn and pushed open the heavy wooden door. "Hello?" I called softly. "Hello? Is anybody here?"

My words echoed hollowly in the hay-smelling half-darkness. They were answered by the scurrying of small animals in the straw, and by the creaking of warped boards. Light filtered weakly through gaps in the walls and roof. In the center of the room I could make out the raised platform of the prize ring. The canvas that had covered it had been stripped away, as had the triple ropes formerly attached to the corner stanchions. The benches upon which confidence men and their marks had sat were now simply bent boards lying across empty boxes.

Walking softly, I moved toward the center of the barn. "Hello?" I repeated more loudly. "Quarrles? Are you here? It's Paddy Moretti."

No human voice answered. I crossed the barn, looking under the platform, and inspected the two cow stalls at the other end, which were empty. I climbed the ladder to the loft and poked around in the dusty hay, to no result. After five minutes I was satisfied that no other person than myself was in, on, or around Eakins's barn.

I sat on the edge of the platform and discussed the situation with myself. *There's one of three conditions that prevails*, I pointed out. *Either Warren Quarrles plans to come here, in which case you are on the edge of the biggest story of your life. Or somebody else plans to meet you here for some deep purpose, nefarious or otherwise. Or nobody at all intends to meet you here, in which case you will sit twiddling your thumbs like the Idiot of the Western World.*

There seemed to be no way to reach a conclusion based on the information at hand, so I waited. After a few minutes the small animals under the straw decided to ignore me and increased their activity. Their rustling sounded like old newspapers blowing in a high wind. The crepuscular light that filtered between the wall and roof boards weakened steadily as the twilight outside advanced to night. Although my eyes acclimated themselves as best they could to the fading light, I soon found myself in nearly total darkness.

I remained where I was in the barn for as long as I could stand it, then felt my way toward the door. After barking my shins on two of the improvised benches and creating a noise that sounded to my ears like a ton of coal going down a chute, I reached the door and slipped through it. There was no moon, but the sky was bright with starlight, bright enough for me to read the face of my watch. The hands said 6:10.

I decided to continue my vigil outside the barn. I leaned against the wall by the door, crossed my arms and tucked my hands under my armpits against the chill, and waited. Rowena nickered softly, and an owl hooted in the distance. After twenty minutes the moon rose. It was gibbous, only two or three days from full, and so bright that it cast shadows.

When I looked at my watch again it was 6:40.

I shifted my position and stretched my arms and legs. *It looks like option number three, Paddy me boy,* I thought. *The Idiot of the Western World.*

Then I heard the sound of a horse approaching.

It was coming from the direction of Cogswell, along the same road I had taken. At first I could see nothing, but in a few moments the horse and rider emerged from the shadow of overhanging trees into the moonlight. The horse was a pinto—I could see the patches of white on his face and chest—and seemed smaller than most. So was his rider, from the little I could make out as he drew closer. He sat straight in the saddle, his face hidden in the shadow of his wide-brimmed hat, his body swaying with the rhythm of his horse.

My heart leaped to my throat, and I pressed back against the barn wall. Was this the Gray Angel of Death riding to meet me at a deserted barn, under a gibbous moon, and me without as much as a pocketknife to defend myself with? *Jesus, Mary, and Joseph, be with me now and at the day of my death, which I profoundly hope are not the same!*

The horse drew up ten feet from the barn door and whinnied at Rowena, who whinnied back. The rider straightened as he studied me. Then he pushed his hat back, and the moonlight revealed a round, snub-nosed face under a shock of tow-colored hair. "Are you Mister Moretti?" he asked in a pre-pubescent voice.

The air rushed out of my lungs with a whoosh, and it was a moment before I answered, "Moretti's my name. What can I do for you?"

"Feller told me you'd be out here at Eakins's. Give me half a dollar to bring you this note. Here." He produced an oblong of paper from his pocket and handed it to me. As I started to unfold it he turned his horse's head and touched his heels to its flanks. "Reckon I'll get me back to town now."

"Wait!" I cried sharply. "Don't go yet! I may have some things to ask you!"

The moonlight was bright enough to allow me to read the brief message, written in the same flowing schoolteacher's script I had seen before:

Dear Mr. Moretti,

Unfortunately detained. Will meet you at Moll Sweeney's sometime after 8:00. Wait till I arrive—much depends on it.

W.Q.

I looked up at the boy, who was waiting impatiently. "Tell me, who gave you this note?" I asked.

"Some feller—I don't know him, never seen him before."

"What did he look like?" I pressed.

"Kind of old. Had gray hair and a kind of droopy gray mustache. And slanty eyes, like you see on Chinamen."

"A big man? Tall?"

"Naw, he warn't much taller than me. But he had real broad shoulders for a little feller."

"What was he wearing? What kind of clothes?"

The boy hesitated. "I don't hardly recollect. They was just clothes. A suit, like. Pants and coat the same color. Gray."

"All right." I was aware of my quickening pulse and the thudding of my heart. "Now tell me this. What did he say to you when he gave you the note? Exactly, now!"

The boy tilted his head back and closed his eyes as if reciting a lesson in school. "He said, 'Boy, I'll give you half a dollar to take this note to a man out at Eakins's barn. His name's Moretti. You ask him who he is, and if he says Moretti, you give him the note, you hear?' "

"That's all he said?"

"That's all. Can I go now, mister? My paw'll whale the tar out of me if I don't get home soon."

I nodded. "Yes, you get on, now. No wait!" I dug into my pocket and withdrew a quarter. "Here—and thanks for your trouble."

He gave a gap-toothed grin, pocketed the coin, pulled his hat down over his eyes, and drove his heels into the pinto's flanks. I watched until horse and rider disappeared into the shadows along the road. Then I unlooped Rowena's reins from the hitching post and patted her on the neck. "Maybe not the Idiot of the Western World after all, old girl," I said. "Maybe the demon reporter you've grown to know and love." I put my foot in the stirrup and lifted myself into the saddle. "Not that either of us had any doubts, did we? Confusion to the enemy!" I turned her head and started back to town.

I returned Rowena to the livery stable and walked to the Barnard Hotel. The temperature had continued to drop since I left the barn, and I decided to get my coat from my room before visiting Moll Sweeney's. I was halfway across the lobby when I heard Ellen Wyeth call, "Paddy! Paddy Moretti!"

She rose from the shabby armchair in which she had been sitting and hurried across to me. Her face was flushed and her eyes were bright with excitement as she clutched my arm. "Paddy, where have you been?" she demanded. "I've been waiting here for you for an hour!"

I told her I had been at Eakins's barn. "Waiting for a gentleman with whom I now have an appointment at an establishment where I fear you cannot accompany me."

She made a gesture of dismissal. "Paddy, this is important. Do you know who I saw riding out of town together, not an hour and a half ago?" I said I hadn't the faintest idea. "Your friend Jack Farringay and Elwood Flocker!" she cried.

"Farringay and Flocker? Riding out of town together?"
I repeated stupidly. "Where were they going?"

"I don't know where they were going! They were heading south on Main Street, just as thick as thieves! Paddy,
why should that confidence man be going anywhere with
the president of the bank?"

I stood for a moment with my mouth open, trying to
think of an answer. Ellen stared at me expectantly. "I was
right to come here to tell you, wasn't I?" she asked. "It
is important, isn't it?"

I took her arm and drew her away from listening ears.
"Ellen, did you track down the source of those rumors
about Warren Quarrles being seen around Cogswell?" I
asked.

She shook her head. "I couldn't. They all ended up with
'I can't remember who told me.' "

I took the two notes from my pocket and handed them
to her. "Well, I think I've been in correspondence with
him," I said.

She read them swiftly and looked up at me, wide-eyed.
"That's what you meant when you came in—about having
an appointment where I couldn't accompany you. Paddy,
do you think it's really him?"

I shook my head. "I don't know. If it is, it certainly
doesn't help to explain anything." I gnawed on my lip.
"One of the problems of a reporter's life that I've never
solved is how to be in two places at the same time."

"I'm a reporter too, remember," Ellen said firmly.

"Somehow I don't think you'd be welcomed with open
arms at Moll Sweeney's. I certainly hope you wouldn't.
And as for the other—no, Ellen, I couldn't let you go alone.
You wait for me here while I get my coat—I'll only be a
minute. Then we'll take us a little ride in the country."

I took the stairs two at a time and threw open the door
of my room. On the bed lay my unfinished dispatch to *The
Spirit of the Times*. I found my overcoat and put it on and

drank two fingers of Mole's Old and Rare from the bottle,
then corked it tightly and slipped it in my coat pocket
against the cold. I trotted down the stairs to the lobby.
"Ellen," I said, "do you have a buggy?"

"Yes—it's in front of the *Free American* office. Paddy,
where are we going?"

"Out to have a visit with Farringay and Flocker—I hope.
Come on, Ellen, they have a devil of a head start on us."

Five minutes later we were in Ellen's buggy headed south
on Main Street, on the road to Hunter's Creek ford. She
held the reins, handling the small roan gelding expertly.
Above us the moon ducked behind silver-edged clouds and
then slid out again to splatter the landscape with moonlight.
After a few minutes the chill began to bite, and Ellen pulled
her woolen shawl more tightly around her shoulders. I addressed myself briefly to my bottle, ignoring Ellen's dis-
approving look.

The lone box-elder tree loomed against the sky on our
left, and fifty yards farther on, the narrow dirt track cut off
to the right. I pointed it out to Ellen and she turned us into
it. For a minute the little gelding picked his way through
almost total darkness, and then we emerged from the trees
into moonlight that seemed dazzling in contrast.

I touched Ellen on the shoulder. "Let's stop a minute
and look where we're going," I said in a low voice. She
tugged lightly at the reins and we came to a halt. Ahead
of us lay an open field that ran a mile to the black treeline
that I remembered marked the creek. The tall grass gleamed
palely in the moonlight. As far as I could see there was no
living creature in sight.

We moved forward again across the luminous field
slowly and uneventfully. It was ten minutes before we
reached the treeline that bordered the creek and entered the
shadow again. The gelding found his way along the path
without effort, and I heard the hollow sound of his hoofs
rapping on the planks of the bridge. *This is the creek that*

almost claimed young Harve Kilpatrick, I thought, where he would have died if Warren Quarrles hadn't dared to pull him out.

Then we were back on solid ground again, moving out of the shadow into the moonlight. But just as we started across the open fields the moon disappeared behind a cloud and darkness descended with startling suddenness.

There was a light ahead, a tiny yellow flame gleaming where no light should have been.

Ellen gasped and clutched my arm. "Paddy, look! There's no house where that light is!"

"I know." I took the bottle out of my pocket. "I think you'd better be having a drop to keep out the cold, Ellen."

She shook her head vehemently, so I tilted the bottle and welcomed the burning liquid into my mouth. It was marvelously restorative, but after two swallows I recorked it regretfully and put it back in my coat pocket. "There's a fork in the trail coming up," I said softly. "We bear to the left."

The light ahead grew larger, and soon we could make out the jagged walls of the burned-out barn that sheltered it. I touched Ellen's wrist. "Stop here," I whispered. "You stay here with the horse—I'll go ahead and scout out the situation."

I slipped down from the buggy seat and moved silently through the tall grass toward the barn. As I drew closer I was able to discern movement close to the light. It was a man's body, now in silhouette, now lit by yellow lantern light, bending and straightening in deliberate rhythm. Digging.

I stopped in the shadow of the barn's front wall and studied the scene before me. The man with the shovel was Elwood Flocker. In spite of the cold he was in his shirtsleeves, and beads of sweat stood out on his forehead. His coat hung from a charred board near him. He was standing calf-deep in a hole three feet across, and fresh earth rose in a pile behind him. A lantern sat on the floor next to the dirt pile, and beyond it Jack Farringay squatted with his back against the wall. He seemed to be cleaning his fingernails with a nail file.

Elwood Flocker drove the blade of the shovel into the pile of loose earth and stepped awkwardly out of the hole. "All right, Farringay, I've done my share. It's your turn now," he said in a complaining voice.

"After everything I'm doing for you? Shame on you," Farringay said suavely. "Put your back into it, Croesus."

"I mean it," Flocker said. "I'm not used to this kind of work. I've got blisters on my hands. Come on now, be fair."

"Where did you ever get the idea that life was fair?" Farringay asked. "Dig in, old socks, make the dirt fly, and maybe we'll get out of here tonight."

With a sigh Flocker reached for the shovel. I drew a deep breath, recited to myself the words *Confidence men never shoot people*, and stepped into the lantern light. "Good evening, gentlemen," I said conversationally. "Can a stranger buy into the game?"

Flocker gave a whimper of consternation, lost his balance, and sat down heavily on the edge of the hole. Farringay glanced up sharply. For a moment his handsome face was absolutely expressionless; then he smiled coolly and put his nail file away. "Well, Bunkie, this is a surprise. To what do Mr. Flocker and I owe the honor of this visit?"

"I hoped that you might be digging up a story for me, Jack. Something about Warren Quarrles and the Drovers Bank money. Imagine me gratification to find that's exactly what you *are* doing."

Flocker regained his voice. "Drovers Bank money? What are you talking about?" he blustered.

A pained expression crossed Farringay's face. "Oh,

please—don't you see he knows, Flocker?'' He sighed. "All right, Moretti, what do we do now?''

"Just what you've been doing. Just keep digging in that hole and see what we come up with. Don't worry about me, Mr. Flocker. I have no designs on the money. It's just the story I'm after.''

The banker stared at me in indecision, then turned to Farringay. Farringay shrugged. "You heard the man, Croesus,'' he said. "Unless you want to shoot him, I suggest you begin to wield that shovel again.''

"Confidence men don't shoot people,'' I said confidently. "I'm reasonably sure that bankers don't either.''

Farringay smiled brightly. "But you're not positive, are you? Well, wait and see. Flocker, let's see some dirt fly.''

The banker said something under his breath and took up the shovel. As he began to dig I squatted down beside Farringay. "The money is here, isn't it, Jack? This is where your father buried it.''

"Yes, I thought you were on to that. I tried to steer you off, you know.''

"With all that flapdoodle about your one-legged Daddy who was shot at the Battle of Fredericksburg? I might have believed it if I hadn't seen the land title records at the courthouse.''

"That's what I thought you went there to check,'' Farringay said. He shook his head. "I should have used another name entirely. But who would have thought my grandmother's maiden name could possibly get me into trouble? I guess if it had been Smith or Jones it wouldn't have.''

Flocker stopped digging. "What are you talking about?'' he asked in a harsh voice. "What do you mean about your father burying the money?''

Farringay spread his hands apologetically. "Oh, did I neglect to tell you that, Mr. Flocker? My father was the definitely uncelestial Gray Angel of Death, General Warren Quarrles.''

"Then it was *you* who knew where the money was all along," Flocker cried. "It wasn't Moretti like you said—"

"Dig, Flocker, dig," Farringay said firmly. "There's no help for it now, don't you see?''

For a moment the two men stared at each other. Flocker's expression was one of helpless consternation, and Farringay wore a smile of gentle irony. Then the banker took up his shovel and began to scoop out dirt. A clod fell from the shovel and broke on the floor beside my foot. I picked up some of it and held it to the light. It was clay, reddish in color and adhesive to the touch.

For a minute or two the confidence man and I sat side by side, watching the perspiring banker dig. Then I said, "How about dotting some i's and crossing some t's for me, Jack? Is Warren Quarrles dead or alive?'' He didn't answer, so I went on. "Did your father tell you where the money was buried?'' When he remained silent, I hardened my voice. "Did he say he wanted to hide his loot in the barn where he found true love—with another man's fiancée? Under the dirt and straw where his son was conceived?''

Farringay turned slowly to look at me. His face was calm; only his blazing eyes showed his rage. "I'd be careful what I said if I were you, Moretti,'' he said lightly. "We're alone out here, and there are two of us and only one of you, and while what you said about confidence men and bankers not killing people is generally true, I don't think I'd want to stake my life on it." He paused, then went on in a voice that had become full-timbred with emotion. "Yes, I was conceived here, Moretti, in the dirt and straw, as you so happily put it. Conceived out of wedlock, a bastard. Shameful! What would you do to the man and woman who did such a shameful thing, if you were a good Christian citizen of Cogswell, Moretti? Tar and feather the man? Ride him out of town on a rail? Point the finger of scorn at the woman until she was forced to take her swollen belly away and follow her lover to a guerrilla camp? What form would your Christian outrage have taken, Moretti?''

I answered carefully, ''Catholics are a bit less likely to cast the first stone, I think. I'd not be about to blame your father or your mother for doing things I've done myself.''

''You!'' Farringay cried passionately. In the yellow light his face was suddenly diabolical. ''You'd compare yourself to Warren Quarrles and his wife? You'd *presume* to give them absolution—you damned Papist mongrel! There was greatness in my mother and father that you couldn't recognize in a thousand years! She was an angel, generous and loving, wanting only to give everything she was and ever would be to her husband and her son! And he—he was thunder and lightning! He was the Wrath of God! And yet I can remember him taking me on his lap and letting me pull his mustache while he told me fairy stories and Greek myths—''

''Like Cadmus and the dragon's teeth,'' I interrupted softly.

He continued as if he hadn't heard. ''—and stories about his battles in the War for the Confederacy—about his triumph at Cogswell, when he gave the Yankees what they deserved!''

Flocker said in a strangled voice, ''He was a damned rebel, a thief and a fornicator!''

''Don't lose your head, banker—remember what's at stake here!'' Farringay snapped. ''Keep digging!''

''And the money, Jack? He told you where he'd hidden the money?'' I asked.

In the darkness a horse whinnied.

Farringay's expression became somber. ''Yes, just before he died. They brought me into his bedroom. He was very weak—I had to bend down to hear him. 'It's your money, Jack,' he said, 'and it's buried where you began, in a burned-out barn outside of Cogswell. When you're a man, go get it, son!'' His expression changed again, and he was once more the mocking swindler I had gotten to know and like. ''And that's just what we're doing—me and this banking gentleman here—although your irritating little investigation forced me to move my calendar up a bit. When I saw you coming out of the courthouse today I knew I didn't have any time to waste.''

Suddenly there was the sound of a commotion from the darkness outside the barn. A male voice cursed and Ellen Wyeth's voice cried, ''Paddy, watch out!'' Farringay stiffened, his face suddenly expressionless, and Flocker froze with his shovel suspended in the air. A moment later three figures entered the circle of lantern light within the barn. First came Ellen, her bosom heaving, her eyes dark with anger, and her hands pinioned behind her. Immediately behind her and holding her hands was Hamilton Yarnell, looking as if he had arrived for tea at some mansion in Saratoga or Newport, his linen snowy, his suit crisply pressed, and his shoes gleaming in the yellow light. His thin, patrician lips curled slightly. ''Look who we found eavesdropping, gentlemen,'' he said. ''A deplorable lack of attention to detail, right, Tommy?''

''Right,'' said Tommy Tompkins, who followed Yarnell into the barn. The fight-store manager had none of Yarnell's sartorial elegance—his suit was rumpled, his gray hair disheveled—but he had something else perhaps more valuable: a big black Colt revolver, the muzzle of which moved restlessly from Flocker to Farringay to me. ''Hello, Jack,'' he said. ''Hello, Flocker. Hello, Moretti. You do get yourself involved in things, don't you?''

''Paddy, they sneaked up on me,'' Ellen cried indignantly. She twisted her hands free and spun around to face Yarnell. ''And kindly stop manhandling me like I was some kind of package!''

"I asked you to stay in the buggy, Ellen," I sighed. I looked at the gleaming black pistol in Tompkins's hand. "So much for that business about confidence men and guns, Jack," I said.

He shrugged. "As a confidence man I'm sure Tommy wouldn't touch the things. But as a veteran of Quarrles's Raiders he has every right. You win some, you lose some."

Tompkins gestured with the Colt. "Sit down there next to Moretti, miss, and keep quiet. All of you keep quiet. And you, Flocker, let's see you start digging again."

Flocker buried his shovel blade in the reddish earth, his breath bursting in explosive gasps as he lifted shovelful after shovelful and dumped them on the growing pile. Tommy Tompkins hunkered down on his heels, his pistol held ready. Yarnell remained standing with his back to the wall, an expression of patient boredom on his face. Ellen sat beside me, her arms hugging her knees, her eyes as attentive as only a cub reporter's can be. My mind raced like a rat in a maze, driven by desperation to find a solution where a solution probably didn't exist.

After a minute or two Tompkins began to whistle through his teeth. The song was "Goober Peas."

I cleared my throat and said to Yarnell, "You and Tompkins—both of you rode with Quarrles during the war?"

He shook his head. "No, Tommy was with Quarrles, but I was in a somewhat more—ah, *orthodox* command." He drew himself up proudly. "I had the honor to serve under General Wade Hampton, sir."

"Then where did you hear about the Drovers Bank money?" I asked.

"Tommy and I became friends in New Orleans after the war. The town was full of Yankees and the pickings were easy." He chuckled reminiscently. "There's no Mr. Bates in the world as generous and cooperative as a self-righteous Republican Mr. Bates from New England. He almost forces the money on you, right, Tommy?'' Tompkins grunted in agreement. "At any rate, Tommy and I became confidants. And that's when Tommy told me about the Quarrles bank money, which he was sure was hidden somewhere near his dear old hometown of Cogswell. We used to wonder how we could get our hands on it—but of course no opportunities occurred.''

Farringay spoke. "Until you happened to meet me, that is.''

Yarnell chuckled again. "Imagine our surprise when we encountered a neophyte in our own profession with the highly unusual name of Farringay. Tommy recognized it instantly, and we made our plans accordingly. I took Jack into partnership, and Tommy returned to Cogswell to establish a fight store there. Then Jack and I made our leisurely and profitable way to the Midwest. Neither of us was in any hurry—each of us being sure the money was waiting for him—''

Tompkins interrupted. "That hole's pretty deep. How do we know we're digging in the right place?''

Farringay said, "My father told me it was four paces in from the southeast corner of the barn. It's there, all right.''

"Keep digging, banker,'' Yarnell said. "As I was saying, Moretti, neither of us was in a hurry. Jack knew where the money was, and I knew as sure as Fate that all I had to do was keep an eye on him and he would lead me to it. And that's what happened, isn't it? In spite of that unfortunate brouhaha when the Kid died in the ring—by the bye, Moretti, I'm sorry you weren't able to come up with any other possible causes for the Kid's death. I really would have paid you off if you had.''

I opened my mouth to answer, but before I could speak Tommy Tompkins cried, "There's something there!'' He pointed down into the hole and ordered, "Careful, Flocker! Dig real careful! Do you see that leather strap there?'' He seized the lantern and held it over the hole as the banker bent to his work.

Farringay's hand clamped down on my knee. "It's now or never, Moretti!" he hissed. "There's a derringer in Flocker's coat. I'll go for it—you douse that lantern!"

"But—"

"He'll kill you, you fool!" In one sinuous movement he was on his feet, his body aimed like an arrow at the banker's coat hanging from the wall. "NOW!" he shouted, lowering his head and thrusting his hands before him.

I stumbled to my feet half a second later, just as Tompkins spun on his heels and fired. His shot was poorly sighted, and because he was off balance he sprawled backward and sat down on the ground before he could fire again. He was bringing the Colt up for a second shot at Farringay when I lurched into him and knocked him into the hole. The lantern flew out of his hand and the barn was plunged into darkness.

For a moment I was deafened by the roar of the Colt; then, as my hearing returned I heard Ellen call, "Paddy! Are you all right?", Farringay shout, "I've got it, Moretti!", Flocker squeal, "Don't shoot! Don't shoot!", Tompkins curse foully, and Yarnell order crisply, "Careful, Tommy! No more fireworks just now!"

For ten seconds or more there was silence in the barn, broken only by the sound of heavy breathing and careful movement. Overhead the sky became softly luminous as my eyes became acclimated to the starlight again. I kept close to the ground so my silhouette would not be visible. Everyone else did likewise. Just as I began to make out specific black shapes in the general darkness around me, Yarnell spoke again. "Jack, I assume you've got a pistol now, so it looks like a Mexican stand-off. I guess it's time for a little cooperation."

From the darkness beyond the dirt pile Farringay answered, "I guess it is, Hamilton. Cooperation is always possible between reasonable men. Moretti, see if you can get that lantern going."

I felt around on the ground and located the lantern. It was undamaged, and in a few moments we had light in the barn again. I looked at the people who emerged from the shadows around me. The two combatants, Tompkins and Farringay, faced each other from positions of partial concealment; Tompkins, his revolver in his hand, was hunched in the hole like a soldier in a shallow trench, only the top of his head showing over the edge. Farringay was on the far side of the pile of red clay, holding a small-caliber pepper-box pocket pistol that just peeped over the top. Ellen sat with her back to the wall, her eyes wide but her expression more interested than frightened. Yarnell stood in a position of relaxation, a hint of a smile on his lips, and stroked the lapel of his coat with one hand. Flocker, eyes bulging and jaw slack, struggled to make himself invisible in the hole behind Tompkins.

Farringay spoke. "Hamilton, Tommy, listen to me. I said I'm a reasonable man, and I am. I know when a deck's cold, and when it is, I take a walk. That's what I'll do now. You put your gun away, and I'll put mine away, and then I'll walk right out of here. Right out of this barn, and then right out of Cogswell and right out of your lives. I swear to God I'm telling you the truth."

Yarnell raised his eyebrows. "Astonishing," he murmured. "Out of the goodness of your heart you'll leave us whatever's buried there, and just disappear forever."

"He's lying, Hamilton," Tompkins growled.

"The goodness of my heart has nothing to do with it," Farringay answered. "I don't like the odds. I'm not a gunfighter, and I don't feel like betting my life on this peashooter against that cannon Tommy's waving around. Would you, if you were in my place?"

"And you'll just walk away? Walk away from all that

lovely money your daddy buried in the ground for you?''
Yarnell asked mockingly.

Farringay's voice was resonant with sincerity as he replied, ''Hamilton, you know that in all the time we've
known each other I've never lied to you. Well, believe me
when I tell you that if I leave here now, I will never, never
give a single thought to the money you and Tommy dig
out of that hole. I swear it on my father's grave.''

Yarnell hesitated a moment, then asked, ''What about
these people—Flocker, and Moretti and the girl?''

Farringay's eyes flicked across the three of us and returned to Yarnell. ''That's up to you, Hamilton. You handle it any way you see fit. All I care about is that I walk
away from here now.''

Yarnell and Tompkins exchanged glances. Yarnell
frowned and scratched his chin. ''If I thought you'd really
leave, Jack, and that would be the end of it—'' he said
uncertainly.

''I swear it! As God is my judge!''

Yarnell nodded slowly. ''I think you mean it, Jack, I
really think you do.'' He hesitated another moment, and
then said decisively, ''All right, it's a deal. Tommy, put
your gun down. You too, Jack—that's it. Nice and easy.''
Both armed men slowly lowered their pistols to their sides
and straightened up. Farringay stepped out from behind the
pile of dirt and moved toward the barn door. Ellen turned
her head to me. ''If he leaves—'' she cried suddenly.

''Wait a minute, Jack,'' I said. ''You know what you'll
be doing if you duck out and leave us here as their prisoners?''

He gave me an apologetic smile. ''No, not really, Bunkie. It seems to me Hamilton has a number of options, and
I wouldn't presume to predict which of them he'll exercise.
Whichever it turns out to be, I'm sure it will represent his
best thinking.'' He bowed to Ellen and said, ''Your ser-
vant, ma'am,'' nodded to Flocker and said, ''Don't look so

sad, Croesus—you had twenty-five good years," waved his hand in farewell to Yarnell and Tompkins, and stepped through the barn door.

Two shots blasted from the outside darkness, and a voice called, "You with the guns—just let 'em drop on the ground real careful-like."

Farringay froze; only the fingers of his right hand showed any movement, as they opened to allow his pepper-box revolver to fall to the ground. In the barn Tompkins straightened his arm and dropped his Colt on the dirt floor. "Pick up that feller's forty-some-odd, Mr. Moretti," called the voice from the darkness. I scooped up the revolver and tucked it into my belt, as Sidewinder Sam Sallee and Charlie Moon stepped into the lantern light, each with a pistol in his hand. "We seen that dude fixing to pull up stakes and figured it was time to make our play," Sallee said to me. "We ain't queered the game, have we?"

I let my breath out in a long sigh. "Oh, no, Sam, you haven't queered the game. In fact, you arrived at the exact right moment for the showdown." I put out my hand to Ellen and helped her to her feet. "Are you all right?" I asked her. She nodded. Her eyes gleamed with excitement and she squeezed my hand. With a gesture that included Farringay, Flocker, Tompkins, and Yarnell, I said, "Then, gentlemen, I suggest we continue with the exhumation."

Each one of the four of them opened his mouth to speak and then apparently thought better of it. Yarnell assumed an expression of politely concealed boredom, Tompkins glowered at the ground, and Farringay raised his chin and squared his shoulders. Flocker's eyes raced from one of us to the next as if seeking an ally and failing to find one. After a moment he picked up the shovel.

I picked up the lantern and held it over the hole. "Just a second, Flocker," I said. In the yellow light I could see the scrap of leather protruding from the dirt. I beckoned to Sidewinder Sam. "I think that's part of the saddlebags that

Warren Quarrles filled with the Drovers Bank money twenty-five years ago, Sam," I told him.

"Well, I'll be dogged!" He gestured with his pistol to Elwood Flocker. "You be careful with that shovel, you hear? It'd be a shame to bust open them saddlebags and have greenbacks blowing everwhichway."

Flocker carefully spaded the clinging dirt away from the scrap of leather. In a few moments it was revealed to be a strap connecting two large leather pouches still anchored in the clay. Too impatient to wait for the shovel to do its work, I shouldered the banker out of the way and, falling to my knees, clawed the saddlebags free and raised them close to the lantern, where the faded letters "C.S.A." showed beneath the patina of dirt and age.

"The Drovers State bankroll—courtesy of Death's Gray Angel," I said.

"It's here, after all these years—you'll see!" cried Elwood Flocker.

"Open it, Paddy! I can't wait!" Ellen pleaded.

The buckle-strap on one saddlebag broke as I tried to unbuckle it. I opened the flap and dug my hand into the packets of dry, crackling paper inside. I pulled one packet into the light. It consisted of U.S. bank notes in fifty-dollar denominations. They seemed in excellent condition after two and a half decades underground.

I reached farther into the pouch and pulled out another packet. It was also made up of fifties, but these seemed much more affected by their quarter century's interment; their edges were black with mold, and the faces of the outer bills were badly stained. I put my hand in a third time, all the way down to the bottom, and withdrew a third packet. It appeared to be made up of rectangles of cut-up newspaper.

"Sam," I said sharply, "you and Charlie keep your eyes on these birds. There's something peculiar going on here." With Ellen at my elbow, I opened the other saddlebag and dumped the contents of both pouches on the ground beside the lantern. Then, in silence except for the hushed breathing of the seven people who watched me, I took inventory.

When I finished I straightened and looked at the faces around me. "Very interesting, friends. Warren Quarrles's saddlebags apparently contain twenty-five thousand dollars in very well-preserved bills, two thousand dollars in very poorly preserved bills, and sixty-odd packets of bank-note-sized newspaper, which, from some of the datelines printed on them, have been assembled in the last month."

The first one to reply was Elwood Flocker. His eyes starting from his head, his hands clutching like talons before him, he screamed, "You son-of-a-bitch, you tricked me! God damn you, I'll kill you for this!"

Sidewinder Sam caught him around the neck and held him quivering in the air.

13

Pigeon Drop
and Chicken Blood

By the time we all got back to Cogswell it was almost midnight. The deputy on duty at the jail went to rouse Sheriff Bybee, and fifteen minutes later he appeared, wiping mucus from the corners of his eyes. I gave him the saddlebag and explained briefly that Farringay, Flocker, Tompkins, and Yarnell had been involved in their exhumation, and that Sallee, Charlie Moon, Ellen, and I had also had our roles to play. "I know you want the whole story tonight, Sheriff," I concluded, "but would you mind if we went through it at the *Free American* office rather than here? There's more room there, and besides I want to show you some things from the files."

"It's all right with me, as long as we get it done," he rumbled. "Let's get on down there."

"I'll meet you there. There's something I've got to pick up at the hotel first."

In my room I checked on the item I had come for, found that my suspicions were well founded, and tucked it under my arm. Then, pausing only to down two fingers of Mole's One and Only, I hurried to the newspaper office.

When I opened the door I felt as if a convention were in

session. In addition to Bybee and his deputy, the banker and the three confidence men, and Sidewinder Sam and his tubular sidekick, the long, disorderly room contained Hamp Wyeth behind his desk reading a month-old copy of the *New York Herald*, Ellen Wyeth listening submissively to the opinions of her lymphatic fiancé Harold Anspaugh, and Oscar the printer and Doc Bennigsen lying on the floor in a position of repose suggesting that Oscar had already fallen off that wagon whereon he had only lately been coaxed by the daughter of his employer.

As I entered there was a moment of silence. I set the object I was carrying on a pile of newspapers and returned Jack Farringay's ironical look.

"All right, Moretti. It's your party—get on with it," Sheriff Bybee said.

"And remember what I told you before," added Elwood Flocker in a warning voice. "The press in this country is governed by the laws of libel!"

"I'll be keeping that in mind, Mr. Flocker," I assured him. I paused a moment to get my thoughts in order, and then began. "It all begins with the Gray Angel and the Drovers Bank money, of course. Quarrles buried it in the old burned barn on the Korshak farm, which had been the Kilpatrick farm, and before that the Farringay farm. It was a place that had—ah, deep associations for Quarrles. When he was dying, he told his son, Jack, here—" I interrupted myself to ask, "Is Jack your real name, or is that an alias too?"

Farringay smiled coolly. "Jack's as good a name as any other. Let's leave it there."

I resumed. "Quarrles told Jack where the money was hidden. He also told him something else—he told him exactly *how much* money was hidden there. You see, Quarrles knew how much money he had gotten in the robbery, and he also knew how much money was reported stolen. There was a considerable discrepancy."

"Remember what I told you about libel, Moretti!" Flocker cried again.

"Believe me, I will," I said. "So this was the situation a few days ago. Quarrles had hidden eighty-five thousand dollars in bank funds at the old barn. His son knew where and how much, and also knew that the man who audited the books at the Drovers Bank had embezzled an extra twenty-five thousand dollars and concealed the theft by blaming it on Quarrles."

"You're my witness, Sheriff!" Flocker was on his feet shaking one fist in the air. "Everybody in this room is my witness!"

"Shut up and sit down, Flocker." Bybee growled. "Go on, Moretti."

"Farringay knew where the money was, but there were other people who knew who *he* was. Tommy Tompkins and Hamilton Yarnell knew Farringay was Quarrles's son, and had been expecting him to lead them to the saddlebags for months. Tompkins had been a member of Quarrles's raiders during the war—as had Kid Slaughter, by the way. Or Josef Korshak, to use his real name. The main reason Tompkins set up his fight store here in Cogswell was to have reason to be here when Farringay dug up the money. He and Yarnell figured that once Jack led them to it they could take it from there."

Hamp Wyeth and his daughter were both taking notes rapidly. Sidewinder Sam shifted in his chair and belched softly. Charlie Moon blew his nose. On the floor Oscar turned over in his sleep and Doc Bennigsen drew himself into a sitting position, his shabby black bag between his knees.

"The death of Kid Slaughter and my arrival in Cogswell complicated things for Farringay, and forced him to act more quickly than he otherwise might have. When I found that the Kid had ridden with Quarrles, and that his mother and brother still lived here, I mentioned it to him. He realized he couldn't wait any longer, and made his plans to visit the burned-out barn that very night.

"By now Farringay might have been a little suspicious of Yarnell and Tompkins—were you, Jack?" I paused and he nodded sardonically. "At any rate, he faked a marathon visit to the second floor of Moll Sweeney's, where he was supposed to have remained for the balance of the evening. Actually, he went to the barn and dug up the saddlebags, which were exactly where his father had said they were."

"Goddamn!" said Tommy Tompkins. Hamilton Yarnell stroked the lapel of his jacket thoughtfully.

"Wait a minute," Sheriff Bybee protested. "If he dug up the saddlebags, how come you all found them out there tonight?"

"Sheriff," I asked, "have you ever heard of the pigeon drop?"

"Pigeon drop," he repeated, frowning. "Ain't that some kind of big-city bunco game?"

"That's right." Remembering the explanation Lieutenant Costigan had given me before I left New York City, I paraphrased. "It's a swindle where the mark is persuaded to put some of his own money along with the money that's to be divided up, as a gesture of good faith. Then later he finds that all the money has disappeared, his own included.

"All right, here's what Farringay decided to do—correct me if I'm wrong, Jack. He realized that Elwood Flocker must have been living in fear for the past twenty-five years, afraid that someone would dig up the Drovers Bank money and discover that it was only eighty-five thousand dollars instead of the one hundred and ten thousand it was supposed to be, and then everyone would know that Flocker had stolen the other twenty-five thousand and built his career on it. And Jack decided to play on that fear and clip Flocker for another twenty-five thousand in the interests of poetic justice and simple acquisitiveness.

"Jack was absolutely right. Flocker had become more

and more nervous with each passing year. He had even planted rumors about Quarrles's curse to discourage treasure hunters. (Not too successfully, however, as you'll see if you take a walk across Shep Fothergill's pasture.) So Jack convinced Flocker that I, Paddy Moretti, had come here to Cogswell to dig up the money, and that I was on the verge of doing it.''

"That's a lie!" Flocker squealed. "Tell them that's a lie, Farringay!" Farringay's smile broadened, and he didn't speak.

"After Jack dug up the saddlebags, he took out almost all the money and refilled them with packets of cut-up newspaper, leaving only two of the original packets on top, the way you'd salt a bogus gold mine with real gold nuggets. Then he buried the saddlebags again, and in the process got some red clay on his shoes.''

"Ouch!" said Farringay, grinning.

"Next he persuaded Flocker that I was on the verge of uncovering the bankroll. How did you handle that, Jack? Did he really believe you and I were on such confidential terms I would tell you when I had located the money? And what reason did you give him for being so solicitous of his welfare?''

Jack's eyes sparkled. There was no doubt about it; he was enjoying himself enormously. "I told him you talked in your sleep—the poor fool believed it," he said. "And he thought I only expected a couple of thousand dollars for my cooperation, and no doubt he could swindle me out of that when the time came.''

"Get on with this pigeon drop thing, Moretti," Bybee demanded. "I don't want to spend the night here."

I reflected that exposition is a thirsty business, and wondered whether or not it would be expedient to ask Hamp Wyeth for a taste of his twelve-year-old Kentucky bourbon. I decided it wouldn't, and continued. "Farringay decided to pull the pigeon drop tonight. He convinced Flocker that

I was going to the barn tomorrow morning, with witnesses, to dig up Quarrles's saddlebags. He laid out a paper chase to get me out of the way, with notes supposedly from Quarrles himself asking me to meet him at Eakins's barn, and then at Moll Sweeney's. He even bribed the boy that brought one of the messages to lie about who gave it to him, and give a physical description of Quarrles instead. My compliments on that, Jack." Farringay gave me an ironical bow.

I continued my story, telling how Ellen had met me at the hotel with the news that Farringay and Flocker had driven out of town together, heading south; how we had followed them and found them at the barn. "Flocker was standing in a hole with a shovel in his hands, and I assumed he was digging for the saddlebags. But he wasn't—he was burying them. He and Farringay had already uncovered them, and Farringay had taken the two authentic packets of bank notes out of them to convince Flocker that the bags contained the Drovers Bank loot. Then Flocker added the twenty-five thousand dollars he had brought with him—the pigeon drop, Sheriff—and they put the bags back in the hole. Flocker had the hole half-filled when Ellen and I got there."

"Wait a minute, Moretti," Bybee said. "You're saying Flocker would put twenty-five thousand dollars of his own money into a hole in the ground, and then leave it there?"

"How much risk did he think he was running, compared to the risk of letting me dig up the money before witnesses and prove that he had embezzled twenty-five thousand dollars? Once it was buried, he and Farringay would go back to town, and the next morning, I would dig the saddlebags up and return all one hundred and ten thousand dollars to the Drovers Bank. Flocker would be proved to be as honest as the day is long, and if he couldn't get his twenty-five thousand dollars back from his own bank at a later date, he isn't the financial manipulator I take him for."

Bybee tugged his nicotine-stained mustache thoughtfully. "And after Flocker and Farringay got back to town, then Farringay planned to sneak back to the barn, dig up the saddlebags again, and take off with Flocker's twenty-five thousand dollars?"

"Of course—along with the eighty-five thousand dollars that had been in the bags to begin with."

"And just where is that eighty-five thousand dollars now, Moretti?"

"He thought you'd never ask," said Farringay. "Show the man, Bunkie."

I picked up Farringay's valise, which I had carried from the hotel under my arm, and unpacked it quickly, setting the neatly folded clothes on a barrel of printer's ink. Then I upended it in front of Sheriff Bybee. Packets of bank notes, dark with stain and mold, cascaded onto the floor. "Here it is, less the two thousand dollars Farringay used to salt the packets of newspaper. All packed and ready to go."

A gasp went up from around the room. Sheriff Bybee picked up one of the packets and tossed it in his hand. "Sure looks like it's spent twenty-five years underground, all right," he said. He flipped the money back on the floor. "I reckon I got some sorting out to do, figuring which of these fellers to lock up and which to escort out of town and which to give a medal to."

"Well, Flocker should look pretty good in court facing an embezzlement charge, assuming the statute of limitations hasn't run out. If you have any trouble making a case, I'm sure Jack Farringay will be glad to help you, especially since you haven't got a case against him for anything, as far as I can see. Yarnell and Tompkins are probably wanted somewhere, but you'll have to decide whether to hold them or let them leave. I'd suggest you let them leave. I don't see how Yarnell's going to raise the money to buy me a case of Irish whiskey if he's behind bars."

"A case of Irish whiskey? What in tarnation are you talking about?"

I explained how Yarnell had offered me a reward if I could find evidence that Kid Slaughter's death had not been the result of the blow he received in the ring. "And if I can show how he was deliberately murdered, that should fill the bill," I added.

"What's got into you, Moretti?" Bybee asked gruffly. "Kid Slaughter wasn't murdered. He was killed by a wallop in the chest. Fifty people saw it happen."

"Fifty people saw him get a wallop in the chest, true enough. And fifty people saw him spout blood like a harpooned whale. But it wasn't his own blood he was spouting—and it wasn't the wallop in the chest that killed him, either."

Doc Bennigsen opened his black bag with shaking hands and reached inside it. I smiled at him. "Faith, Doc, you're not the first medical man to make a mis-diagnosis. I doubt if you'll lose your professional reputation over it."

"All right, stop this damn toe-dancing, Moretti!" Bybee barked. "If the Kid was murdered, how was it done, and who done it?"

"He was murdered, and it was done by the same man who later killed the private detective, Magruder." I turned toward Ellen Wyeth. "The last time I was in this office, Miss Wyeth said something very interesting. Remember, Ellen? You were scolding your father for taking a little nip, and you repeated a quote from your mother—"

" 'To think that a man would put into his mouth that which will steal away his brain,' " Ellen finished.

"A deep thought, and one we could all stand to turn over in our minds every so often," I said.

"Moretti—" Bybee grated dangerously.

"And that's what I kept doing—turning it over in my mind. Then after a while it changed to 'To think that a man would put into his mouth that which will steal away his *life*.' Could Kid Slaughter have put into his mouth something that stole away his life? Well, he certainly put something into his mouth, at any rate.''

"You mean the—the—'' Hamp Wyeth groped excitedly for the word.

I supplied it. "Yes, the cackle-bladder, of course. He had it in his mouth all during the fight, full of chicken blood and ready to bite down on when the time came for him to take the fall. And nothing happened to him as long as the bladder stayed intact. But once he bit down he was dead in thirty seconds.''

"Poisoned? Was there poison in the bladder along with the chicken blood?'' Ellen asked eagerly.

"There had to be—that's the only way things make any sense. The murderer was someone with access to the cackle-bladder, someone who could have added a lethal dose of some quick-acting poison without attracting any attention.''

"Who?'' Sheriff Bybee demanded.

I hesitated. "Give me a minute or two. The second murder was Magruder's. It took place in a—your pardon, Ellen—house of ill fame, under cover of a brawl that put out all the lights. The man was stabbed in the back with some kind of knife, and died instantly. The *dramatis personae*—''

"The what?''

"The cast of characters, the possible suspects—were much the same as at the boxing match in Eakins's barn. The weapon wasn't found. But as for the motive, I thought I had a clue to it. A few minutes before he was killed Magruder came to me demanding that we have a talk. I refused; I didn't like the man, and I was thinking about other things at the time. Maybe if I had listened to him he'd be alive today, not that that would be a particular benefit to anyone. Anyway, I think I know what he wanted to talk about.

"He said we were after different things, but that didn't

mean we couldn't help one another. 'One hand washes the other' was the way he put it. And he promised he'd give me a story if I just played along. But if we were after different things, then what thing was *he* after? He knew what *I* wanted—to catch a couple of confidence men and write a story about Kid Slaughter's death in the ring at Tommy Tompkins's fight store—so what *he* wanted had to be something different. It couldn't be identifying the other two con men, Faro Ed Wheeler and the Bushy-Tailed Kid, because I knew he had already told Sheriff Bybee about them.

"So what was it? The only thing I could think of was Cogswell's story of the century, the unsolved mystery of the Drovers Bank money.

"The next question I asked myself was, What could he tell me that would help me get what *I* wanted? He said he'd give me a story. What story? I had no idea then—but someone overhearing our conversation—someone with a murder to hide—would have guessed Magruder meant the facts about Kid Slaughter's death."

"You think Magruder was killed to keep him from telling you who put poison in Kid Slaughter's whatyoumacallit?" Sheriff Bybee's tone was skeptical. "Hell, if he knew so much, why didn't he tell *me*?"

"Because he wasn't interested in catching a murderer, he was interested in finding a hundred thousand dollars. And I didn't say he knew who put poison in the cackle-bladder. He must have learned about the connection between Kid Slaughter and Tommy Tompkins and Warren Quarrles, and perhaps Jack Farringay too. Anyway, by the time he spoke to me at Moll's that night, he had decided we should pool our information. The important thing isn't what his information was; it's that he made the mistake of mentioning it out loud. That's what got him killed."

Sheriff Bybee set his jaw decisively. "And for the last time, Moretti—who's the killer?"

I sighed. "All right, Doc, I guess it's time. Do you want to tell them, or shall I?"

Doc Benningsen raised his head and looked at me with eyes that had seen a good deal of the horrors of human life. His mouth twisted ironically as he said, "You're doing fine so far."

Sheriff Bybee's jaw dropped, Hamp Wyeth's pencil snapped in his fingers, Ellen Wyeth gasped in disbelief, Elwood Flocker's eyes bulged like a trout's, and Sidewinder Sam Sallee said, "Well, I'll be buggered!"

"Old Doc?" the sheriff said incredulously. "Why in the world would Old Doc kill anybody? He ain't never done no harm to nobody but hisself!"

I stepped over to the stack of bound back issues of the *Free American* in the corner and tugged out the volume labeled 1863. I leafed through the pages until I found the first article I wanted. "Dateline, February, 1863," I read aloud. "Headline, MATTMILLER-BENNIGSEN NUPTIALS. Story begins as follows: 'Miss Esther Mattmiller, lovely daughter of Mr. and Mrs. Chester Mattmiller, and Doctor Rolf Bennigsen, the popular young physician who began practicing in Cogswell last year, solemnized their vows in a candlelight ceremony last Friday at the Grace Methodist Church, the Reverend Howland Clegg officiating. The bride wore—"

Doc Bennigsen, head lowered, mumbled, "That's enough. Read the other one." He cradled his black bag on his lap as protectively as though it were a baby, with one arm around it and the other hand inside.

I turned the pages until I came to the description of Quarrles's raid on Cogswell four months later. "Here's the description of Quarrles and his guerrilas on their way out of town after the robbery. It tells how they brained an old man with a thrown whiskey bottle, and shot down a young boy on his own doorstep—" My finger ran down the column of type until I found what I wanted. "And then this happened: 'As Quarrles led his murderous band toward the edge of town he surprised Doctor and Mrs. Rolf Bennigsen crossing Main Street. Realizing that one of the guerrillas intended to ride them down, Doctor Bennigsen pushed his wife to the safety—as he thought—of the curb, only to fall himself beneath the hoofs of the raider's horse. The gray-clad murderer then reversed his steed's direction several times, passing back and forth over the body of the uncon-scious doctor. Mrs. Bennigsen, horrified at the savagery of this deed, cried down the wrath of the Almighty upon its cowardly perpetrator, whereupon the scoundrel deliberately drew his pistol and shot her dead.'' I paused and looked around the hushed room. ''The man who shot Doc Bennig-sen's wife was Kid Slaughter. I recognized him from a picture I saw in Miss Carrie Heckman's room. You rec-ognized him when he came to box at Tommy Tompkins's fight store, didn't you, Doc?''

''She was three months pregnant,'' Bennigsen said. ''We were going to have a baby. She wanted it more than any-thing in the world.'' He sat with his chin on his breast, cuddling his black bag; beside him the supine body of Os-car the printer twitched in its sleep, as if he were troubled with bad dreams. Ellen Wyeth, an expression of intense sorrow on her face, reached for the hand of her fiancé. ''When I recognized Slaughter, I decided to kill him,'' Doc went on. ''I used hydrocyanic acid because he wouldn't have to swallow any of it—any little cut in his mouth or on his tongue would be enough to let it into his blood-stream, and he'd be dead in half a minute.'' He looked up and grinned mirthlessly. ''When I saw that chicken blood coming out of his mouth, I thought, 'That's his own heart's blood, but he doesn't know it yet.' ''

Hamp Wyeth had found a new pencil and was writing furiously. Farringay, Tompkins, and Yarnell stared at the hunched figure in rapt fascination; Elwood Flocker wore an expression of fastidious disgust.

"And Magruder?" Bybee asked tersely.

Bennigsen shrugged, as if suddenly bored with the subject. "I was afraid he knew enough to stop me. I still had Tompkins to settle with—he was one of Quarrles's men too. And maybe some of the others; they were all singing 'Goober Peas' at Moll's that night, God damn them!"

"So when the fight started and the lights went out, you put one of your doctor's knives into Magruder's back," Bybee said.

Bennigsen nodded. Then, raising his head, he said decisively, "I think that's enough, Sheriff. Mr. Moretti there can fill you in on any other details, I'm sure." His hand suddenly appeared from his bag, an open paper packet held between his thumb and first two fingers. Although I had half-expected the action, its suddenness caught me by surprise, and before I could move Doc Bennigsen had conveyed the powder to his mouth and swallowed it.

He dropped his hand to the floor and released the black bag, which slipped sidewise from his lap. Ellen gave a cry and Bybee swore as he made a futile clutch at Bennigsen's hand. Doc leaned his head back against the wall and surveyed us from his wounded eyes. "Don't bother trying to do anything," he said. "There's nothing now that would do any good. Maybe there never was." He closed his eyes, the lids coming down like shades over broken windows. "Ah, Essie, Essie—I wonder if you're really there," he whispered.

And then he died.

Twenty minutes later Sheriff Bybee left the *Free American* office. His deputy, assisted by Sidewinder Sam Sallee and Charlie Moon, carried along the body of Doctor Rolf Bennigsen. Accompanying them were Jack Farringay, Tommy Tompkins, Hamilton Yarnell, and Elwood Flocker, "so's I can sort you out and figure who's going to end up in the calaboose, and for how long," as the sheriff said. Ellen

Wyeth, her father, her fiancé, and I remained, together with the gently snoring Oscar.

I shook hands with Hamp Wyeth. "Thanks for your help," I said. "Maybe the story will sell a few papers for you."

He shook his head in embarrassment. "You got more help from Ellen than you got from me," he said. "I'm going to have to give her a by-line on this, and that'll probably spoil her for life."

"Don't you worry, Daddy," Ellen said, tucking her hand firmly under Harold Anspaugh's arm. "This will be my swan song. Harold doesn't think a career in journalism is fitting for someone planning to be a wife and mother." She regarded the smug lout fondly. "Harold says a woman's place is in the home." She turned to me and, unmindful of the coals she was heaping on my head, continued. "It was a wonderful experience working with an experienced older newspaperman like you, Paddy. I'll think about you covering all those glamorous stories in New York while I'm bouncing babies on my knees here in Cogswell."

It took me two hours the next morning to write my story for *The Spirit of the Times*. When I had finished, I appended three suggested headlines. They were:

BOXER, DETECTIVE MURDERED
IN WAKE OF BARE-KNUCKLE FIGHT

GUERRILLA QUARRLES'S $100,000 BANKROLL RECOVERED

and

S.O.T. REPORTER SOLVES MURDERS, RECOVERS MONEY

The more I looked at the third one, the more I thought it might be inexpedient to use its initial letters to represent the name of the newspaper, so I crossed it off. I was about to take the completed story to the railroad station for transmittal East when Jack Farringay entered the room.

"Ah, Bunkie, I'm glad you're here to receive my fond *adieux*," he cried cheerily as he sailed his homburg onto the bed. "I couldn't have stood for you to steal off like a thief in the night—not after all we've been through together."

"Hello, Jack. So Bybee let you out. I assume it's on condition that you stay in town and testify against Flocker."

"Well, the man *did* cost me a hundred and ten thousand dollars. I thought it was the least I could do."

I regarded his smiling face curiously, aware of conflicting feelings within me. "Before we get chummy, tell me something, Jack. Back there in the barn last night, when you were ready to leave Ellen and me with Tompkins and that Colt of his, didn't you know you were probably signing our death warrants?"

He looked grave. "The possibility did occur to me, although I must say I thought wiser counsel would prevail." His face lighted with a smile. "But what would you have wanted me to do? I mean, I had eighty-five thousand dollars waiting in my suitcase!"

I nodded. Then I found the bottle of Mole's Ne Plus Ultra and poured us each a finger and a half and added water. I toasted him with my glass. "Happy days, Jack."

"Happy days, Bunkie." He drank half his drink. "Perhaps we'll meet again one day, Paddy," he said, his eyes sparkling. 'I certainly hope so.''

"So do I—I think," I replied.

I took my story to the train station for the telegrapher to transmit. A small group of people were waiting on the platform for the train from Chicago. Among them were Faro Ed Wheeler, Tim the Tiger O'Meara, and the Bushy-Tailed Kid. They looked at me coldly, and I decided there was nothing to be gained by engaging them in conversation. While I was arranging for the transmission of my dispatch the Chicago train arrived and left. When I stepped out on the platform again, there was only one person on it.

"Moretti? Moretti, is that you?" called a petulant voice I recognized.

"The very same, Bertram. Welcome to Cogswell." I joined him and put out my hand, which he took after a moment's hesitation and pumped only once. He regarded me suspiciously as I offered to carry his suitcase and show him to the hotel. "You'll enjoy yourself here. The people are the salt of the earth," I told him as we walked toward the Barnard Hotel. "I only wish I could stay here with you while you dig out your story. It's my misfortune that I have to leave for New York tomorrow."

His suspicions did not diminish as I showed him into the hotel lobby, introduced him to the desk clerk, made pleasant conversation while he signed the register, and carried his suitcase up to his single room. He took off his overcoat and hung it carefully over a nail on the door and then turned to regard me from pale round eyes that seemed pasted on the surface of his pale round face. "I'm sorry about this, Moretti, but you know I have to ask you for your notes. Mr. Hochmuth specifically instructed me to utilize them in the composition of my story."

"And of course you shall!" I said cheerfully. "And how is Mr. Hochmuth, by the way? Enjoying vibrant good health and high spirits, I hope? A darling man he is, and that's a fact, Bertram! I count the days as wasted until I see him again!"

"And you'll give me your notes?" he asked, his dumpling face creased in a frown.

"Why, of course I will! Unfortunately I've already written my own story based on them and sent it off to the paper twenty minutes ago, so I don't know what good they'll do you, but you shall have every jot and tittle, I guarantee!"

His mouth dropped open. "You've—you've already written your story and sent it in?"

"Complete with account of swindle exposed, treasure recovered, and murderer unmasked. You'll see when I give you my notes." I rose and opened the door. "Sure and you must be dead tired from your trip, Bertram. Why don't you take a nap? Then later we'll have a bite to eat, and maybe I can put you on to a *real* story."

After dinner an uneasy Bertram and I strolled out Center Street, crossed the tracks, passed the warehouse, and climbed the steps to the front door of the house with the green shutters. Moll Sweeney greeted me warmly, and simpered when I introduced her to my associate, the well-known aquatic journalist of *The Spirit of the Times*. We gave our coats to the white-jacketed Maurice and entered the parlor.

My luck was in. "Hellfire, Mr. Moretti, Charlie and I was hoping you'd be here dipping your wick tonight!" cried a huge figure in a tight swallowtail coat, a dirt-glazed shirt, and faded jeans. "Let's have us a drink and get on with our business!"

"Sam, Charlie, I want you to meet Bertram McAnly," I said, pushing my startled colleague forward. "Mr. McAnly is one of the top reporters in the East, and he's come all the way out here for"—I lowered my voice and said significantly—"the *big story!*"

Bertram's eyes widened in shock as the indescribable emanation from Sidewinder Sam Sallee reached him. I waited until I saw that he was safely immobilized by Sam's giant arm around his shoulders, and then sought out Moll Sweeney. She adjusted her Marie Antoinette coiffure demurely and asked if I would care to converse with any of the young ladies in particular.

"To tell you the truth of it, I've a hankering to make the acquaintance of Miss Billie Mae, if you'd be so kind," I replied. "I was inclined in that direction the other night, but things didn't work out."

Moll gave a moue of distress. "Oh, I'm so sorry! Billie

Mae isn't receiving any company for the next few weeks. When Doc Bennigsen saw her yesterday he said the poor girl had been working too hard and she needed a nice long rest. Isn't there someone else you'd enjoy socializing with?''

Thanks, Doc, I said to myself. *That's a favor I owe you, if I ever get a chance to repay it.* "I think not, Moll. I have a long day tomorrow—I'll just have a glass of your champagne and toddle back to the hotel. Make a short night of it.''

I settled myself in a comfortable wing chair, took a sip from my glass, put my head back, and closed my eyes. The piano player began to play "Believe Me If All Those Endearing Young Charms,'' and there was the sound of rustling taffeta and the odor of perfume in the air.

A soft voice close to my ear said, "I don't believe we've been introduced. My name is Peggy, and I just love Eastern gentlemen.'' Her warm breath tickled my earlobe.

It was the beginning of a very long night indeed.

Author's Note

The inspiration (if that's the word) for the character of Warren Quarrles is, of course, William Clarke Quantrill, who, like Quarrles, was a schoolteacher before becoming a guerrilla leader. The raid on Cogswell was suggested by Quantrill's raid on Lawrence, Kansas, although the theft of the Drovers Bank funds more nearly resembles the looting of the bank in Mount Sterling, Kentucky, by John Hunt Morgan's command than it does any recorded robbery of Quantrill's. (Morgan and his men got eighty thousand dollars at Mount Sterling; Quantrill's biggest haul, at Huntstown, Kansas, was only thirty thousand.) But Quantrill, unlike his fictional counterpart, did not survive the Civil War—he was killed in Kentucky in the spring of 1865.

Con game buffs will find very little material on the fight-store grift in print. David W. Maurer gives a brief description of it and its sister swindles, the wrestle store and the foot-race store, in his wonderful book *The American Confidence Man*, and it is mentioned by name in two or three other works. But as Maurer says, ''The best source of information is the memory of old-timers—if you can find any still alive.'' Quite a problem, since the fight-store con was superseded by the more sophisticated Rag, Wire, and Pay-Off before World War I.

The Pigeon Drop, however, is widely practiced today, generally by very sleazy operators and in a wide variety of forms. One of the most common is persuading an elderly person to draw his or her savings out of a bank so that the serial numbers of the money can be checked. When the money is returned, the victim discovers that worthless paper has been substituted for the bank notes. Respectable con men do not practice the Pigeon Drop, considering it a pure swindle unredeemed by the element of poetic justice that enhances the better bunco games.

The venerable device of Finding the Leather is also in regular use today, in exactly the same form described in the first chapter of this book. The next time you find a wallet under your table while you are having drinks with a stranger, be very careful.

The Spirit of the Times (subtitled "A Chronicle of the Turf, Field Sports, Aquatics, Agriculture and the Stage") was an actual newspaper published during the late nineteenth and early twentieth century, although I don't believe any of the characters in this book was on its payroll. The paper's loss, I say.

J.S.

About the Author

JAMES SHERBURNE, a well-known historical novelist, has turned to mysteries with the acclaimed Paddy Moretti series, the first two volumes of which became Detective Book Club selections. He lives in Midway, Kentucky.

MYSTERY, ADVENTURE and THE WORLD of HORSE RACING

DICK FRANCIS

A fascinating blend of horseracing and international intrigue—high finance, detectives, and skullduggery—wrapped up in six thrilling novels.